## Praise for the National Bestselling
## Chocolate Covered Mysteries

"Kathy Aarons has penned a delectably devious mystery. . . . Best friends and amateur sleuths Michelle and Erica make a formidable duo as they unwrap their first chocolate-covered mystery. Any lover of chocolate and books will find this story the perfect combination of savory, sweet, and deadly."

— Jenn McKinlay, *New York Times* bestselling author of *Dark Chocolate Demise*

"Aarons's deft blend of delicious chocolate and tasty mystery will delight the reader's palate."

— Victoria Hamilton, national bestselling author of *Death of an English Muffin*

"This delectable new series is well written, and I found I could not put it down. . . . Mystery lovers will eat up this yummy story." —MyShelf.com

"This mystery blends chocolate with murder and continues to surprise. . . . Delicious descriptions and recipes enhance this smartly written debut mystery series."

—Kings River Life Magazine

"[A] sweet treat, indeed." —Lesa's Book Critiques

"[*Death Is Like a Box of Chocolates*] quickly caught my attention with all my favorites: a mystery, chocolate, and a hilarious assortment of characters! This mouthwatering story line has all the appeal of a marvelous mystery series in the making."

—Fresh Fiction

# BEHIND CHOCOLATE BARS

## KATHY AARONS

**BERKLEY PRIME CRIME**
New York

BERKLEY PRIME CRIME
Published by Berkley
An imprint of Penguin Random House LLC
375 Hudson Street, New York, New York 10014

ISBN: 9780425267257

First Edition: October 2016

Printed in the United States of America
1 3 5 7 9 10 8 6 4 2

Book design by Laura K. Corless

This book is dedicated to the love of my life—Lee Krevat— who supports me in everything I do. I'm the lucky one!

# ACKNOWLEDGMENTS

I'd like to thank Jessica Faust, my awesome agent, and Robin Barletta, my wonderful editor, for making my publishing dreams come true.

Thanks so much to cover artist Mary Ann Lasher, who brought my scenes to life in each book. I'd also like to thank copy editor Courtney Vincento, who made this book so much better!

Once again, this book wouldn't exist without the help of my critique group, the Denny's Chicks: Barrie Summy and Kelly Hayes.

I would not be writing today if it wasn't for the gentle editing of my first critique group, Betsy, Sandy Levin and the late Elizabeth Skrezyna.

I can never express the gratitude I feel toward all of the family and friends who bought books across the country, attended my book signings and spread the word, especially Jim and Lee Hegarty, Pat Sultzbach, Manny and Sandra Krevat, Donna and Brian Lowenthal, Patty Disandro, Jim Hegarty Jr., Michael and Noelle Hegarty, Matthew and Madhavi Krevat, Jeremy and Joclyn Krevat, Lori and Murray Maloney, Lynne Bath and Tom Freeley, David Kreiss and Nasim Bavar, Lori Morse, Amy

Bellefeuille, Sue Britt, Cathie Wier, Joanna Westreich, Ssusan O'Neill and the rest of the YaYas, my Moms' Night Out group and my book club.

Thank you to Simone and Julia Camilleri, for continuing the CCA Writers' Conference, and to Cecelia Kouma and Laurel Withers of the Playwrights Project. Both of these organizations are close to my heart.

A special shout-out to Terrie Moran, author of the Read 'Em and Eat mystery series, for her friendship and encouragement, and to Dru Ann Love, for her friendship and support of the cozy mystery community.

Special thanks to the following experts for unselfishly sharing their knowledge:

Isabella Knack, owner of Dallmann Fine Chocolates, the best chocolates in the world.

Kaylee Brogadir and Donna Martel, for their accounting expertise.

Jim Hegarty Jr., for his technical expertise.

Dr. Josh Feder, for his expertise in treating PTSD and depression, and Caron Feder for her event-planning knowledge, and both of them for being untiring cheerleaders for my writing.

Jill Limber, for her cat knowledge, which led to Coco's multiple identities.

Dr. Susan Levy, for her medical knowledge.

Lori Morse, for her support and years of friendship.

Judy Twigg, for her expertise in the world of academia and being a typo-finding guru.

Kristen Koster, for her Maryland knowledge.

Annette Palmer, co-owner of Earth Song Books and Gifts.

## ACKNOWLEDGMENTS

Christine Hajak, president and founder of Gentle Giants Draft Horse Rescue.

Any mistakes are my own.

And most important, mountains of gratitude and love to my brilliant, beautiful and creative daughters, Shaina and Devyn Krevat. You make me proud and grateful every single day!

"We need more zombies," I said, sliding a latte across the counter.

It was Sunday morning at Chocolates and Chapters and we were about to open. The sun was shining, and the crisp, cool fall air wafted in from the open door. Homemade tortes had been delivered, and fresh coffee was ready for the first wave of customers who stopped by after church. I'd turned on the small chocolate tempering machine used to dip strawberries and other fruits, sending the tantalizing scent throughout the store.

My business partner and best friend, Erica Russell, sat at the counter, staring at the spreadsheet on her laptop. She'd placed Halloween-themed books on the side tables in our dining area, and we'd plumped the couch cushions. The welcoming glow from the small lamps decorated with black and orange scarves tempted our customers to take a leisurely break.

"Can't have too many zombies," Erica agreed with absolutely no sarcasm. She sipped her coffee and looked at me over her glasses. "Four more? We've got enough volunteers. I'll ask Janice if she can make more costumes."

I nodded, considering the space available in the Boys and Girls Club. The new director had provided an entire wing for this year's haunted house, which would be the centerpiece of the West Riverdale Halloween Festival. We had less than two weeks until opening night, and again, the amazing Erica Russell had been talked into taking the reins. If she wasn't careful, she'd find herself in charge of the Thanksgiving Parade and Winter Holiday Fair too.

I watched her smile as she updated the staffing spreadsheet. She'd love taking on all of them.

"Hey, Michelle. Can I be a zombie?" Dylan Fenton carried a small box of books from the back of the store.

Dylan was Chocolates and Chapters' new high school intern, a position Erica had invented when she'd heard about his plight from our teacher friends. After a scandalous affair with the married soccer coach, Dylan's mother had left West Riverdale over the summer and moved to Florida. Dylan had started skipping school to avoid the snide comments from fellow students. The job gave him a safe haven and access to his most favorite thing in the world—comic books. He didn't mind my chocolates either.

"Sure thing," I said.

Erica made a note on her computer.

"Cool!" He dropped the box on the stool beside her.

Dylan was small for his age, taking after his mother, with dark hair that fell over his eyes.

"Are those the new Superman?" she asked.

He tilted the box to show her the shipping label, and they both grinned. "Upstairs?" he asked.

"Put some aside for the club," she said.

Dylan was an enthusiastic member of Erica's comic book club. She'd started it when she realized a bunch of high school students drove every month to Frederick to get the latest comic books. They'd dubbed themselves the Superhero Geek Team, and Dylan and a few other members had volunteered for the Halloween Festival, looking forward to it with the eagerness of toddlers waiting for Christmas. Or Disneyland. Or Christmas at Disneyland.

I rolled my eyes at their passion for superheroes in skinny books and grabbed another cup of coffee. We'd been up late hammering nails into too many realistic-looking coffins from the time our store closed until after midnight, and my body was protesting.

Erica returned to her laptop and frowned. "Maybe we should get a few more volunteers to help the Duncans with the last stage of construction. They're a day behind."

I waved my hand. "They'll catch up." Harold and his son Sammy ran Duncan Hardware Store and had donated most of the supplies.

"Probably," Erica said. "But Harold hurt his back yesterday building the guillotine. He might appreciate the help."

I smiled at her proper accent—gee-a-teen—and gave in, of course. "Go for it," I said.

Harold and Sammy had already worked wonders. They'd

built a false floor out of acrylic. When customers walked on it, lights flashed, showing motorized rats underneath. A mechanical spider the size of a small cow peered from a storage closet and clacked its legs when people passed by, and a hallway had been transformed into a zombie prison, where our volunteers would reach through the bars as customers walked by.

The booth for Chocolates and Chapters was carefully placed right outside the exit, like the gift shops at entertainment parks, where it was guaranteed to get a lot of traffic. I'd had a lot of fun creating my "spooky" truffles, especially Booberry Whites, creamy white chocolate filled with tart blueberry-infused milk chocolate ganache in the shape of blue-eyed ghosts. The Screamin' Orange Milks were filled with tangy orange ganache that made taste buds pucker before flooding them with sweetness. And the Mummy Wraps had the same biting cherry ganache as my Black Forest Milks, but were covered in white icing ribbons to look like mummies with tiny black eyes peeking through.

"What's on the list for me?" I asked. We were hosting another committee meeting at the shop in just a few hours, and I liked to know what to expect.

We heard a screech and turned to see a hearse park in front of the store. I'd almost gotten used to seeing it there, especially since Dylan had started working for us. The owner, Tommy Voltz, had bought the thing at auction as soon as he got his driver's license. He decorated it in year-round Halloween glory, like the neighbor who never took down his Christmas decorations. Today, he'd placed a fake skeleton in the backseat with its arm hanging out the window.

We weren't surprised to see both Tommy and Quinn Perch get out of the car and come in. They were good friends of Dylan's and members of the comic book club. Tommy wore his trademark black T-shirt, black jeans and black biker boots. Quinn was about half his size with big eyes that reminded me of a cartoon character. She wore a bright red coat that swung around her knees.

"It smells amazing in here," Quinn said.

"Thanks," I said. "It must be your lucky day, because I need a taste tester for these." I put a few Booberry Whites onto a plate and handed them to her. "Dylan's upstairs."

Quinn thanked me profusely and they headed up the wooden staircase that led to the second floor. Erica and I were both grateful for their steadfast friendship with Dylan, especially defending him against the bullies at school. Tommy was the size of a small grizzly, but he was as gentle as a teddy bear. He'd still used his bulk to intimidate Dylan's tormentors, while Quinn had fought back with scathing sarcasm.

Their efforts must have worked, because Dylan stopped skipping school and had lost the haunted expression he'd worn after his mother had left.

Erica stood and picked up her laptop. "Nothing new for your festival to-do list," she said. "But on a different note, we're meeting with Phoenix on Thursday. He needs both of our P&Ls from this quarter. He also wants a projection on our marketing plans running up to the holidays."

"Ugh." I liked to complain about getting the numbers ready for our accountant, but unless we were having a hard month, like when no-carb diets were all the rage, it was helpful and kinda fun to get a financial snapshot of how my business was doing.

Erica and I had joined together my chocolate shop and her family's bookstore over a year before to create Chocolates and Chapters, a match made in heaven that no one could resist. I loved making and selling my delicious truffles, while she enjoyed managing the bookstore and running a rare and used book business on the side.

Erica had been one of Phoenix Keogh's earliest clients when he started his accounting business five years ago, and even now, when he had customers all over Maryland who were much larger than us, he treated us like VIPs.

The jingling of the bells on our doorknob announced the arrival of our first customers, if we could call them that. Bean Russell came into the shop with Bobby Simkin, and my brain instantly melted, along with various other parts of my body.

Bean was Erica's older brother, a world-renowned reporter and author. His first book had become a freakin' bestseller. He was also one of my brother, Leo's, best friends, and was staying with him since he'd come back home. And I was dating him. "Complicated" wasn't a complicated enough word to describe all the relationship issues that might entangle us. But it was worth it. Or at least I hoped it was.

Bobby touched the strand of gold on Erica's neck and ran his hand down her arm before sitting beside her at the counter. He was one of West Riverdale's police officers, as well as Erica's boyfriend. He'd just given her the gold necklace with a gold pendant in the shape of a book, which was perfect for her.

How I felt about seeing Bean must have been obvious, because he grinned. He may have even blushed a bit. "Good morning," he said in a rough tone, reminding me of our make-out session in a dark room of the Boys and Girls Club the night before. Since Erica and I were so busy with the store and the Halloween Festival, Bean and Bobby volunteered for haunted house construction duty whenever they could.

"The usual?" I asked them both, feeling a little breathless.

"Sounds good," Bean said, and Bobby nodded.

I started on their coffee.

"You guys busy today?" Erica asked.

Her innocent tone didn't fool them for a minute. "No way," Bean said. "We're going fishing with Leo, not working on that haunted house."

Erica was about to protest, until she heard my brother's name. "How's he doing?" she asked.

"Getting better," Bean said, but I could tell he wasn't being completely honest.

Leo had been back from the war in Afghanistan for a few years. Physically, he'd healed from the loss of his leg, but his fight against PTSD would probably last a lifetime. In the last several months, he'd actually been happy. But something changed a couple of weeks ago. He had a motorcycle accident, and even though he and his girlfriend, Star, had walked away with only minor injuries, Leo seemed to be on the brink of depression once again.

"It'll be okay," Bean said. "We'll cheer him up today."

I nodded as the first customers drifted in after church in their Sunday finest, but my concern about Leo clung like a black cloud in the back of my mind.

. . . . . . . . . . . . . .

We'd scheduled our Halloween Festival meeting for one o'clock, when our assistants came in to take over.

Yvonne Nicola was the first to arrive. "Good afternoon!" she called out as she set down two bags from Hole in One Donuts along with her huge purse filled with papers on the back table we'd reserved for the festival committee meeting.

My mouth watered instinctively. Hole in One had opened in the town of Normal, where Yvonne now lived, and she liked to thank the committee with treats. Even though Chocolates and Chapters sold tortes along with our truffles, we all loved those glazed and filled pastries.

Yvonne was the new director of the West Riverdale Boys and Girls Club and was thrilled about all aspects of the festival, especially the money we predicted it would raise. She was over forty years old, and had the body and energy of someone fifteen years younger. She had shiny eyes that looked like someone had painted a white sparkle right on her eyeball. It made her enthusiasm even more engaging. Her children had gained a great deal from the club's after-school programs when they were younger, and she worked hard to make it just as valuable for the next group of kids.

Erica set down a huge three-ring binder full of printouts of the project plan, opened her laptop, and took a seat.

Jolene and Steve Roxbury came in, Steve wearing a *Doctor Who* TARDIS T-shirt that made him look like a blue phone booth. They both taught at West Riverdale High School, and were regularly drafted for Erica's projects, especially those involving students. Jolene always did an excellent job motivating her drama kids to volunteer, and Steve did wonders with his science club students.

By the time I served them their favorite truffles—the Bacon and Smoked Salt Milks, a sweet and salty mix they both adored—Janice the Costume Lady had arrived. I put a few Irish Cream Milks on a plate for her, and brought the decaf coffee she preferred.

"Hi, Janice," I said. "Thanks for coming to the meeting. Please keep all of the gore out of sight." She nodded her head, not at all offended by the reminder. Maybe because she realized the error of her ways at the last meeting, when she'd pulled out samples of zombie T-shirts with what looked like bloody intestines made out of pink material hanging from them. My next-door neighbor had been about to buy a dozen of my mummy-shaped Black Forest Milks and had bolted out the door instead.

Erica started. "Let's talk about the haunted house first," she said, "because that's the biggest part of the festival." She unfolded a layout of the Boys and Girls Club. "The guillotine room, the chain-saw massacre room and the rat floor are done."

Steve pointed to an unused room near the vampire corner on the layout. "Should we stick something in there?"

I blushed when I realized that's where Bean had kissed me last night.

"One of the students suggested we should use it as a quiet room, where the volunteers can take their breaks without coming outside in costume," Erica said. "It has a refrigerator, and the students dragged some beanbag chairs into it."

Jolene and Steve looked at each other and laughed. "You

better give them strict rules for that room and make sure a parent is around so there's no funny business going on in those chairs."

Good idea. Maybe some rules for the adult volunteers too.

Erica made a note. "The TV room is working well." Aside from the usual vampires, chain saws and mummies, Erica's tech guy and assistant for her rare and used book business, Zane West, had hung a bunch of huge TVs by the entrance with "terrifying" social media posts. As customers waited they'd see messages like *OMG! John posted that photo of you at the party. Hurry and untag it before your mom sees it!* or *Click here to see Winston's missed shot at the buzzer again!* or *Your sister's YouTube song about your wreck of a love life is trending on social media!*

She spread out the very complicated schedule of festival volunteer assignments. "I'd like to get more adults to participate."

The outside festival, with booths and games for smaller children, would run every night from five to eight, but the haunted house would be open for the teenagers and adults until ten on Friday and Saturday nights.

I noticed that a line of customers had grown and excused myself to help my assistant. Someone asked for Balsamic Dreams, truffles with dark chocolate ganache that perfectly balanced the rush of balsamic vinegar, and I went to the cooler in the kitchen.

Dylan stuck his head in the doorway, his backpack on his shoulder. "Had an idea for tomorrow's recipes," he said. "What about crushed pumpkin seeds?"

Dylan had somehow wormed his way into my Monday early-morning routine, the one day I banned everyone from my kitchen and went into creative mode, trying new recipes and finalizing the week's offerings. He'd quickly learned to stay quiet and not interrupt my thought process, just observing unless I asked him to help. Lately, he'd been making suggestions for ingredients. I was both amused and impressed that he was so interested.

I pulled out a tray of chilled truffles. "With or without shells?"

He looked uncertain. "Without?"

"Bring some by tomorrow," I said, "and we'll give it a shot."

He flashed me a delighted grin and then the phone in his hand pinged. He looked at the screen and his face turned red with anger.

"Everything okay?" I asked.

"Just fine," he said, his teeth clenched. "I gotta go."

"Are you sure you're okay?"

He clicked off his phone and shoved it in his pocket. "Just peachy."

By the sound of bitterness in his voice, he was anything but peachy.

2

Dylan's dad, Oscar, arrived right before closing. Erica had kicked out Tommy and Quinn right after Dylan left, with the admonition that they finish their social studies papers due the next day.

Oscar had a much larger build than Dylan, with a big head to match his big body. It looked even more square with his John Deere hat. He was a talented carpenter, and his big hands were scarred by his work.

"Hi, Oscar," I said. "Are you looking for Dylan? His shift ended hours ago." I debated mentioning that he'd seemed upset, and decided to keep my nose out of it.

"Uh, no," he said, as if embarrassed. "Dylan was supposed to bring home a box of your chocolates but he . . ."

"Forgot?" I said. Oscar wasn't a big chocolate fan, something I couldn't begin to fathom. The only time he came to Chocolates and Chapters was to buy books.

"Yes," he said, anger flashing across his face.

It reminded me a lot of Dylan's expression when he left. Uh-oh. Could Dylan have been mad that his dad asked him to bring home chocolate? But why?

"Well, you know kids," I said. "They'd forget their heads if they weren't screwed on." Which made no sense but I'd heard it often enough to use it to defend Dylan.

At his nod, I asked, "What can I get you? A box of nine, sixteen, twenty-five or thirty-six?"

Oscar hesitated, and then said, "Twenty-five."

We discussed some options and then I probed, using my special chocolate insight. "The Spicy Passion Darks are filled with a zesty passion fruit ganache and chili flakes, with a dash of sea salt on top. Very romantic."

Maybe that last part wasn't very subtle. I rushed on. "Our Cherry Ambrosia truffles have tangy kirsch and dried cherries in the ganache." I remembered that they were in the shape of a heart. "And our Champagne Milks are deliciously light and perfect for any celebration."

He raised his eyebrows and didn't answer.

I backed off, pointing to the ghost and mummy shapes. "We also have a selection of Halloween-themed truffles." I pulled out a sample of my annual protest against the indignity of candy corn that was all over the place during Halloween. I'd spray-painted candy-corn-shaped molds with white, orange and yellow cocoa butter, poured delicious chocolate inside and filled them with vibrant vanilla ganache that I hoped would ruin children's taste buds for that fake stuff forever.

He shook his head. "Four of the Spicy . . . Passion ones."

Ah-ha! It was a date!

He made the rest of his selections, none potentially romantic, to my disappointment. Maybe it was too soon to think he'd begun dating. When I was wrapping up his order, he surprised me by asking, "Dylan doing a good job?"

I paused, sensing there was a lot more to the question. "Yes," I said. "He works hard and seems happy to be here." I swiped his credit card through the machine.

He paused. "I wanted to thank you two for helping him out during our . . . difficult time."

"No problem at all," I said.

He seemed to struggle with his words. "The thing is, we don't have any family close by. You've made him feel at home, and I'm grateful."

My throat closed up. "We love having him here too," I managed.

"Oscar!" Erica called from the hallway. She was using the mop to push our bucket on wheels. "How nice to see you."

He nodded. "You too."

"Did you get that last Jack Reacher book?" she asked.

He shook his head. "No time right now. Maybe during the holidays, when things slow down."

We both said, "Good night," and I closed the door behind him. It was already dusk and the air outside had chilled, sending in an icy breeze to swirl around me.

"Everything okay with Oscar?" Erica asked.

"Yes. He just said the sweetest thing." I took the mop from her, ran it through the wringer and started mopping while I told Erica about our conversation. "At first, I thought he and Dylan were fighting, but then he thanked us."

"Dylan was rather preoccupied today," Erica said. "Maybe you can ask him during your Monday madness tomorrow and see if he's ready to talk about it."

I shook my head. "We only talk about chocolate. Sensitive stuff is your thing."

Bean opened the door, sending the bells on the knob jingling. "Ready?" he asked.

"Yep," I said. I couldn't help the smile on my face. We closed up the shop early on Sunday nights, so it had become our designated date night, often our only date night, given our crazy schedules.

Erica grabbed the mop from me. "You guys get out of here. I'll finish up."

"Are you going out with Bobby?" I asked.

"No, he had to cover for someone tonight," she said, slapping the mop around the stools at the counter.

"Do you need to stop at the Boys and Girls Club?" I asked, feeling a little guilty that she'd still be working and I'd be having fun.

"Harold said they've cleaned up for the night, but I may check it out for a few minutes," she said.

"Did they get the ghost catapult done?" I asked.

"Yes, they did. I'll let you know how it looks." She made a shooing motion with one hand for us to leave.

"Where are we going?" I asked Bean as we went out the front door. The comforting scent of wood burning in someone's fireplace drifted down Main Street.

He seemed a little nervous as he opened the car door for me. "It's a surprise."

"The diner?" I joked.

He didn't even smile. "We'll get some food after."

We got in the car and he headed toward the highway. "Frederick?" I asked.

"No," he said.

"Wait," I asked. "Is Leo okay?"

He took a breath. "He tried to have a good time fishing today, but he's not . . . in a good place."

I bit my lip. "Is it because of the accident?"

He kept his eyes focused on the road. "I got the impression that it brought up some old stuff. From Afghanistan."

"I knew it," I said. "Do you think he's getting better or worse?"

He shrugged. "Hard to tell. He's not sleeping much. Waking up pretty early to ride his motorcycle for hours."

"Is he eating?" I asked even as I worried that I shouldn't be invading Leo's privacy by asking his roommate, my boyfriend, questions I should be asking Leo himself.

Bean stopped in front of a small one-story house. The porch light was on and a real estate agent's sign marked *Sold!* hung from a pole by the street.

I pushed aside my worry. "Who lives here?"

Bean pulled a key out of his jacket pocket and grinned. "Me."

"You bought a house?" I knew Bean couldn't stay forever with Leo, but he hadn't said anything to me about getting his own place.

"Yep," he said, as he got out and led the way up the walk toward the tiny porch. "It's been on the market a while. It was the Yerricks' house."

I took in the large oak trees and trim flower beds. "It's so cute."

The Yerricks had moved to South Carolina to be closer to their grandchildren months ago. Bean opened the front door and flicked the light switch. A small chandelier hung in the entranceway, and a short hallway led to other rooms.

"Pretty." My voice reverberated in the empty house.

Bean opened the door on the left. "My office will be here." We walked in and I looked out the front window. Lights twinkled from homes across the street. "It's small but it'll do the trick," he said, his voice excited.

He walked out into the hall and stuck his head in the next room. "Workout room."

I peeked in the small square room with mirrored sliding doors on the closet.

He took a few more steps. "And bedroom."

A delicious shiver crept up my spine. It was an L-shaped room that had windows on two sides. One window faced tall hedges and the other looked out toward a stand of trees that made it seem all too secluded. With Bean staying at Leo's and me living in the same house as his sister, we hadn't been alone much.

I coughed. "Nice."

"You'll like this," he said, and then led the way to the kitchen.

I stopped in the doorway, immediately falling in love.

The Yerricks had built a long, high-tech, deluxe kitchen. It was tricked out with an endless stainless steel counter, an industrial range hood that would whisk away the fishiest of smells, and a deep farmer's sink. Even the pendant lights hanging over the island were gorgeous, made of rainbow-colored glass.

"Check it out." Bean pushed a button and I heard a machine sound. The whole counter moved sideways, revealing an electric stove top.

"Are you kidding me?" I said. "This must have cost a fortune," I said. "How did she ever move away from all this?"

"Grandchildren," he said simply.

I ran my hand over the counter. "It's beautiful." I imagined making chocolate, spreading out my ingredients on that wide expanse, and then pulled my brain up short. Was Bean thinking of me cooking here?

"I knew you'd like it," he said.

"So you cook?" I asked, hoping I didn't sound like I was fishing for information.

"Of course I cook," he said. "Not like you, but I can handle a real meal now and then."

Then he opened the door to the basement. "Wait until you see what they did down here." We walked down the wooden stairs to a deep carpet that was black with orange circles, which looked like the Baltimore Orioles logo. "Is that . . . ?" I asked.

"Yes," he said. "Mr. Yerrick was a huge Orioles fan."

A small counter lined one of the walls, with a sink and small refrigerator. I imagined it was normally filled with beer cans. And then we came to the pièce de résistance. "Four TVs?" I asked. They took up a whole wall. Four movie-style La-Z-Boy chairs were centered in front of them.

"Are you keeping them up there?" I asked.

"For now," he said.

"You'll probably have all the cable news shows playing."

He laughed. "Probably." He looked at me. "So you like it?"

"It's great," I said.

He walked toward me and ran his hands down my arms. "Now we can be alone."

I smiled, suddenly nervous. Was I ready for *alone* alone? "Especially when you get some furniture." I pulled away and he watched me. "I can see why it was on the market for so long. They made it perfect for just them."

"You okay?" Bean asked.

"Fine," I insisted and then changed the subject. "Is Erica going to help you decorate?" I wanted to make sure he wasn't counting on me for that. My decorating skills were limited to painting truffles. At home, I barely replaced chipped coffee mugs.

"Nah. I can handle it," he said. "I talked the real estate agent into letting me rent until escrow closes. I thought it was a good idea to get out of Leo's hair. I won't do any major work until it's all official, but I think I can handle painting a few rooms, just to start."

"Do you think Leo will be okay living alone?" I asked without thinking.

Bean's smile faded and I felt bad for changing his happy mood. He took a moment to answer. "One of the reasons I'm moving out is because he was getting more concerned about our relationship."

"Really?" I was astounded. "Yours and mine?"

He nodded, watching for my reaction. "I'm hoping that getting a break from me as a houseguest and getting his privacy back may help him."

"That makes no sense. He loves you like a brother," I said. My heart thudded. "Okay, how bad is he?"

"I'm not sure," he said. "But I think the accident caused some kind of . . . resetting, for lack of a better word."

"Resetting?"

"Figuring out what his life should be," he said. "And if Star fits into it. He feels responsible for Star getting hurt, which really shook him up."

"He's thinking of breaking up with Star?" I asked, stunned.

He held up his hands. "I really don't know. I'm just speculating," he said. "You need to ask Leo yourself."

"I will," I said.

"You know what?" he said, drawing me into his arms. "Leo's not here now."

My nerves evaporated. "No, he's not." I pulled him closer.

We ended up eating dinner at the West Riverdale Diner, looking a little disheveled, I was sure. Who knew what would've happened if Bean owned furniture?

"Look what the cat drug in," Iris, my favorite waitress in the world, yelled when we arrived. She picked up two plates of the dinner special—a slab of meat loaf and mountain of mashed potatoes—from the serving window to the kitchen. "Sit right 'ere." She pointed with her chin to an empty table in the back, and delivered the specials to another table.

"Thanks, Iris," I said. I slid over to avoid the duct-taped cracks in the leather, while Bean sat across from me.

"I'm heading over to Frederick to check out couches tomorrow," he said. "If you can get away in the afternoon, maybe you want to come too?"

I nodded. "Sure. If it's not busy. Kona opens on Mondays."

Iris interrupted by slapping two menus down on the table. "I recommend the special," she said. "But stay 'way from the seafood tonight, if you know what's good for ya."

"Thanks," I said. "How are you, Iris?"

Iris had been a waitress at the diner for as long as I could remember. She must have been at least eighty years old and still smoked like a chimney and tanned herself to a deep bronze year-round. "Jus' same as I was last time you ate here," she said. "Except I'm missin' my *60 Minutes* tonight to cover Janie Lee's shift. Dat twit gone and eloped wit' dat idiot Jensen boy."

"Sorry," I said, "but it's nice to see you."

She blew out her breath in a "pshaw," pretending she didn't believe me. "So, two specials?"

We both knew to give in. "Sure," Bean said good-naturedly.

I waited for Iris to head over to the kitchen and yell our order to the cook. "What else are you buying?"

He'd already ordered the basics to be delivered the next day. A bed and dresser, desk and chair, breakfast table and bar stools. Little pieces of life. "But I wanted to see the couch first."

Iris returned, holding our waters in one hand. She set them down and sat beside me. "What you two lovebirds up to?"

"Bean bought a house," I said.

She gave him a long look. "Ain't that nice," she said. "You settin' to stay, then?"

I held my breath, and then Bean's phone pinged. He pulled it out and then a few more phones buzzed, vibrated and rang around us.

"What is it?" I asked him.

His face turned grim. "Someone found a body here in West Riverdale."

"Who?" I asked, my voice faint.

"A woman," he said, focused on his phone. "No identity yet."

Iris pulled her phone out of her apron pocket and tapped at it. "Dat's right. They found 'er at Green Meadows Estates."

She looked up, eyes narrowed. "Beaten to death."

3

Another murder in our small town? Green Meadows Estates was on the outskirts, close to the highway, but still technically part of West Riverdale.

After a fitful night of sleep, rolling over several times to grab my phone and see if anyone was sharing anything new, I'd abandoned my morning run in favor of another cup of coffee before heading into Chocolates and Chapters.

The police were keeping a tight lid on the details, not allowing neighbors or the press anywhere close to the crime scene. I was sure that Reese Everhard, owner of the town newspaper, was gnashing her teeth about that. She'd decided long ago that lurid headlines like *Are Drones Spying on YOU?* and *Keep Your Children Safe from Predators on Halloween!* were the best way to bring readers to her newspaper website. She'd probably been pacing at the crime scene tape, badgering the young officers assigned to watchdog duty. From past experience, I knew that woman would stop at nothing to increase her viewership.

I even stooped to reading Reese's news blog. The headline was *Murder Streak Strikes Fear in West Riverdale* with a photo of the small crowd around the police station. Then she went for broke. *Once again, someone was viciously murdered in our sleepy little town of West Riverdale, Maryland. Just hours ago, the battered body of Faith Monette, a resident of Frederick, was found in an abandoned building in the defunct Green Meadow Estates.*

*Is the killer living among us?*

Even though I knew Reese dramatized anything and everything, her words made me uneasy as I drove to the store.

Monday was usually the best day of the week, when I put aside all of my worries and focused on the chocolate plans for the next seven days, including the new flavors I would create. I juggled making enough to meet the demands of my regular customers—like my hotel and gift basket clients, or like Tonya, who bought exactly six Green Apple Indulgences every Tuesday—with bringing back seasonal favorites—like pumpkin, which everyone fell in love with in late September and discarded like a summer romance in early December. And of course I introduced other recipes to see if I could create new favorites for my customers.

I stood in my storeroom and inhaled the scent of my supplies, which never failed to inspire me. The mellow cocoa fragrance of Felchlin milk chocolate and the sharper bite of their dark chocolate, both from Switzerland and the base of all of my truffles. The nuts and dried fruits that added flavor and texture. The spices with the right amount of magic to bring them all together. I'd learned long ago that no amount of talent could make up for low-quality ingredients, and I used only the best.

Then I realized that Dylan hadn't arrived yet. He was never late for our early-morning sessions, which continued to surprise me. When I was that age, nothing could've gotten me out of bed before I absolutely had to. And he was supposed to bring pumpkin seeds to incorporate into new recipes.

I waited a few minutes and then went into action. Dylan would just have to miss the fun.

For some reason, I was drawn to bitter flavors today. Dark chocolate, licorice and coffee, with a little sour lemon thrown in. Not all together of course. I went into mad-scientist mode, pulling out my recipe binders and spreading out all kinds of ingredients on my counter.

I quickly chopped up the dark chocolate tabs and added cups of them to the double boiler. I was going to push the envelope today, which meant I needed a lot of tempered chocolate to work with, because some of my experiments might not be successful. As the first batch of dark chocolate melted, I stirred, releasing the intense notes of coffee and nuts, and even a hint of citrus into the air.

Maybe the bitter flavors meant I was feeling a little unsettled. A murder in town could do that to a person.

It took me far too long to shut off my mind and lose myself in my ingredients. But eventually the beauty of making chocolate—the action of mixing and pouring the delicious mixture in molds, adding the nuts and fruits, and finishing with decorative touches—soothed me, and I relaxed.

..............

I didn't talk to anyone until after we opened, when I grudgingly rejoined the human race. Kona had followed our normal Monday process, setting up the store on her own and leaving me to work alone in the kitchen.

"What's new this week?" she asked, her brown eyes shining. She and Kayla would be helping me make the chocolates throughout the week, but Kona got as excited as I did about the new flavors.

"Lemon Zest Darks, Anise Stars, Cocoa Bean Drops, and Nutty Turtle Milks."

"Only one new milk this week?" She looked at me. "You okay?"

"What do you mean?" I asked.

"Just wondering if you're, I don't know, in a mood," she said, frowning.

My assistant knew me far too well. "You got that just from the chocolates I made?"

"I calls 'em as I sees 'em," she said flippantly, and then her eyes became worried. "Wait. You're not going to get involved in that murder, are you? I mean, I like the extra hours, but you guys can't keep risking your lives like that."

It was unusual for her to be so serious, and I felt a pang. "We have no reason to get involved." I tried to change the subject. "How are things at Kona's Kreations?"

Kona had started a website to sell anything anyone could want for a bachelorette party—except for male strippers—and business had been booming. Her company was the only place to get anatomically correct chocolate party favors that actually tasted like chocolate.

But she wouldn't be distracted, and she handed me her phone. "Look what crazy Reese wrote."

Reese had added on to the article I'd read earlier, including a long rant about how the West Riverdale police were failing to keep our town safe. That might rile up some of the townspeople but it could also make the police mad enough not to give her any information.

Several people had posted comments below the article. Most were simple *May she rest in peace* remarks about the poor woman who'd been killed. Almost all of them were anonymous, one of them saying, "A bright light is now among the stars." The rest of the comments were spam promoting websites offering financial advice, miracle diet pills, and scam businesses offering high incomes working from home.

Erica quickly walked up to the counter from the back. "Oscar just called me," she said in a concerned voice. "Dylan's been taken in for questioning, and Oscar is on a job an hour away. He wants us to get Dylan out."

"Questioning?" I asked. "For what?"

Just then Quinn and Tommy ran through the front door. "Erica! You have to help Dylan!"

Erica raised her hands. "It's okay. We're going there now."

Kona pointed to the door. "Go!"

"I'll drive," I said, still confused. "Come on."

The teens and Erica rushed out the back with me and piled in my minivan. I'd taken the backseat out to put in shelves for truffle delivery but could fit three passengers.

"The police station?" I asked.

When she nodded, I asked again, "What is he being questioned about?"

"They think he's involved with that woman," Quinn said, agitated.

"What woman?"

"The dead one they found last night!"

"What do you mean by 'involved'?" I asked. "Do they suspect him of something?"

"I'm sure it's some kind of misunderstanding," Erica said, dialing the phone. "Oscar. I have a lawyer friend who can help. May I call him?"

We could all hear his panicked "Yes, of course."

They said their good-byes and Erica clicked on the contact list on her phone. Someone answered in a clear, businesslike tone. "Law offices of Antony Marino. May I help you?"

"Who's that?" Quinn asked me.

I met her eyes in the rearview mirror. They were wide with worry. "A great lawyer," I tried to reassure her while Erica told Marino's assistant who she was and that she needed to speak to her boss immediately. Antony Marino was the criminal defense lawyer we'd worked with before. He was A Big Deal in Washington, DC, and I knew our little West Riverdale police department would not be happy to face him again. "He'll be able to help Dylan."

A few months earlier, Bean had called in a favor to get Marino to take the small-town case pro bono. I just hoped there was some debt left to repay, or better yet, that Erica was jumping the gun and Dylan wouldn't need Marino to get involved at all.

I turned the corner onto Cedar Lane and could see a small group of teens standing in front of the police station. A few of them were members of the comic book club. How had they all heard about this so fast? And why weren't they in school?

As soon as I came to a stop, Erica jumped out.

"Erica!" The teens all tried to speak at once. I thought I heard the word "thugs" a few times, but no way could that apply to West Riverdale Police Chief Noonan. He was way more grandfatherly than thuglike.

Then I noticed the state police car parked on the street. Which probably meant that Homicide Detective Roger Lockett was inside.

Lockett could definitely seem a little thuglike, but I'd had enough experience with him to know how to handle him. Most of the time.

Erica got control of the group. "It's okay. I'm getting Dylan out." She looked at me and jerked her head toward the kids before going inside.

It took me a second to realize that Erica wanted me to see what I could find out. I joined the group of teens. "What's going on in there?"

"The police came into school this morning to arrest Dylan!" Trent's thin shoulders shook with outrage. He was a freshman at West Riverdale High School, one of the younger club members, and along with Tommy and Quinn, one of Dylan's good friends. "They think he had something to do with that woman they found at Cuesta Verde."

Townspeople had nicknamed the Green Meadows development "Cuesta Verde," the name of the housing project in the *Poltergeist* movies. With the development's half-finished abandoned buildings, it had gained a kind of haunted-house status in the town.

"That's not true," Quinn said. "They're just asking him questions."

"Right, that's all." Trent managed to sound sarcastic and worried at the same time.

"Why are they questioning him?" I asked.

Quinn was about to say something and stopped.

Then Trent started to say something, and Quinn shook her head at him.

"Trent?" I asked.

He looked at Quinn and then Tommy. "I don't know."

"Quinn? Tommy?" I asked, my worry coming through. "What do you know?"

"Nothing," Quinn said, but her eyes slid away.

"Stay here," I said, and went inside.

Unfortunately, or fortunately, Erica's boyfriend, Lieutenant Bobby Simkin, was working at the front desk. He'd recently gotten a military-short haircut and looked even more imposing in his uniform.

That hadn't stopped Erica. "I need to see him," she said in an angry voice that meant she'd already said it more than once.

When he shook his head, she grabbed his hand across the counter. "Now."

He glared at her with no hint that they had a personal relationship, even though the whole town knew they were dating.

Another deputy, who everyone called Junior, stood by his desk as if to back him up if he needed help. He looked like he couldn't be older than eighteen, but he could be counted on in tough situations.

She shoved a few pages of club paperwork at Bobby. "Call his father. He told me to come down here. And technically,

I could be considered his guardian, based on what his father signed."

Bobby glanced at it and handed it back to her. "That's a permission form. He's not on a field trip."

She tried another tactic. "His lawyer is on the way. He instructed me to tell you that all questioning of this minor must cease immediately."

"I'll take that under advisement," Bobby said. When Erica eyed the trapdoor that she'd have to lift to get past the counter, he warned, "Don't."

The door opened to the interrogation room, also known as the lunch and dinner room for the police department, and Erica gave up the legal maneuvering. She yelled, "Dylan. This is Erica. Do NOT answer any questions! A lawyer is on the way."

Detective Roger Lockett stuck his head out with an incredulous expression. His eyes zeroed in and he realized it was Erica yelling. And I was standing beside her. The same two people he'd warned before to stay away from his homicide investigations. And here we were interfering with his interrogation.

His eyebrows slammed together so fast, I almost heard the boom. Okay, that was a bit of an exaggeration. But he definitely looked thunderous. Then he was joined by West Riverdale's chief of police, Eric Noonan, wearing the same expression, with white hair instead of brown.

I grabbed Erica's elbow to drag her away. "We'll wait outside for the lawyer."

When she protested, I muttered, "Don't worry. I'm sure Dylan heard you." The whole building had heard her. "He won't say a word."

A camera flashed as soon as we reached the door, and we held up our hands like pop stars fending off the paparazzi. It was not far from the truth. Reese Everhard was clicking away with her camera as if we'd personally confessed.

"Really, Reese?" I said. "It's light out, for heaven's sake. You don't need that stupid flash."

She lowered her camera for a minute while pulling out a microphone and pointing it our way. "Do you know the identity of the woman who was found dead at Green Meadows?" she hammered away, pretending to be impersonal, like a real journalist. "Was it a crime of passion?"

Since Reese was generally in contention for the most idiotic reporter of the year, we ignored her.

She gave up on us and shoved her microphone into a teen's face. "Is the suspect a friend of yours? Is he capable of cold-blooded murder? Or are you here to make sure your friend isn't the victim of police brutality?"

When the boy simply scowled at her, she turned to another. "What do you think about this crime wave hitting our sleepy little town?"

She certainly had a point there, but Erica moved in between Reese and the kid.

"I believe that *child's* father owns Geppetto's Shoe Store, one of your advertisers," Erica pointed out. "Perhaps you should try to find someone over the age of twelve to harass."

Reese actually looked concerned for a moment and then saw Tommy, who had a full beard. She took a step toward him, microphone extended.

"I'm eleven," he said, with a straight face.

Reese, who already resembled a tall awkward bird, stuck out her lower jaw, looking for a moment like a pelican. Then a van from a Baltimore news station turned down the street and she scampered off, elbows flapping, without a word. Most likely, she wanted to get to her office to post her version of the story online first.

Two more vans from rival stations drove up as well. Detective Lockett was not going to be happy about any of this attention.

Erica and I herded the teens away from the growing media. I was sure a few of them would have loved to be on TV, but not in this situation. Once we had them around the corner, Erica answered her phone and listened intently.

I took a few steps away from the group. "What's happening?" I asked when she hung up.

"Marino's almost here and as much as he'd love the publicity for himself, he wants to keep Dylan away from the cameras," she said. "So he's going in to arrange for Dylan's release. Then he'll exit through the front door, and make a statement to draw their attention, while I take Dylan out the back door. You bring the car there and wait, so we can jump right in."

"Sounds good," I said. "What about the kids?"

"Hey, guys." She moved into the center of the pack. "It may be a while, but we're taking Dylan out another way and bringing him to our house until his dad shows up. Can you keep those reporters toward the front of the building? And, Quinn and Tommy, can you get back to your car on your own?"

The group responded with enthusiasm and I slid away to move the minivan into position while Erica went back inside. As I waited behind the police station, I couldn't stop thinking about Dylan. He was only sixteen and already had to deal with so much. He shouldn't have to handle being accused of something so terrible.

And he was a good kid. A hard-working employee, genuinely helpful to customers. The way his friends rallied around him was proof. Then I thought about their reluctance to answer questions. Were they hiding something?

Erica walked out with Dylan in a dark sweatshirt with the hood pulled around his face. They both rushed into the car and I took off as fast as I could go.

"You okay?" I asked Dylan as he pulled his hood off his head and squished himself into the back corner of the car, seeming even smaller than before.

He answered with an automatic "Yes" that he couldn't possibly mean.

"Marino's the best," Erica said over her shoulder. "He'll fix this." If I knew Erica, she was already figuring out how to find out more about the victim, the first step toward uncovering suspects other than Dylan.

"Thanks for calling him," Dylan said politely. He certainly didn't look like a murderer, with his hands scrunched up in his jacket pockets and his brown shaggy hair falling into his eyes.

"I missed you this morning," I said.

He looked surprised, as if he'd forgotten all about coming in. Then his phone rang and he looked down at it. His face hardened. "I'm out," he said into the phone, his tone flat.

I could hear that it was Oscar's voice, but I couldn't make out his words.

"I'm fine," Dylan said. After a few "okays," he hung up.

"Was that your dad?" Erica asked.

"Yes," he said. "He'll meet us at your house."

There was something definitely wrong between Dylan and Oscar, but now was not the time to pry.

We made it back to the house and walked into the kitchen. Erica gestured for Dylan to sit at the table and she sat opposite him.

"Hot cocoa?" I asked.

"No, thanks," he said.

When I just stood in front of him, surprised, he relented. "Okay, sure."

Erica started in gently. "Dylan. What did Detective Lockett tell you about . . . what happened?"

He shrugged his shoulders, in that teen way guaranteed to drive adults crazy.

I moved over to the stove and put my cow teakettle on to boil. My Tropical Cream hot cocoa was Dylan's favorite, sure to soften him up for Erica's questions. I used the best cocoa powder, measured in only enough sugar to make it this side of sweet, and added dried orange zest and a little cayenne pepper for kick. It was like a warm chocolate volcano in your mouth.

Dylan took a deep breath. "He said a woman named Faith Monette was killed at the community center of Cuesta Verde, I mean, Green Meadows Estates, and that something that belonged to me was found near the . . . body."

4

My hands shook and I banged the mugs together, the clang causing both Erica and Dylan to look at me from the kitchen table.

"Sorry." You'd think I'd be used to dead bodies in West Riverdale, the way the last few months had gone.

"Did you answer any questions?" Erica asked.

"I just said that I didn't know anyone with that name," he said, choosing his words carefully.

His tone had changed. We both knew he was lying.

Erica paused. "You're sure you don't know her?"

I peeked out of the corner of my eye while I stirred my homemade mix into the mug.

He glanced up at her, with a hint of helplessness. "No."

She looked at him steadily, an accepting expression on her face.

"I don't know." He moved his eyes to the ground, but his voice wavered.

We heard car doors slam outside and saw that Tommy, Quinn, Trent and two others had arrived, their cars lined up behind Tommy's hearse. I guess they'd decided to skip school. They gathered on the porch, and Dylan went out to join them, probably to get away from us. Erica followed him out to the porch while I got more hot cocoa ready.

I could hear them talking self-consciously about upcoming comic book releases, ignoring the elephant in the room, or on the porch. I brought out a tray of steaming mugs, the sweet fragrance of cocoa filling the air. The railing groaned under the weight of two of the boys reaching for mugs. Erica waved them off and they hopped down to sit on the stairs.

Erica gave them a moment to sip at the cocoa, but before she could ask questions, Oscar arrived, screeching his pickup truck to a diagonal halt in front of the hearse. Oscar ran toward the porch but slowed when he saw Dylan hadn't moved. Then as if something broke inside him, Dylan dashed down the stairs and hugged his dad in a way I was sure he'd be embarrassed about later. We couldn't hear their short conversation, but it was punctuated by some forceful questions by Oscar and sniffled answers by Dylan. We all stood rather awkwardly on the porch, wavering between joining them and staying out of the way.

Erica walked down to greet Oscar and they talked, again in a frustratingly quiet way so I couldn't hear. She handed him a card, most likely Marino's, and Oscar and Dylan headed for the car.

Dylan turned, his eyes sweeping over all of us on the porch, and said a heartfelt, "Thanks."

We watched them drive away. The rest of the teens seemed unsure if they should still be there. They sent meaningful glances at one another over their mugs of hot chocolate, and then looked away. None of them met Erica's eyes. They knew something. What could it be?

The ever-observant Erica didn't miss any of it and got to the heart of the matter immediately. "The only way to help Dylan is to tell us everything you think might be relevant," she said.

Silence. Tommy peered sideways at Quinn, who gave an almost imperceptible shake of her head.

Erica didn't let up. "Tommy? Quinn? No ideas?"

Nothing.

I stayed out of it. Erica was the one they knew well and trusted from their comic book club meetings.

"That doesn't sound like you guys at all," Erica said. "You're usually full of ideas, all kinds of ideas." Her intense expression betrayed the cheerful tone she used.

Still silence.

"Wow." She sounded so disappointed in them that I couldn't imagine how they weren't spilling everything they knew. I was ready to make something up to avoid her sad expression.

"Who's up for more hot cocoa?" I asked in an effort to alleviate the uncomfortable silence on the porch.

Quinn stood up. "Not for me. Thanks. I gotta go."

The others shot to their feet with a bunch of "Me toos" and they started placing their empty mugs on my tray.

Erica let her shoulders drop. I thought it was a little dramatic, but maybe that's what worked on teens. "I guess when you're ready to help your friend, you'll tell me what you know," she said. "In the meantime, the police will come to their own conclusions." She went inside totally composed, not even letting the screen door slam.

I stayed behind as they all shuffled away with guilty backward glances.

Their silence made me even more nervous for Dylan. What were they hiding?

Erica didn't speak until we'd cleaned the mugs and headed back to work. I recognized her deep-thought expression and waited until we were almost at the shop. "So, do you think we should look into this?"

She blinked a few times from the passenger seat, as if not sure where she was. "First, we need to find out why the police are interested in Dylan. And if that's easily resolved, we have no reason to investigate."

I nodded. "That makes sense."

"But if Detective Lockett persists in this line of inquiry, we may have no choice," she said.

Uh-oh. The more upset Erica got, the more snotty she sounded.

It wasn't her fault. She'd always been the town genius who aced high school, college and grad school, and she was expected to talk that way. Sometimes I still wasn't sure how she and I, the community college dropout, became best friends.

"What did Oscar tell you?" I asked.

"Just that he's keeping Dylan at home, from school and the store, until this all blows over," she said.

I hoped that would be soon.

The store was bustling with gossiping customers when we arrived. "Thank goodness you're back," Kona said. "It's been crazy."

Erica stopped to talk to her sister, Colleen, who was working on the bookstore side, and then headed toward her office in the back. She was most likely typing "Faith Monette" into her computer as fast as she could open it.

I grabbed an apron from behind the counter and asked the next customer, my neighbor Henna, "What would you like?"

Henna was the poster child for finding yourself at any age. After her husband's death, she'd re-created herself as an artsy hippie. Today she'd wound tiny flowers through her now-blond hair, and wore several silver bracelets on each arm. "A chocolate torte, please."

"Coffee?" I asked. Henna had recently let up on her health food habits to include caffeine.

She nodded. "Have you heard anything about that poor woman?"

I shook my head. "Just what everyone else knows. Why?"

"I thought Erica might have learned something from Lieutenant Bobby," she said in a conspiratorial whisper.

I didn't mind gossip, especially when it brought in customers, but not when it came to my best friend. "I don't know what you're talking about."

She snorted. "Right. I know you two are going to get involved in this. It's in your blood."

I curled my lip. "Ew. It is not."

Then Detective Roger Lockett came into the store and my brain went on high alert.

Henna looked over her shoulder and turned back with a

smirk. "I'll bet you five dollars that you two are investigating it by the end of the week."

I thought about Erica's comments in the car and the look on Lockett's face. "No bet."

"Good morning, Detective," I called out cheerfully. "Coffee? Chocolate? Both?" Maybe I could find out something to clear Dylan so we wouldn't have to get involved.

He sat down on a stool at the counter, his eyes shadowed with exhaustion. Even that tired, he emanated a tough energy, with his wide shoulders and long-ago-broken nose. "The largest coffee you got."

Henna lingered by the cash register until I shot her a *get lost* look. She smiled knowingly and went out the front door.

I poured coffee for the detective and slid the creamer over. He reached for it and I noticed a ring on his left ring finger. The wedding ring finger.

Whoa. I thought about how to ask him about the ring. It wasn't that I couldn't imagine any woman being interested in him. He was attractive in a rumpled big-guy kinda way, and when you threw in that authority-figure thing, it even overcame his somewhat surly nature. It's just that he'd never talked about his personal life with me.

I pulled out some of my Wild Huckleberry Milks and put them on a plate in front of him. "Yinz guys have a tough night?" Lockett had a strong Pittsburgh accent and I had picked up some of the region's unique expressions from an ex-roommate who was also from Pittsburgh. I enjoyed trying them out on the detective, but he might not appreciate it as much as I did.

He gave me a sardonic look. "You could say that."

I leaned my elbows on the counter with chin in my hand

like I was listening intently to whatever he had to say. "You're not here for the coffee or the truffles, even though those Wild Huckleberry Milks are awesome, if I do say so myself. We put the preserves on the top, and the berry flavor is intense. So what's up?"

"Can I just drink my coffee in peace before you harass me?" he asked. "Actually, I'm here to speak to Erica."

"Okay," I said, "but I think she's in her office talking on the phone with Marino." That was a lie, but I knew mentioning Dylan's lawyer would bother him.

"Great. A media circus is the last thing this town needs." He bit half a truffle. "Awesome," he said grudgingly, as if not wanting to admit it. Then he popped in the rest.

I let him savor it for a minute, giving it the right amount of respect before asking, "You mean we should count on Reese's journalistic standards to get our information?" I was sure he'd already read her insulting column.

He shook his head. "Yeah. We really enjoyed her 'Keystone Cops' line."

"She's a wordsmith," I said with sarcasm.

"I was told that Dylan worked here." He looked down at his truffle. "Do you know him well?"

That got me ruffled. "Really? You're here looking for gossip?"

His jaw tightened, probably gritting his teeth like he usually did around me. "It's called an investigation."

"He's a good kid," I said in a flat tone, and then changed the subject. "I like your ring." Just then it glinted in the light coming through the front window. "Are those diamond chips?"

"Yes," he said, looking wary.

"So, you're married?" I probably shouldn't have used that slightly incredulous tone.

He raised his eyebrows. "This is so sudden," he said. "Aren't you taken?"

I tilted my head. "Actually, crotchety, reclusive older men aren't my type."

He winced. "Ouch. You went for crotchety *and* old?"

"Okay," I said. "I'll stop being nebby about your personal life." I paused. "Nebby" was Pittsburgh-ese for "nosy," and I wanted to get it out there before he used it on me.

"You're going to be nebby your whole life," he said.

I realized that could have two different meanings. "You mean, like, *curiosity killed the cat* nebby?" I asked.

"No," he insisted. "Like *old lady spying on neighbors* nebby." He took a sip of coffee. "You okay? You don't usually focus your annoying questions on me."

I pursed my lips, as if considering which way I wanted to go. "You'd rather I ask questions about that dead body at Cuesta Verde? I mean Green Meadows?"

"You're calling it that too?" He glanced around to see if anyone was close enough to overhear. A couple of customers looked away, trying to seem uninterested. "If Erica is done with her phone call, perhaps we can talk in the back."

I glared at several of my nebby customers.

Lockett picked up his coffee, his ring sparkling again, as if begging me to ask.

"So, a promise ring?"

"Let it go," he said.

I smirked. I'd get it out of him soon enough. I led the way back to Erica's office.

Erica shut her laptop as we walked in. She must have

already started researching the murder victim. "Detective Lockett," she said. "How nice of you to stop by and give us an update."

He ignored her maneuvering. "Ms. Russell. Want to show me what you're hiding on your laptop?"

"Of course," she said with such warmth that I thought she meant it. "As soon as you show me a warrant."

He smiled, as if he knew he never had a chance.

"What can I help you with?" she asked. "You'd like some information on Dylan, I suppose. Can you tell me why you'd even begin to suspect a young boy like him?"

"First of all, he isn't so young," Lockett said in his tough-guy voice. "He's just small for sixteen. But plenty big enough to use a bat and kill someone."

A frisson of alarm went through me, and not just at the word "bat." Lockett seemed to have his sights set on Dylan, and he had chosen his words to deliberately scare us.

"A bat?" I asked.

Erica went into investigation mode right away. "Was the murder weapon found?"

"No," he said.

"But you found *something* that led you to Dylan," she said.

"Yes," he said. "His Green Lantern key ring."

My heart stopped for a moment before speeding up. The *Green Lantern* was Dylan's favorite comic book series. I knew his mom had given him a key ring with the superhero's symbol on it. He'd never talked about it, but I suspected that was one of the reasons he carried it every day.

Erica's face went still for a minute and then angry. "There must be thousands of those. How do you know that one is Dylan's?"

"It has a Duncan Hardware Store rewards tag that we traced to his father and his house key on it," he said in a no-nonsense tone.

Erica shook her head. "He could've lost it or loaned it to someone."

"Yes," he said. "That's what we were trying to find out when we were talking to him at the police station. Unfortunately, we were interrupted by a disturbance in the lobby."

Erica didn't react to his dig. "He was talking to you before that?"

"No," he admitted. "But he would've." At her skeptical look, he added, "Believe me. I know how to handle a sixteen-year-old kid."

"And it's legal to question a minor without his parent present?" she challenged.

He scowled. "There are gray areas, and this was one of those."

"So the victim's name is Faith Monette?" I asked, trying to get them off that topic. I wondered if Erica had already told her assistant and tech guy, Zane, to research the victim. He was an online wizard who could dig up all kinds of information, maybe something to take the heat off Dylan.

"Yes," he said. "Did you get that name from Dylan?"

He sounded like he was going to try to lead us somewhere. To shake up his rhythm, I spoke quickly. "It's not a secret. Reese blabbed it to the universe." When he scowled, I changed the subject. "Most of Green Meadows was abandoned when the developer went out of business. What could the victim possibly be doing there on a Sunday night?"

He frowned. "We don't know," he said. "But it's not where she was killed."

"What?" I asked.

"Her body was left at the Green Meadows community center," he explained. "We're looking for the original murder site." He used our stunned surprise to ask his own question. "So what do you know about Dylan and his family?"

Erica shrugged. I could see that she was taking time to figure out how much to tell him before she could ask more questions. "He's a bright kid. A straight-A student who's planning to go to college for electrical engineering. Obviously I know him as an employee and a member of the store's comic book club, and he's fantastic at both of those—committed and caring. He's close to his father. You're probably aware that his mother moved to Florida this summer, after somewhat of a scandal. He's a devoted son. His friends love him." She paused. "I'm not sure what else I can add, except that I know he's not capable of killing someone, especially with a bat."

I held back a shudder.

"We have reason to believe there was more than one assailant," Lockett said, carefully watching her reaction.

Suddenly the room felt absolutely airless. Was this why the comic book club members weren't talking?

5

Detective Lockett was not happy that we rushed him out of there soon after he dropped his second bombshell. Before he left, he informed us rather emphatically that whoever was responsible should come forward before the police found the site of the murder. That it would reveal more clues and make it harder for him to offer any kind of deal to the killer. "Or killers," he'd added.

"This isn't good," I said to Erica. "We have to help Dylan."

"Absolutely," she said.

"Time for a project plan?" I asked.

Erica thought any problem could be solved with a ruthlessly organized project plan. "Of course."

Zane West walked in, sighing with a put-upon air. "I know," he said. "You want me to look into that woman's murder. What do you have?" Today he wore his usual boating look—a green and white striped T-shirt with matching green long shorts and a bright yellow windbreaker, collar up. He pushed his hipster glasses up on his nose with one finger and sat down at his desk, which was wedged into the small office next to Erica's.

Zane studied computer science in college and was the tech expert of most of the Main Street shops. His burgeoning, not always quite legal, skills to access information us normal people couldn't get to had come in handy before.

"I'm so glad you're here," Erica said. "You know we can't do this without you."

He looked pleased even though he knew Erica's tactics as well as the rest of us. "Name? Age? I don't suppose you have a Social Security number."

Erica smiled. "Faith Monette. She lived in Frederick."

"That's it?" he said. "Wunnerful." That last part must be sarcasm.

I left them to work their computer spelunking magic and stopped over to see how Colleen was holding up. Just a few months before, we'd had our town's first murder in a decade, and the victim had been Colleen's best friend.

"Can you believe we have another murder in West Riverdale?" she asked. She'd recently started highlighting her light brown hair, which made her face seem brighter somehow. Or maybe it was because she was happier in general after ditching her cheating husband.

"I know," I said. "It's terrible. Are you okay?"

She nodded. "Did you see the news coverage of Marino?" she asked. "He zoomed up to the police station in that stretch limo, wearing that bowler hat and brandishing his cane at the reporters."

He must have done a good job drawing attention away

from Dylan's escape out the back. "He does arrive in style," I said. "Did he talk to them?"

"Of course," she said. "His usual, 'While the death of this beautiful woman is certainly a tragedy, let's not compound the tragedy by rushing to judgment of an innocent young boy.'"

Her pretend-deep voice caught me by surprise and I laughed.

"I can just imagine his courtroom bellow booming down Cedar Lane," I said. "Did he use his 'In this great country of ours, everyone is innocent until proven guilty' bit?"

"Oh yeah," she said, and then we both sobered.

"What do you know about Dylan?" I reached over to straighten an already neat stack of the latest Michael Connelly book, feeling uncomfortable that I was essentially inviting gossip about one of our employees and a child. And I'd given Lockett a hard time for exactly that.

"He's been great here," she said. "His mom, Gilly, was in my Bunco group, but I never knew her very well. We were all completely surprised that she, you know."

That she ditched her family and ran off with a married man?

"Does she keep in touch with them?" I asked. "Or anyone around here?" Maybe now would be a good time for her to provide some support, to her son at least.

"She used to be friends with Yvonne, but they had a falling out," Colleen said.

"Boys and Girls Club Yvonne?" I asked.

She nodded. "Some of the Bunco moms thought Yvonne was letting Gilly know what was happening with her son."

"What's wrong with that?" I asked.

"Oh, you know how judgmental people can be," she said.

"A bunch of them said that Gilly didn't deserve to know what was going on after what she did."

"That's too bad," I said.

"Personally, I think they're happy Gilly's gone and Oscar is single," Colleen said.

"Really?" I asked.

"Oh yeah," she said. "He started dating right after Gilly left, but nothing ever worked out," she said. "Some of the Bunco crowd say he's still hung up on his ex-wife."

"A few?" I asked.

"It's a small town," she said. "A nice guy with a decent job? He's a great catch."

I felt my phone buzz and looked at the screen. It was my brother, Leo. I waved my cell at Colleen in the universal "I have to get this" symbol and answered it. "Hey, Leo."

"You're not investigating this thing, are you?" he demanded without a greeting.

"What are you talking about?" I winced at my defensive tone.

Our parents had died when I was fourteen and Leo was eighteen, and even though he'd officially been in charge of parenting me, he'd always acted like a big brother and not a "parent."

"Don't play dumb," he said. "I know the kid works for you, but that doesn't mean you need to get involved." He sounded almost frantic.

"Leo, are you okay?" I asked. "You never worried like this before."

"I'm fine," he said, with so much emphasis it couldn't be true. "This isn't about me. It's about you and your safety."

"Why don't you come to the store and see that I'm totally safe," I said, trying to sound reasonable.

"Just promise me that you're staying away from this whole mess," he said.

"Leo," I said. "This isn't like you. What is going on?"

"Promise me, Michelle," he insisted.

I took a deep breath. "You know I can't do that," I said quietly. "Why don't we have dinner tonight and talk about this?"

He hung up.


Just like always, whenever something newsworthy happened in our town, we had more customers than our usual Monday. They ate my Booberry Whites and pretended to browse books, but inevitably joined together in little chattering groups. As I served coffee and chocolate, making my way around the tables and chairs of the dining area, I overheard snippets of conversations. "And after all he went through with that nasty divorce, to have his son accused of something so awful. Such a shame . . ." and "I can't imagine that boy doing something that terrible. He just cut my grass and refused to take money!" and "Superman would pull his freakin' head off!" Okay, the last one probably wasn't about the murder.

May Jensen, owner of the Enchanted Forest Flower Shop next door, bustled in after her lunch break, the scent of roses trailing after her. She'd always worn clothes the color of whatever flower she had on sale—today's outfit was a pumpkin scoop-neck shirt along with a rust-colored corduroy skirt—and she'd recently started wearing flowery perfumes to add to her marketing ploy.

"Orange roses?" I predicted, automatically getting her usual order of Spicy Passion Darks ready. She loved any of my chocolates that had a zip, but especially this combination of spicy and tangy.

"Oh!" she exclaimed, bringing her wrist to her nose. "Is it too strong?"

"No," I said. "You know me." Erica liked to say I was hyperosmic, because of my ability to distinguish between scents. It was a curse in the gym, but was a huge asset in making chocolate.

"Whew!" she said. "I wanted to invite you to the Coco Kitten Lottery party on Saturday."

"Wow! That time went by fast. Are the kittens old enough to leave their mother already?" Coco had started off as a stray cat that visited a bunch of the Main Street shops for meals, and wormed her way into the affections of the whole town. She had given birth to six kittens and we were all enthralled by their adorable behavior. My favorite was Truffles, one of the boys that May had let me name. He was always the first to come to me, climbing up my pants with his tiny claws, demanding my attention. He was also the one who seemed to take after Coco the most, trying to get out of anyplace May attempted to keep them. The only thing that seemed to work was a closed door, and he was most likely working on a way to escape that too.

Coco had finally settled down in May's home with her kittens, and we hadn't seen her wandering Main Street since then.

"Yep, the vet said this week is fine," she said. "I'm going

to pull names from a hat, and the winners get to pick their kittens."

I felt a pang of regret that I wouldn't get one of Coco's kittens. But neither Erica nor I were home enough to take care of one and there was a long list of West Riverdale citizens who were dying to get one of the well-loved Coco's babies.

"What time is the lottery party?" Maybe one of my assistants could close up on Saturday. And since I was free early, maybe after May's lottery party I could have a Saturday evening date with Bean to make me feel better about not getting a kitten. And maybe— I stopped myself right there. We were still new to this dating thing.

"Three o'clock," she said. "Are you sure you don't want to throw your name in the hat?"

I sighed. "Just can't."

During a lull later in the afternoon, Kona was preparing a tray of smaller sample-sized versions of our Fleur de Sel Caramels, the scrumptious, mouthwatering bestsellers and what we readily admitted were our gateway drug. "The Knit Wits Yarn Store is demonstrating a new loom," she said. "I'm going to take these over to get a few more of their customers hooked."

"Great idea," I said. Once people tasted their perfect combination of sweet chocolaty exterior and smoky, liquidy caramel inside with a sprinkle of sea salt on top, they'd be totally addicted and come into the store for more.

Of course, as soon as she left, a group of ultrarelaxed customers who had just finished their yoga class came in, quickly followed by a group of moms who'd just dropped off their children at the dance studio in the same rec center. I rushed around until they were all served and happy.

Our friendly neighborhood accountant, Phoenix Keogh, strolled in, and I almost wished I'd been the one to take the tray to the yarn store. I hadn't yet compiled the end-of-quarter financial reports he wanted. We weren't scheduled to meet for a few days, but sometimes he asked questions ahead of time so he could prepare. I needed my own time to get everything ready, at the last minute, if past performance was any indication, so it always flustered me when he showed up. Like when I saw my dentist in the grocery store and checked my flossing job with my tongue before talking to him.

"Good afternoon, Michelle," he said, radiating a calm joy that was uniquely Phoenix. "Your business is booming, I see." He looked around with satisfaction as if he was personally responsible for it. He wore his normal businesslike attire, a gray suit, a blue button-down shirt that matched his eyes and a colorful tie pulled loose.

Now that I knew him better, I realized that being one of his clients probably had helped us along. He was the best networker I knew, regularly updating us on the business news of other clients through his newsletters and social media. He was his own public relations firm, free to his customers.

Phoenix had been one of the first openly gay students I'd known in high school, invigorating the Gay and Straight Alliance Club with his bright energy and skillful handling of the bullies. He'd started blogging back then, before everyone in the world was doing it, and had won national awards for encouraging diversity and acceptance, all of which had paved the way for his Ivy League education.

A lot of us were surprised when he'd returned to West Riverdale after grad school and a stint in a public accounting firm to set up his own accounting business. Erica's store had been one of his first clients, and luckily, he'd given me the same "old friend" discount when I signed on with him.

"The regular?" I asked, already moving to make him a cappuccino.

"Absolutely." He sat at the counter. "I wanted to thank you for your referral. It looks like we'll be working with May."

"That's great," I said. "She's a very cool lady. I guess now we'll be hearing all about peonies and poppies in your newsletters."

He smiled. "Whenever the poppies are on sale or otherwise newsworthy."

I kept my eyes on the machine while it steamed the two-percent milk he preferred. "Before you ask, I'll have that P&L you want before we meet, so don't worry."

"You mean, don't nag," he said with a rueful expression. He reached into his pocket and slid a wrapped box toward me.

"You didn't need to do that," I said. I poured the milk into the wide-mouthed mug and spooned the foam onto the top, the coffee scent filling my senses and making my mouth water.

I handed him his coffee.

"Open your present," he said. "I hope you like it."

I tore off the paper and opened the box. It was a paper-weight molded to look like my chocolate bars. I traced my logo, *Chocolates by Michelle*, below the *Chocolates and Chapters* one. "It's perfect. Thank you!"

He took a sip of his cappuccino, his eyes looking pleased. Then he cleared his throat. "I actually wanted to get your permission for something special."

"What?"

"You and Erica put your stores together more than a year ago," he said in a careful tone. "What do you think about taking it a step further and combining the accounting to make it one business? In a financial sense, I mean."

I stared at him, surprised. While the name on the store was Chocolates and Chapters and our customers could pay for items from both stores at the same cashier stand, we tracked the items independently through our accounting systems.

Erica and I had discussed the idea when we combined our stores, but had decided to keep our actual businesses separate. At the time, I was more worried about being a burden on Erica's family bookstore, which had been running since the 1950s.

He rushed on. "I'm putting it out there, to both of you, as a way to save expenses. There are economies of scale you two may be able to take advantage of, from insurance to taxes, that could reduce your overall costs." He smiled. "Even your accounting expenses."

My mind immediately started whirling with what-ifs.

Phoenix lost his smile when I didn't answer right away. "But if it's not what you want, no problem. We can revisit this in the future."

I bit my lip. "What do you need permission for?"

He waited a moment as if making sure I'd meant it. "I'd like to have my staff prepare an analysis of what I believe you'd save and present it to both of you. If you decide to move forward, you'll form a legal partnership."

I took a deep breath. "If that works for Erica," I said. "It works for me."

"She was next on my schedule," he said. "Is she in her office?"

I nodded.

"Thank you again for your referral to May." He reached out and patted my hand. "Either way it'll be fine."

His soothing tone usually made me feel comforted, but I couldn't let go of the feeling that if we combined our businesses, something might change. And what Erica and I had right now was pretty perfect.

Both sides of our shop were doing fine. I easily met payroll, covered the rent, and even put a little away for that industrial-sized chocolate-tempering machine I'd been pining for.

I watched Phoenix walk down the hall toward Erica's office. I'd always liked that the financial parts of our businesses were completely up to each one of us. Would Erica and I start depending on each other even more than we did now? What if one of us starting having trouble? Would the other one feel resentment?

My brain swirled with possible pros and cons and I pulled out strawberries to dip while I waited for Phoenix to leave. When he waved good-bye, I scooted back to Erica's office to see what she thought of his idea.

She looked up from where she and Zane had been conferring over his computer. "Oh no," she said.

"What is it?"

"Zane found a dating website that Faith Monette used," she said. "It seems like she talked to a lot of men."

"But that's good, right?" I asked. "That's a lot of people who might have had a problem with the victim."

They both had dismayed expressions.

"We thought so," Erica said. "But then he found another dating site, where she had an account under another name—Faelynn Monet."

"Okay," I said, waiting for the other shoe to drop.

"Here is one of her matches." Zane turned the computer around to show me a photo of Oscar Fenton.

6

Dylan's dad was dating the murder victim? I drew in a deep breath.

"Shoot," I said.

This was a connection I didn't want to see. It led to way too many things to consider, things like "motive" and "means." Was Dylan not talking to us because he was hiding something about his father?

"We have to talk to Oscar," I said.

Erica nodded. "I'll call him. But I know Marino told him not to talk to anyone about anything. And I heard . . ."

"What?" I asked.

"The police are searching his house right now."

"Uh-oh." They must have thought that Dylan's Green Lantern key ring was enough evidence to justify a warrant. "What else did you find out about Faith?"

"Just this so far," she said. "Zane's trying to learn more."

"How many men are we talking about here?"

Zane shook his head. "She linked up with at least a hundred."

"She dated one hundred men?" I couldn't keep the shock out of my voice.

He shrugged. "I can't tell how many of them she actually met in person yet."

"So that means there are still a lot of potential suspects, besides Oscar and Dylan," I said.

Erica looked at me. "Only one that we know of with physical evidence near the body. So far."

"Right," I said.

"But it gives the police a lot of people to investigate," she said. "Which will keep them busy."

"What does Faith have in her dating profile?" I asked.

Zane turned the computer around and clicked a few times, and I looked over his shoulder at a photo of a pretty smiling woman with highlighted brown hair and brown eyes. The profile said she was twenty-eight, with an athletic build, that she wanted kids, and that she was "curious, adventurous, entrepreneurial and fun." Her favorite quote was "Life is not measured by the number of breaths we take, but by the moments that take our breath away."

"That quote would appeal to a lot of people," I said.

"Let me try something," Zane said.

I watched as he copied the photo into Google Images search and waited for the results. Several Facebook pages popped up, each with a different name.

His eyes opened wide. "She's a catfish."

"What's a catfish?" I asked, thinking of the ugly bottom-dwelling creatures.

"Someone who creates an online identity different from their real one," Erica said.

"Like lying about your weight and age on your dating profile?" I asked. "Doesn't everyone do that?"

"No," Zane said. "Like pretending to be someone else entirely. Using someone else's photo and lying about everything—your job, your family, your interests." He clicked to the different Facebook pages. "At least she used her own photo."

"Can you find out what she was up to?" Erica asked Zane.

"Yeah," he said, his eyes focused on the screen, filled with thumbnail photos of Faith. "It's going to take some time."

By the next morning, Zane had compiled files on several of Faith's identities. She seemed to have taken catfishing to an art form. She had several different identities on Facebook and dating websites—with different education and job info as well as completely different friend lists and interests.

"Usually catfish develop only online relationships with other people," Erica said while we opened up Chocolates and Chapters. "But Faith 'graduated,' for lack of a better word, to meeting and dating men she met online."

"Why did she do that?" I asked.

"My theory is that she made money from this somehow," Erica said. "It's a lot of work to keep up so many lies, especially in person. She had to have a good reason."

"All that seemed pretty easy for Zane to find," I pointed out.

Erica knew where I was going with that thought. "So Detective Lockett probably has the same information."

"Let's hope he finds something and leaves Dylan alone," I said.

Erica nodded. "I finally got in touch with Quinn. She's the only one who would agree to talk to me about what we found out last night." She stopped in the middle of dusting the dining area.

"What's wrong?" I asked.

She shook her head. "I can't believe my comic book kids don't trust me."

"They're teenagers," I said. "They can't think ahead enough steps to know what's good for them."

I was about to ask Erica what she thought about Phoenix's idea to combine our finances when she asked out of the blue, "How would you like to go to a high school reunion?"

"No way!" I said in mock horror. I couldn't imagine a less fun evening. "It's not time for our next one yet, so whose reunion are you talking about?"

"When I was doing my own research, I saw that Faith's class from Buckey Central High School is celebrating its ten-year reunion," she said. "It's not clear if she was even planning to attend—she came up on their Lost Classmates list."

I made a little map in my head between the high school and Faith's address, which Zane had uncovered. "That's weird," I said. "She didn't live very far from the school. And with Facebook, how can you be lost, unless you want to be?"

"Maybe she had a bad time in high school," Erica suggested.

"Who didn't?" I said.

She looked down and didn't answer. Oh yeah. Erica was the star of our class. She'd had a delightful high school experience. And then she went on to to excel at Stanford and win a freakin' Fulbright scholarship. "There's an email address to ask for info on the event," she said.

"Are you going to be in charge of our next reunion?" I asked, teasing.

"Maybe," she said. "Be careful what you wish for."

"What does that mean?"

She smiled. "When it comes to projects, where I go, you go."

"Noooo!" I gave a dramatic shudder.

"The reunion is next Friday." She handed me piece of paper with a name and phone number. "Here's the person handling all the reservations."

"How does this help us?" I asked.

"I'm not sure," she admitted. "But just because Faith's listed as missing doesn't mean she didn't keep in touch with some of her high school friends."

Then I thought about the timing. "We can't go to the reunion. The festival opens the next day."

"*You* can go. With Bean maybe," she said. "I'll hold down the fort."

"Hold down the fort?" I said. "Are we seventy?"

"Come on," she said. "It'll be like a date."

A date. I could do that. "Are you sure? Would they let us attend when we didn't even go to that school?"

"Talk her into it," she said. "Pretend you're Bean's assistant. Say he wants to do a piece on reunions."

"I'll try," I said. "Worst case, we'll crash." Just like they did on TV. I had a short fantasy of picking up a random person's name tag and talking to "my" fellow classmates as they tried to reconcile their memories with the person standing in front of them.

"Maybe you'll find out something we can use to help Dylan," she said, and went to turn the sign on the front door to Open.

I called the number and a perky voice answered. "Hello?"

"Hi," I said. "Is this Honor Tambor?"

"Yes," the woman said carefully, waiting to see if I was a salesperson.

"My name is Michelle. I'm an assistant to Benjamin Russell, the reporter, and I wanted to find out if I could attend your reunion next weekend."

"Benjamin Russell from West Riverdale?" she asked.

"Yes," I said tentatively. "His book—"

She gasped. "OMG! Is he looking into Faith Monette's murder? I didn't know that was worthy of a Benjamin Russell story!"

"I'm sorry," I said. "Mr. Russell is actually doing a piece on high school reunions in these days of social media."

"That's a great cover," she said enthusiastically. "We'll tell everyone that. But meanwhile, I have some ideas of people who he should look into."

Whoa. I had to back her up. "He's really not looking into this murder you're talking about."

"Right," she said. "I think we should all meet to discuss this in more detail."

"I'm sure that's not—"

"Of course it is," she said. "I talked to her just days before she was killed. She was coming to the reunion."

"You did? She was?" I asked.

"Yep," she said. "I was class president, so I'm in charge

of the reunion. I know *everything*. So how about I meet him and you, if you're in this area, at his bookstore."

"What bookstore?" I said, getting an ominous feeling.

"The one he owns with his family," she said impatiently. "I was there, at his book signing. Are you sure you're his assistant?"

I sighed, knowing a bulldozer when I heard one. "Okay. What time is good for you?"

"Really?" she asked. "I'm going to meet Benjamin Russell?"

"I'll check his schedule, but you and I can get started and see when he can join us."

"Fine," she said. "But it'll be way beneficial to his story if we meet. In person."

Three hours later, Honor Tambor arrived at Chocolates and Chapters, looking exactly like her Facebook picture. Late twenties, perfect hair and big smile. She wore a small pink backpack with some sorority letters on it and pink sunglasses.

"You must be Honor," I said. "I'm Michelle."

"So nice to meet you!" She looked around the dining area expectantly, and then her smile faded. "Is Mr. Russell not joining us?"

"He'll be here," I said. "This story is really important to him." I tried to take control of the meeting right up front by pointing to a table in the corner. "I reserved this for us."

She walked right past me over to Colleen, who was working at the cashier counter on the bookstore side. "Erica!" she said as if they were long-lost friends.

Colleen looked up, startled. "No. Colleen."

"Oh!" Honor said. "So nice to meet you. I'm a huge fan of your brother."

Colleen got a knowing look on her face. "We have some signed books of his if you're interested."

"I already have one," she said. "As do all of my friends. Gifts from me. It's so cool that he's practically from our own neighborhood." She looked around. "Is he here yet?"

"No, sorry," Colleen said. "He's—"

"He's joining us later," I said.

"Are you sure?" Honor took a shaky breath. "I promised myself I wouldn't fan-girl, but I'm not sure I can stop myself."

"Let's get started," I said, leading the way. "Kona, can you take Honor's order?"

"Of course," she said, laughing.

"Michelle?" Colleen said. "Can I talk to you a minute?"

"Sure." I turned to Honor. "I'll be right over."

"Looks like Bean has an admirer," Colleen said. "Maybe we should start a fan club."

"I'm hoping she's an isolated incident," I said.

"Better not tell her who Bean is dating," she said with a smile.

I joined Honor at the small table in the corner as Kona delivered iced tea and Fleur de Sel Caramels. "Before I forget, please keep this meeting and what we discuss confidential. We wouldn't want to influence anyone's behavior."

She opened her eyes in delight. "Oh! I hadn't thought about that." She took a bite of caramel, closing her eyes and giving a long groan. "Now, that's a little bite of heaven right there. The balance of gooey caramel with the chocolate, and the perfect amount of saltiness? I just *have* to bring back a dozen of these for my friends. No, two dozen!"

Okay, maybe I liked her a little. "Mr. Russell would like to write about the experience of high school reunions in these days of social media. Classmates can easily stay in touch these days. How do you think that affects your reunion in particular?"

"It's so helpful!" she said. "We keep up-to-date on each other's lives, so we have more to talk about when we get together." She sipped her iced tea. "Not everybody stays in touch," she said. "We have a Lost Classmates list of people who no one has email addresses for."

"That's understandable, because email addresses change," I said. "But they're not on social media?"

"Nope," she said with a *can you believe it?* look. "Faith Monette was on that list."

"Really?" I acted dumb. "She wasn't on Facebook?"

"Actually, she was," Honor said, "but her profile picture was a photo of her cat or something and she never responded to any friend requests, so no one knew it was her."

"Then how did she find out about the reunion?" I asked, and then realized that I might sound too curious about Faith. "Maybe the article can help others find out about stuff like that."

"She emailed me that she had seen the announcement on some reunion page and asked why she hadn't received an invitation," she said. "I told her she was on the Lost Classmates list and sent her an Evite. She wrote that she was excited to see me, which was total nonsense."

"Did you take her off the Lost list?"

"Oh yeah," she said. "I announced it on the Facebook page."

Interesting. I had to tread lightly here.

"Why do you think some classmates want to stay lost?" I said. "For example, as far as you know, Faith wasn't in contact with her classmates for years. Did she have a hard time in high school?"

Honor let out a scoffing laugh. "Hard time? Hardly." She looked around to make sure no one could hear her. "I hate to speak ill of the dead, but Faith was like, the ultimate mean girl. Really popular." She gave a little sniff. "For all the wrong reasons, of course."

"What do you mean?" Was it a coincidence that as soon as the class mean girl was found, she was dead?

"She was just so nasty to anyone who wasn't in her little group," she said. "Today she'd be labeled the bully that she was, but back then we all just dealt with her the best way we could."

"But you were class president."

She nodded with false modesty. "I know. Lucky for me she wasn't interested in anything like that—just Homecoming Queen. And Prom Queen of course."

"What kind of bullying did she do?"

"She was just vicious. At the time, I thought she could read everyone's mind and know the exact thing they didn't want anyone to know." She stopped to think, with a look of vulnerability. "For me, it was that I was a little overweight. I can't tell you how many times she whispered things like 'fat pig' at me as I walked by. Or she'd make fun of my name, saying things like 'On her tambourine is here.'" She rushed on to add, "But she was much worse to others, especially anyone really on the outs."

"Like who?" I asked, even as I heard Erica's grammar ghost whispering "whom" in my ear.

"Everyone," she said. "The goths, the druggies, the wannabe jocks, the nerds. Even the kids who just wanted to be left alone. *Especially* them."

"Wow." Inside I was thinking, *That's a lot of people with motive*. "Did *anyone* like her?"

"I don't think so," she said. "She went to college in Colorado or someplace out West and didn't even tell anyone when she came home. At least according to her friends. They were all shocked that she lived so close for the last few years and never contacted them."

I realized that we'd been talking about Faith for a long time. "Did you 'find' any other students on the Lost Classmates list?"

She chatted on about several of the "found" students until I asked, "Are you collecting any kind of information about your classmates? Jobs, families, that kind of thing?"

"Oh yes!" she said. "But our survey is way cool. Instead of those stupid questions like 'How many children do you have?' we made it all about high school. Like, favorite lunchtime experience, most embarrassing story, who'd you have a secret crush on, that kind of thing. Someone on the reunion committee is putting together a slide show with photos and answers to the questions for the party."

"That *is* cool," I said casually, even though I was thoroughly excited at what could be a treasure trove of useful information. "Another way social media is influencing reunions. Is there any chance you could send me the questions and responses? We wouldn't use any of it in the story without your permission."

"Sure," she said. "We emailed it to everyone we could find, and it's part of the Facebook page too. I can add you if you send me a friend request." She brought Facebook up on her phone. "Oh wait. You want to be a secret, right? Let me think of a name you can use." She paused to think. "You know, it's too bad you're not taller. We had a Swedish exchange student that you could pretend to be." Her eyes made a sweep of the store. "So when is Benjamin getting here?"

"Let me text him and see," I said. "While we're waiting, did any of the answers to your survey surprise you?"

She frowned as she scanned the answers on her phone. "There was only one. When we first sent it out, Wade Overton emailed it back right away. And he said he had a crush on Faith Monette way back when."

A crush? "Why did that surprise you?"

She shrugged. "He was this really quiet guy in high school, hung out in the machine shop mostly. I doubt she ever even spoke to him."

"Is he coming to the reunion?" I asked.

"Yes," she said. She glanced at the door and her face lit up.

Bean had arrived. I wondered if that's what my face did when I first saw him.

t took all of my control not to slap Honor's hand off of Bean's arm while she finally said good-bye. I'd tried to find Erica while Honor gushed over Bean, but she had run over to the post office. Finally, Honor was gone and Bean told me that the only additional information he'd learned was that Honor was single and her high school crush had been the captain of the water polo team. Not at all helpful. He seemed highly amused by Honor's adoration before he left.

I filled Erica in about Faith's mean-girl reputation when she got back. "She mentioned only one person who seemed to actually like Faith in high school," I said. I explained about the questions for the reunion. "Wade Overton said he had a crush on Faith back then."

She shrugged. "Worth a shot. Should I ask Zane if Wade was one of her dates?"

"Sure," I said. "I wonder why she wanted to attend the reunion after so many years of ignoring her high school friends."

"Maybe she was planning to apologize," she said.

Sheesh. Erica really liked to see the best in people. Even a catfish like Faith.

# 7

Later in the evening, Erica and I were at the Boys and Girls Club, meeting with Harold Duncan about where to place the vampire coffin so it wouldn't hit anyone when it opened. Harold's son Sammy was putting special hinges on it to make it spring closed once the vampire inside wasn't holding it open. I was sure something was going to go wrong with this prop at some point, but we were on a fast-moving train that wasn't stopping until opening night.

The club looked so crazily different from the place where I'd spent so much time growing up. It wasn't just the blackout paper covering the windows, the dark walls we'd built to guide the customers to their next frightening moment, or all the scary decorations we'd placed everywhere. When I'd been at the club, someone else had been in charge of all the kids' safety. Now we were in charge.

But Yvonne was the Boys and Girls Club director, and she didn't seem worried at all. "If we angle it deeper into the corner, and place the glow-in-the-dark tape showing where to walk farther away, it'll be fine."

Quinn had backed out of meeting with Erica at the shop, but she had shown up to volunteer for the festival preparations. We'd asked her to help Janice the Costume Lady spray red paint onto the zombie costumes, so we knew where she'd be all evening.

I noticed her walking toward the now-empty quiet room, so I gestured for Erica to follow me. Quinn set down her backpack, which was covered with patches of superheroes.

She turned to go and saw us in the doorway, and looked trapped. She obviously didn't want to talk to us. Luckily, I'd grabbed her favorite chocolates as a bribe and held out the box. "Watermelon and Cotton Candy Whites?" I didn't work with a lot of white chocolate but some of my customers loved it.

She took the box reluctantly.

"How is Dylan doing?" Erica asked.

Quinn's face froze. "He's fine."

"Have you seen him?" I asked.

"No," she said in a grudging tone. "Just texted."

"We're just trying to help," Erica said. "You know that, right?"

"I can't tell you anything." She took a bite of her truffle and the pink filling oozed out.

Oh man. That meant there was something to tell.

"We know that Oscar was dating Faith," Erica said quietly.

Quinn's eyes widened, but she didn't respond.

"And we know Faith was a catfish," I added.

Quinn pressed her lips together hard, as if forcing herself not to say anything, and stared at the floor.

Erica ducked her head to try to get Quinn to look at her. "Did Oscar know?"

Quinn took a short, fast breath and blurted out, "Oh my God, it was so obvious! She said she was some big-time real estate agent and then Dylan couldn't find anything about her so-called business and told his dad."

"Did his dad ask her about it?" I asked.

"Yes," she said. "And then she pretended to admit that she really was just a secretary to a Realtor and was getting her real estate license, like she was ashamed or something. But even that wasn't true. She didn't even have a job."

"How do you know that?" Erica asked.

Quinn stuck out her chin. "We followed her. A lot. She never went anywhere but her apartment and on dates."

They followed her?

Erica seemed shocked as well, taking a moment to respond. "Who followed her?"

"We all did. Dylan, Trent, Tommy and me," she said. "We took turns so she wouldn't recognize us. And Dylan's dad didn't even believe us when we all told him together that she was a liar."

"What did Oscar say?" I asked.

"He told Dylan to stay out of his business."

"What did Dylan do then?"

"Nothing." We could see her close down. "I have to get to work. Right now."

She pushed past us, and we let her go.

..............

When we opened up on Wednesday, I was surprised and delighted to see Coco sitting on the back porch of Chocolates and Chapters, her brown tabby fur almost blending into the wood. "Are you getting ready for empty-nest syndrome?" I asked her. Maybe she'd resume her Main Street shop visits once she was kitten-free.

She stayed on the porch and waited patiently for me to go back inside and dig up some cat food, just like our old routine. I sat on the little porch and petted her while she purred and ate.

It was amazing how much Coco's visit comforted me. I hadn't realized how much I'd missed her.

When she finished eating, she thanked me by cleaning her face on my jeans. Then, tail high in the air, she took off for her next visit, and her next breakfast.

I grabbed the empty bowl and went back into the store to find Erica rearranging bookshelves. Kona appeared from the back, tying her apron as she walked. "Did you guys see Reese's article?"

Erica pulled her phone out of her pocket while I whined, "Am I going to have to read her blog every day now?"

"You might want to see this," Kona said. She turned her phone around and I took it from her so I could read.

*Murder Victim Victimized Twice!* the headline said. It seemed that Faith Monette's apartment had been ransacked and robbed the same night she was killed. Reese was already predicting that whoever had robbed her had killed her, which to be fair wasn't too far-fetched.

"What could a twenty-eight-year-old own that someone would want to kill her for it?" I asked Erica and Kona.

Kona looked offended. "I have plenty of stuff that people want. TV, my gaming system, computer—"

"Computer!" I said.

Erica's eyes narrowed. "Maybe someone wanted the information she had on her computer."

"Enough to kill her for it!" I sounded way too dramatic, as if I'd just cracked the entire case. "Do you remember when I couldn't find my laptop at the haunted house and Zane tracked it down for me?"

Erica nodded, probably already two steps ahead of my thinking process.

I went ahead anyway. "If what Reese wrote is true—and you can ask Bobby now that it's public—then maybe the police don't have Faith's computer yet. And if the police don't have it, then maybe Zane could figure out where it is."

"If we found it, we'd have to give it to the police," Erica warned while she texted Bobby.

"I know." I smiled. "But maybe we can, you know, at least check out her emails first?"

Kona gave a big sigh. "You guys can't help yourselves, can you?" She grabbed her phone from me, and I pulled mine out of my back pocket.

Erica's phone dinged. "Bobby says it's true and to leave it alone."

"At least he answered you." I was already dialing Zane, not realizing that it was still early in his world.

He answered with a sleepy "Yeah."

"Sorry to wake you, Zane. This is Michelle," I told him,

in case his brain wasn't processing voices yet. "Is there any chance you can use that same app that you used to find my computer and track down the location of Faith's computer?"

He was silent on the other end for a moment. "Give me a minute." He hung up.

I couldn't help my excitement. "If Faith is anything like us, she had her whole life on that computer."

Zane called back. "Luckily for you, she has the same app. And she uses the same password for just about everything. It says the computer is at her home address."

"You're sure?" I asked. "How accurate is that app? If it was at her home, why wouldn't the police have taken it?"

I could almost hear his shrug. "Pretty accurate. The app gives me the address. It's an apartment complex, so the computer could be anywhere at that location." He yawned. "Why? What's going on?"

I filled him in about the burglary, and then realized I'd never learned if the guy who had liked Faith in high school was in touch with her. "Did you find out if that Wade guy was one of Faith's dates?"

"Yes I did. And no, he wasn't," Zane said.

There went that idea.

We said our good-byes, with Zane most likely going back to sleep, and I told Erica what he'd found.

The bells on the front door jingled as Bean walked in.

I smiled. "Hey. Want to take a field trip this afternoon?"

"Sure," he said. "Is this about Dylan?"

I explained about the computer still being in Faith's building.

He got his "on the hunt" look. "Now?"

Amused at his impatience, I said, "No. I have to make a batch of Goji Berry and Himalayan Salt Dark Chocolate Bars."

He relaxed. "Goji berry?"

"Yes. They're amazing for antioxidants," I said, "and delicious." I picked up my phone. "I'll see when Kayla can come in." The call went straight to voice mail and I left a message.

Erica gave me a serious look. "You two need to be careful. Whoever is holding on to that computer may have killed for it."

Kayla wasn't free until one and then Bean got held up on his own investigation, so we didn't get started until late in the afternoon. Bean drove in his nondescript Honda, and we made it to the address of Faith's apartment complex, which Zane had provided before the evening rush hour. It was a series of relatively new two-story buildings along a country road. The first foray of development into the countryside that would inevitably lead to more and more buildings and fewer and fewer trees.

Faith's building was on the end, with a huge banner that said, *First month FREE!* It seemed to contain four nice-sized apartments on two floors. "What do we do?" I asked.

"Let's knock on doors first," Bean said. "We'll see what we can learn from her neighbors."

As we got closer, we could see the crime scene tape fluttering across a door on the second floor. Was that where it happened? Whoa. I had to calm myself down. Detective Lockett hadn't said if the police knew where the murder occurred yet. Her apartment was still sealed off as a crime scene, so we wouldn't be able to get in there.

We split up the downstairs units and each knocked on a door. Nothing.

We both went upstairs to Faith's neighbor. A small dog yapped from inside, but no one answered.

"Let's see if we can find the super," Bean suggested.

Just then I got a text from Leo. *Staying out of trouble?*

That was weird. *I'm out with Bean.*

*And staying out of trouble?* Leo repeated.

I held up the phone to show it to Bean. I could tell we both had the same thought, that maybe Leo was actually following us. We scanned the road and didn't see Leo's car or motorcycle. We shouldn't have bothered. Leo had been a Marine. If he didn't want us to see him, we never would. I texted him again. *Of course. I'll call you in ten?*

He didn't reply. I checked behind us several times as we followed a winding cement path to the pool and barbecue area. We found a door with a Building Manager sign and hours when he was available. Bean knocked and a bow-legged man with a grizzled face opened the door. He could have been anywhere from sixty to ninety.

He frowned. "Not talking to no reporters."

Wow. He had pretty good radar.

He tried to close the door but Bean stuck his foot in. "This isn't about the murder," he lied. "I'm working on a piece about keeping people, especially women, safe. We've learned that your tenant was dating men she found online and that may have led to her death."

The manager stared as if evaluating whether he could trust Bean.

I stepped forward. "Do you have a daughter?" I asked. "I'm only asking because I'm a victim too. Not as terrible as what happened to Ms. Monette, but . . ." I let my voice trail off. "I'm doing what I can to make the world safer." Maybe I was getting too good at lying for an investigation.

The manager scowled, but held the door open. "Come in, I guess."

"Thank you," Bean said and pulled a small notebook out of his jacket. "Could I get your name or would you like to be anonymous?"

"Anonymous," he said. "But you can call me Floyd."

I looked around the living room, where bookshelves filled with models of various NASCAR cars lined a whole wall. The rest of the room was filled with an eclectic assortment of furniture. Maybe he kept what tenants left behind. "Cool collection."

He nodded. "Thanks."

"Thanks for talking to us, Floyd," Bean said. "Since our story is about being safe online, do you have any knowledge that Ms. Monette used an online dating service?"

He shook his head. "Just that she had more than a few fellas sniffing around."

"Have the police given you any information about the burglary that occurred? Do they think it's connected to what happened to her?" Bean asked.

Floyd sat up straight in his chair. "No! And you don't put that in there. This is a safe place."

Bean held up his hands. "Of course. It certainly looks safe. Did they say anything about the murder happening here?"

"No," he said. "They didn't find anything here. Just her stuff missing."

"Okay," Bean said. "Any idea who broke in to her place?"

"No idea," Floyd said, shifting in his seat.

"What kind of security cameras do you have?"

"Why you asking that?" he said, starting to get riled up. "Don't have any. No need."

"Did she have friends here in the complex?" Bean asked. "Someone that looked out for her?"

Floyd reacted with something between a snort and a "pshaw." "There's that Chuck fellow. Total pothead. His folks bought him this condo and every time he gets himself fired, they tell me they're gonna sell it and put him on the street. But they never do."

"Chuck?" I asked. "Where does he live?"

"Next building over," he said. "But he didn't help her none. She probably helped him."

"What do you mean?"

"Just that she paid his rent once in a while. I suspect it was when his folks cut him off," he said.

"Thanks so much for your time," Bean said. "We have to go. We have an appointment with Detective Lockett to see if he can provide any safety information for our piece."

Floyd nodded. "You're plenty welcome."

"I hope it's okay if we come back. My editor may want some more information," Bean said as Floyd walked us to the door.

"Sure, sure," he said.

After quick good-byes he shut it behind us, but we still kept an eye out until we were sure he wasn't watching us. Then we made our way back to the building beside Faith's.

I called Zane. "Any chance your map isn't so accurate?"

"What do you mean?"

"Could it be in the next building over?"

"I guess," he said. "It's not military accuracy or anything."

"Thanks." I hung up.

We went through our knocking-on-doors routine again and got no answer on the ground floor. On the second floor, someone was working out to an exercise video—the pounding music and stomping feet gave that away. We moved to the other door and Bean knocked.

Nothing. The scent of stale beer and pot smoke oozed out. The super had said Chuck was a pothead.

"Chuck?" I called out.

Nothing.

"Pizza delivery." Bean tried the doorknob and then pulled something from his pocket.

"Really?" I hissed as I recognized lock picks.

"Block the view from the street." He pulled black gloves from his pocket, handed me a pair, and put his own on.

I turned my body as I put on the gloves. My heart was beating wildly as I searched the area, feeling like a total criminal. Nothing moved. This was serious breaking and entering, which didn't seem to be outside Bean's experience. In a few clicks, the door was unlocked and we walked into a mess.

The inside smelled like a college dorm, not that I knew much about that. Dirty laundry, rotting food and cigarettes. I was startled to see a young man with disheveled hair sprawled facedown on the couch. He didn't move at all when we entered.

The furniture appeared to be high quality, but was scarred with burn marks, and warped and stained by dark liquids. Beer cans and take-out food containers littered the floor.

"This guy needs help," I whispered to Bean.

He stood over Chuck for a minute and watched him. "Just passed out. He's breathing fine and his color is good," he whispered.

Then he walked to the dining room table, which was covered with electronics. A laptop was open. I typed in the password Zane had given me and the home page appeared.

"It worked!" My voice came out in a squeak. I looked over at the sleeping man. Whoa. We'd found the burglar. Had we also found Faith's killer?

Bean pulled a thumb drive from his pocket and handed it to me. "Copy all of the documents."

Then a loud knock sounded on the front door and I nearly jumped through the roof.

Oh. My. God.

8

I looked at Bean with wide eyes. He shook his head, and then pointed to the computer. With shaking hands, I put the thumb drive in and dragged the mouse over the Documents icon to copy them.

A loud knock came from the door again. "Michelle." It was Leo! "I know you're in there."

Chuck snorted and turned over on the couch.

Panic curled up my stomach.

Bean stayed calm, his eyes on the computer. "Get all the photos and download files too. I'll see if there's another way out." He walked over to peek into the kitchen and pointed. "Back door," he said quietly.

My phone vibrated in my pocket and I pulled it out. Leo was calling me. I put it back.

Leo tried the doorknob. "Bean, if you don't open this door . . ."

"Let's go!" I reached to pull out the thumb drive and he walked over to stop me.

"One minute won't hurt," he said. "Let it finish."

Then Bean went into the bathroom, and I heard water running while I watched the Copying bar slowly fill in until it said *Complete*. Finally!

Bean came out of the bathroom, leaving the water running.

"What are you doing? We have to go." I'd been attempting to play it cool but the screech in my voice negated all that.

"Come on," he said, and headed toward the kitchen.

Then I heard someone stomping up the back steps. It had to be Leo. I pulled Bean back and we went out the front door, running down the stairs to the car. For some reason, I felt like giggling, like a kid getting one over on a parent.

As we drove away, I looked back and saw Leo limp around from the back. My breathless laughter died. I called him. "What are you doing?" I asked with no attempt at pretending we hadn't been there.

"Having fun running from the cripple?" Leo said, making my whole body burn with shame.

"I'm—"

He interrupted me. "Tell Bean his ass is grass." He hung up.

We stayed quiet on the drive back to West Riverdale.

"I guess it's a good thing you moved out," I said.

Bean nodded. "As long as we're in trouble," he started, trying to sound lighthearted, but I could hear the strain. He wasn't happy about upsetting Leo either.

"What?"

"Let's go check out Green Meadows Estates," he said. "Maybe the police finished the investigation of the site."

"What?" My voice was a little alarmed. I cleared my throat and knocked my tone down an octave. "It's getting dark."

"You know, they have these newfangled things called flashlights," he reached into the floor of the backseat and pulled out a huge Maglite, put it on my lap, and then pulled out another one.

He brought two of them? "You planned this?" I asked.

"No," he said. "I'm just always prepared."

I raised my eyebrows at him.

"Okay," he admitted. "I thought it would be a good idea if we had the time."

"Can't it wait until tomorrow?" I definitely sounded wimpy.

"Sure," he said, and then clucked like a chicken.

"Wow. Peer pressure." I laughed. "Okay, let's go."

He smiled like he'd won. "Let's stop for dinner first and wait for it to get darker, so it'll be harder for anyone to ID us."

We went through a drive-thru, and then parked to eat in the car. It was dusk when we made it to Green Meadows Estates. The lights that would have shone on the entrance sign no longer worked, but a street lamp showed us the way. Most of the homes were empty, but it looked like a few brave souls still lived there, their houses lit against the oppressive dark.

The half-built houses were even more depressing, looking like the contractors had left in mid–hammer hit, with half-done roofs, partial walls and muddy yards.

We drove by a house that was actually lived in. It was

close to the community center, where Faith had been found. The owners had put out pumpkins for Halloween, but there wasn't a chance of them getting any trick-or-treaters.

The unfinished community center loomed ahead, the car's headlights casting spooky shadows on the wooden framing, reminding me of the skeletons in the Halloween Festival.

Bean parked, leaving his headlights turned on, and we got out. I took a deep breath and let it out slowly. The ground around the building was crunchy with overgrown grass that had folded over and dried out in place. Wind whispered in the trees overhead and I jumped when I saw one end of the crime scene tape flap around.

"What are we looking for?" I asked, my voice sounding too loud in the hushed quiet. "All the evidence must have been prepped and taken by the crime scene techs already."

"I just want to see where she was found," he said. "Maybe something will pop out that helps us clear Dylan."

I tripped over something, and when I shined the flashlight on it I saw that it was a white hose from the no-longer-functioning sprinkler system. We walked up the simple wooden steps through what looked to be the main doorway, and went into the lobby area.

It would have been grand, I thought, with a soaring atrium and ballroom beyond. But now it was rotting away, open to the elements for far too long.

Bean followed the crime scene tape. "Here," he said.

Even with the strong flashlight beams, I couldn't see anything different. Until I focused on a dark spot on the floor. "Is that . . . ?"

"You don't have to look," he said, but I couldn't keep my

eyes off it. I knew Faith hadn't been killed here, but all the evidence tags left behind meant something had happened. Right there.

Bean examined the site from all angles, shining his light along the walls and even getting his face close to the floor to check every inch.

He walked back to the doorway, and then all around, looking at the floor. "Any idea how much she weighs?"

"She claimed one hundred and ten on her dating site," I said.

"Does Dylan work out?" he asked.

I shook my head. "Not that I know of."

"What does he weigh?"

"I don't know. One twenty-five?" I answered. "Soaking wet."

"There aren't any drag marks," he said. "She was carried in."

I shuddered at the thought of someone carrying the lifeless woman into the building. Completely in the dark. But I saw what he was getting at. "So even if she was telling the truth about her weight, there's no way Dylan could've carried her in."

"Lockett must realize it as well," he said, his face lost in the shadow of the flashlight.

"He said there might have been more than one assailant," I said slowly, wondering if two boys could carry a dead body. Like Tommy, who was big but not necessarily strong, and Dylan together.

"Lots of footprints here," Bean said. "Could be the police, but that might be the reason Lockett is looking for more than one killer."

Just then a minivan drove toward one of the few houses

with lights on. It paused as it drove by, clearly checking out who was at the crime scene at night. The woman driver looked vaguely familiar. "Shoot," I said.

"It's okay," Bean said, turning his flashlight to peer at the doorway once again. "It's too dark for anyone to recognize us."

"Are you sure?" I asked, not wanting to be that obvious about our investigation.

"Yep," he said. "And we're done here anyway."

Before sunrise the next morning, Reese knocked on the front door as soon as I stumbled my way to turn on a light in the kitchen. She must have been waiting for some kind of indication that Erica or I was awake. If I'd been alert enough to check who was at the door at such an ungodly hour, I certainly wouldn't have opened it.

She was wearing a pen camera in her front pocket, even though the whole town knew what it was by now. "What do you think of the arrest of Chuck Sinsle for the murder of Faith Monette? Are you going to stop messing around and let the real police do their work?"

No one should have to face that nonsense so early in the morning. I shut the door in her face without a word and went back to the kitchen to put water on to boil. I'd had a tough night, worrying about Leo. He hadn't taken any of my calls and hadn't responded at all to my apologetic messages or texts.

"You have to come out sometime," Reese yelled from the porch.

I pulled my laptop out of my backpack and found an article on what Reese was talking about. Chuck had been arrested last night, based on the discovery of Faith's belongings in his apartment. It seemed his super saw them while responding to a minor flood in the apartment below.

I winced, hoping the flood had been caught before causing too much damage.

Erica walked down the stairs, ignoring Reese's repeated knocks, and looked over my shoulder. "Nice work."

"It was Bean's idea." I got up to grind the beans and pour the boiling water into a French press. "I just hope that the files tell us something. Did Zane tell you what he found?" I'd decided the night before that I didn't want any evidence of our little B&E on my computer, and Bean and I had delivered the thumb drive to Zane.

"Not yet. He'll call me when he wakes up." She got the cream from the refrigerator. "What does Reese want?"

"Not sure," I said. "She wants to know what I think about this arrest. Maybe she thinks she's rubbing it in that we didn't help figure out whodunit?"

Erica shrugged. Even a genius like her couldn't figure out Reese.

I sat down and read the article again. Something didn't feel right. Maybe because I wasn't sure this answered all of our questions.

"So, mystery solved?" Erica said, watching me.

We should be counting our lucky stars, but I couldn't quiet the sense that we weren't finished. "Do you think so?"

She shook her head. "I wish it was solved, but there are some remaining questions. And Lockett won't stop until he answers them."

"I'm sure he wants to find out what Dylan's Green Lantern

key ring was doing there," I said. And I wanted to find out what the comic book club was hiding.

She sighed. "To say the least."

We were both silent as I pushed down the press and poured the coffee.

"Did you get in touch with Leo?" she asked. I'd told her the whole story the night before.

I shook my head. "Bean told me that before he moved out, Leo had started getting up really early and taking long motorcycle rides for hours. I was thinking of trying to talk to him when he comes back."

"Sounds like a plan," she said. "You go out the back and I'll distract Reese. Maybe you can catch Leo before we open."

I knocked on Leo's apartment door but he didn't answer. His motorcycle was gone from his assigned parking spot in the garage. I waited on the steps leading up to the second floor for over an hour, the coffee cup I held for him getting cold, but he never showed up. I watched many of the apartments come to life with stirrings of his neighbors getting ready and leaving for work. Where was he?

I headed in to Chocolates and Chapters, feeling overwhelmed by my worry for Leo, on top of the investigation. Something was going on in his head about my investigation—following Bean and me to Chuck's proved that—and I couldn't help wondering if I was letting my brother down by helping Dylan.

The news of the arrest of Chuck Sinsle for the murder of

Faith Monette was the topic of conversation all morning. I kept my mouth shut about what had happened with Bean. Admitting to criminal activities was never a good idea, even to our closest friends and customers.

The bells on the door jingled, and Leo's girlfriend, Star, walked in. She was in dark blue workout clothes, which probably meant she was on her way to a personal training client.

"Hi!" I always acted too enthusiastic around her, like a mom trying to marry off her kid. "Latte this morning?"

"Sounds great. Nonfat please." She took a seat at the counter, moving the silverware around nervously.

"Torte? Chocolate?" I asked while working on her espresso drink. "I have your favorite Dark Chocolate Lava Cakes." She'd said many times that she loved the sensation of the chocolaty liquid center melting so quickly on her tongue and spreading its intense cocoa taste.

She seemed tempted, but shook her head. "I'm actually here to ask if you know . . ." She trailed off and then cleared her throat.

It was unlike Star to be so uncertain.

"How Leo is?" I prompted.

"Yes." She took a deep breath. "I seriously debated discussing this with you, but I'm a little worried. He hasn't seemed happy lately. Since the accident really."

"Did you ask him about it?" I asked.

She nodded. "I tried. Several times. He never wants to talk. I thought you might know . . . something."

"I'm sorry. He hasn't told me anything. But I noticed he's been acting strange," I said. "Like worrying way too much."

She bit her lip. "He freaked out when he heard about this woman."

I went still. "Do you know why? He's never worried much before."

Star twisted her hands together. "He's been kinda messed up since the accident." She met my eyes. "I'm concerned."

I covered her hands with one of mine. "Me too. I'm going to call his therapist. He won't tell me anything that Leo told him, but I want to make sure he knows that we're both concerned."

She nodded, still worried, and then a group of preschool moms came in, with their passel of kids noisily lightening the mood. I served a bunch of coffees and warm cocoa, along with pastries and the last of my Earl Grey Tea–Infused Milks.

Star finished her coffee and waved good-bye as she left. I started formulating what I'd tell Leo's psychologist.

Then Detective Lockett walked in.

"Good morning," I said, pouring him a coffee and wondering what he wanted. It was definitely not a social call.

"Thanks," he said, pouring cream in and stirring.

"I hear you got a break in the case," I said. "Congrats on winding up the investigation so quickly."

He didn't even crack a smile. "I got a phone call this morning."

Uh-oh. That couldn't be good. My satisfaction went out the window.

"Someone told me you and Mr. Russell were at the scene of our suspect's apartment yesterday afternoon." He took a sip of his coffee, keeping his eyes on me.

I leaned oh-so-casually on the counter. "Yinz guys can't always trust those anonymous calls, you know dat, right?" Distracting him with Pittsburgh-ese expressions didn't seem to be working.

"This one wasn't anonymous," he said.

I straightened.

"It was your brother," he said. "Seems he was sure you and your boyfriend were inside Mr. Sinsle's apartment. He's concerned about your safety."

"That's . . . interesting." I gritted my teeth, my earlier worry now morphing into anger at Leo's meddling. "He's having some overprotectiveness issues lately." To say the least.

"I get it. The whole big-brother thing." Lockett nodded.

"Yeah, but that's going overboard," I said, not regretting throwing Leo under the bus. I pulled out a tray of Lemon Zest Darks and quickly put them on a plate. "You should try these new truffles—they have an amazing citrusy zing."

He raised his eyebrows. "Zing?"

"Zing," I repeated.

"You know what else I heard?" He took a bite of the truffle and savored it for a minute before continuing, probably knowing the waiting drove me crazy. "The building super was happy to confirm that the two of you visited him at the same time that Leo said you were there, breaking into an apartment. And that you were asking questions about Faith's friends. How lucky was it that said friend had a mighty convenient flood that brought the super to the door so he could see the items missing from the victim's apartment and call the police?"

I'd planned for this. "Wow, what a coincidence. Bean interviewed the super for his new article on Internet security," I said. "I just tagged along." Shoot. It came out in my *I'm telling a bald-faced lie* voice, not anything like I'd practiced. I blamed Leo—his tattling put me off my game.

"Sounds like a great date night," Lockett said, with obvious sarcasm. "Find anything interesting on that computer?"

"What computer?" Shoot! My eyes slid away at the last second.

He shook his head. "Look. I'm never going to give up on telling you guys to stay out of my police business, and don't think for a second that I won't arrest you for obstruction if you screw up my case." He paused as if not sure he wanted to tell me something. "Just so you know, the papers got it wrong. We arrested Sinsle for burglary, not murder."

I took in a quick breath. "He didn't do it?"

"We don't know for sure yet," he said. "But we don't have any evidence linking him to the murder. Right now the only thing we have on him is burglarizing the victim's apartment."

I blinked at him.

"I'm definitely getting him for obstruction as well." He took a sip of coffee. "So maybe you want to stay out of my way so I don't do the same to you."

"Don't you have a ton of paperwork to do with that arrest?" I asked, wanting to get rid of him so I could tell Erica the news.

He smiled and then his phone rang. "Lockett," he answered.

I watched his face change and his whole body tense as he listened to whoever was on the other end. I'd seen that look before. It was his *time to hunt a killer* expression. "I'll be right there." He hung up and got to his feet. "Gotta go."

It looked like he'd caught another break in the case.

9

I waited for him to leave and rushed back to Erica's office, where she and Zane were poring over the information Bean and I had "found."

"Something's up." I told them what Lockett had said, about Chuck being arrested for burglary and not murder, and about the phone call. "Can you, I don't know, call Bobby or something?"

"No," Erica said. "He won't tell me anything."

Zane clicked on a website that offered a live feed of what was being broadcast on the police scanner. He bypassed the Listen Here button and read from the transcribed information at the bottom of the page.

"There's nothing here," he said. "They're keeping it off the radio."

"Did you find anything yet from all that?" I asked, looking at Zane's computer.

"Yes." She looked up, troubled. "She juggled quite a few men."

"How many?" I asked.

"A lot," Zane said. "Like thirty. So far."

"Thirty?" I asked. "At the same time?"

He shook his head. "Over the last couple of years."

"Anyone stand out?" I asked. "Who's got the highest MQ?" Erica had probably already started some initial estimates of what she called each suspect's "murder quotient."

"I'm working on it," she said. "I just need more time." Her voice grew distant as she sat down and focused on her screen.

I went out on the back porch to get some amount of privacy so I could leave a message with Leo's therapist. I outlined what Star and I had discussed, knowing he wouldn't be allowed to call me back. I still felt better.

I took a deep breath and headed inside, but stopped for a moment to send my traitorous brother a text. *You're tattling on me?*

He texted back immediately. *You doing something you shouldn't be?*

The relief I felt when I saw the three dots that indicated he was responding was short-lived. *Lockett told me what you did. Stop it.*

*I'm still your big brother. My job is to keep you safe.*

I didn't answer.

*I care about you.*

He knew that would work. *Don't do it again,* I sent back and put the phone in my pocket. The rest of what I had to say to him would have to wait until we were face-to-face.

I went back out front, where Kona had propped the door open, taking advantage of the warm October day. I thought about trying to find Leo at his work, to apologize for running away from him at Faith's apartment building, and also to tell him that following me was not okay. But his hours were so flexible that it would be hard to catch him in his cubicle. It was one of the reasons his job was so perfect for him. As long as he got all the data input on time, he could be there any time, day or night.

There was plenty of whispering among our customers, with a lot of glances at their phones, as if they were waiting for news that hadn't come yet. I couldn't shake the ominous feeling that something bad was about to happen.

Sure enough, May stuck her head in the store while I was serving my more traditional truffles to a group of seniors who'd taken the bus from their assisted-living center to shop Main Street. After the complaints they gave me about the Coconut Curry Bonbons I'd served two years before, I never went more edgy than goat cheese in their chocolates.

May was wearing lavender today. She waved me over while she kept an eye on her store. "Sorry I can't come in. I swear that new admin at Dr. Dwyer's has been stealing a purple flag stem every week for the past month, but I haven't been able to catch her in the act."

"Vanilla latte, extra hot, with two Splendas?" I asked her.

She shook her head. "I just wanted to tell you that I heard from a customer that they found that poor woman's car."

My heart started beating faster. "Okay," I said, my worry about Dylan turning into something more concrete, like a bunch of aimless bees joining together in a big cartoony arrow, buzzing over my head.

She looked over her shoulder and said in a stage whisper, "And the murder weapon!" Her volume rose toward the end, drawing the attention of the closest customers. She saw someone approach her store and dashed back out.

I made a beeline for Erica and waited impatiently for her to finish recommending *The Artist's Way* to a middle-aged man. He looked a little unsure about adding more art to his life, but she pointed him in the direction of creativity books and said, "I'll just let you browse. Let me know if you have any questions."

"They found the murder weapon," I hissed once he was out of earshot. "Which probably means they found the original crime scene."

"That's good news," Erica tried to reassure me. "The weapon and the crime scene could point the police away from Dylan and to the real killer."

"What should we do?" I asked, feeling useless.

She shook her head. "Nothing we can do."

But I could tell she was worried. "Look," she said, "we know Dylan. He's not capable of something like that. Just hold on to that thought." Was she trying to convince herself?

"Have you and Zane found out anything new?" I asked. The *that would clear Dylan* was left unsaid.

"Just a few more of her fake identities," she said. "And not all on dating websites. She joined different online support groups too, like for people who had anxiety or depression."

"Why do you think she did that?" I asked.

"It seems like she integrated herself into the group, for

months even, and then started talking about financial problems she was having. The other people on the loop would try to help her out."

"With money, I assume," I said.

"Yes," Erica said. "By then, they felt like she was a real friend."

"Did she ever help them?"

"Yes," she said. "But never even close to the same extent, and perhaps just to keep up appearances."

"Did anyone seem mad about that?" I asked.

The man returned before she could answer. He was holding *The Artist's Way*, *Steal Like an Artist*, and *Art Before Breakfast*. I guess he really did want to be creative.

"Have Zane show you what we dug up," she told me, and turned to her customer.

Kona tried to hide her phone when I got to the front. "What?" I asked her.

She puffed up her cheeks and then blew out the air. "I got a text from a friend."

"What is it?" I asked.

She pulled showed me the screen, and what it said chilled me to the bone. *i saw the police with the murder weapon of that woman. it was a bat. creepy.*

"I'll be right back," I said, and took the phone back to Erica. Even though Lockett had told us Faith had been killed by someone wielding a bat, I was still freaked out.

I showed Erica the message.

"I'll call Bobby," she said.

I waited while she called him. She shook her head at me to let me know he wasn't answering, but she left him a message to call her.

"I'll make him tell us what he can," she said. "And Zane and I will keep working on her files."

The late-morning crowd spilled over into the after-lunch rush, and I didn't get back to the office for a while. When I did, Zane brought up his research on his computer, including a whole screen of photos of Faith with different names. Each one seemed to have a distinct personality that went along with the name. "Faith" went with the girl-next-door look. "Faelynn" seemed to be the artsy one, wearing an off-the-shoulder tie-dyed shirt and a rainbow-colored headband. Plain ol' "Faylinn" wore a business jacket over a red tank top and librarian glasses. She'd even modified her makeup for each personality.

"Is this for real?" I asked.

He nodded. "Look at this one." He brought up a photo where she was wearing a wig and makeup that made her look at least fifty years old.

"Holy cow," I said. "What was that for?"

"She went after seniors," he said. He clicked on the dating website for mature adults. "She listed her age as fifty-seven. And said that she wanted to date men sixty and above."

"Did she actually go on dates with them?" I asked. That would be hard to pull off.

"No," he said. "She just talked to them online."

"So she really was a conwoman," I said. "How could she do that to people?"

He realized that was a rhetorical question and clicked a few buttons. Faith's emails appeared on the screen. "Look

at her Outlook. She had it meticulously organized by whoever she was supposed to be."

Each folder had a different variation of Faith's identities.
He clicked on the Faelynn folder—it had subfolders broken
down into different men's names. "She kept copies of every
conversation."

He opened Excel spreadsheets. "Then she transferred the
important information and tracked everything in these files."

Holy cow. Her organizational skills rivaled Erica's. What
a waste of talent.

"She was trying to get money out of all of them," he said.
He brought up a spreadsheet with the money given by
various contacts, as well as gifts and their estimated values.
"When she got a gift, she noted it here. And she kept track
of when and where she sold them—usually on eBay or to a
pawnbroker—and how much she got."

"Which broker?" I asked, adding a visit there to our list
of things to do.

"Freddy's Fast Cash," he said. "In Baltimore."

I looked at the spreadsheet. How did she keep track of
all of this? "Wart Nose Guy? Chipped-Tooth Guy? Some of
the men don't have real names."

"Yeah," he said. "I checked that out. She used code
names sometimes."

"So we don't know who the code names belonged to?" I
asked.

He shook his head. "No, it doesn't say." He pulled up
another page. "It seems like that's how she handled men
until they were deeper in the process. Maybe until she was
sure they were using their real names." He clicked on a

subfolder labeled *Duds* and pointed to it. "Here are her rejects."

"What made them rejects?" I asked.

"Not sure yet," he said. "We can probably assume that they either didn't have money or weren't immediately taken in by her story."

The sheer amount of information was staggering. And our list of potential suspects was already huge. "Let's get started on the ones with actual names." Then I had a terrible thought. "Is Oscar in there?"

He nodded, and brought up the emails they had written to each other.

I felt a sense of dread climb up my spine. "Did he give her money?"

"No," he said. "Just a necklace. That he made himself. She wrote down that it was made of wood with a gold clasp. But that's not what's interesting."

"What?"

"I was double-checking her entries against the contact information, and I found something unusual about Oscar's Facebook account." Normally impassive Zane looked upset.

I waited.

"It seems like Oscar started a second Facebook account to communicate with only Faith, who he thought of as Faelynn."

"Why would Oscar do that?" I asked.

He hesitated. "It's been my experience that second accounts are usually fake."

"And why would someone do that to Oscar?"

"It's more like, someone was doing it to Faelynn."

"Why?"

"I'm assuming that someone who knew Oscar well enough to know he was dating Faelynn wanted to interact with her," he said. "Someone was catfishing the catfish."

"Oh no." I could think of only one person who would be upset enough about their relationship to do that.

He scrunched up his face. "It gets worse."

"What is it?"

"The account was deleted right after her murder."

I found Erica upstairs adding books to her Classics section. "We need to speak to Oscar," I told her once I'd filled her in on Zane's latest discovery. The police were sure to know all about it by now, but from what we'd heard, Oscar wasn't talking to them.

I hadn't noticed Kayla working in the next aisle. She popped up, her curly blond hair pulled off of her face with a colorful scarf. "Should we just assume you will need us, like, all the time until you wrap this up?"

"Um," I said. "I guess?"

"Kona and I talked last night, and we know we can't talk you out of it, but we're going to use this on you the next time you start acting like our mom, okay?"

I must have looked pretty sheepish, but she laughed. "Don't worry. I'm going to Hawaii for Christmas and can use the extra money." I still felt guilty as Erica and I drove off.

Oscar and Dylan lived close to the elementary school, in a small redbrick house with white trim. Oscar had converted an old barn into a workshop where he did woodwork. His bread and butter was making custom kitchen cabinets for local contractors, but he also created more elaborate furniture for a high-end shop in Frederick.

As we parked in front of the house, we heard the high-pitched whine start up from some kind of saw. We followed the noise around the side of the house to the workshop.

Oscar was guiding wood through a huge saw, following an intricate pattern, until a piece of the wood fell off. Playing it safe, we waited far back until he stopped the machine and blew on the wood to see the result.

The smell of the sawdust brought back a vivid memory of my own dad working in his garage. My mom had called it puttering, because he rarely finished what he started, never adequately happy with his workmanship. The memory was so bright, I had to blink to bring myself back to today.

"Hi, Oscar," Erica said.

He set down the wood and took off his goggles and safety headphones and set them on a table. "Erica. Michelle," he said with a curt nod. "What can I help you with?"

Erica dove right in. "I know Marino said not to discuss this case, but we're hoping you can answer just one question."

He stood still, not giving any indication what he'd do.

She went on. "Do you have more than one Facebook account under your name?"

His face changed, looking frightened for just an instant, and then it went straight to angry. "You have to leave."

"But . . ." Erica tried.

He put his goggles and headphones back on. "I'm sorry."

He picked up the piece of wood and started the saw, preventing any further conversation.

I caught a movement out of the corner of my eye and saw Dylan standing in the window. I waved and he gave an uncertain wave back, and then backed away from the window, disappearing from view.

10

"What do you think about bailing on the rest of the afternoon and checking out that pawnshop, Freddy's Fast Cash, in Baltimore?" I asked, wanting to make some kind of progress. "Before we head over to the Boys and Girls Club, I mean."

"Good idea," Erica said. "We could leverage the travel time if we picked up my laptop and you drove, so I could finish up a few items on the way."

Erica spent most of the trip east making notes on her various to-do lists.

I tried to figure out why Oscar blocked us. He had to know we were trying to help Dylan. Why wouldn't he tell us anything? It seemed like more than just his lawyer telling him not to.

Soon we were leaving behind the rolling hills filled with

quilts of autumn colors and heading through the suburban developments to approach the real city, something I avoided as much as possible.

As we got closer to Baltimore, I asked, "How do you want to handle this guy?"

"What do you mean?" Erica asked, blinking as she came back to reality.

"We should have brought something to pawn," I said.

"We can stop at another pawnshop," she said. "But the difference between what they charge and what they pay is significant." She pulled off the necklace Bobby had given her, the book pendant swaying.

"That'll work," I said. "I'll pretend to be Faith's friend who recommended him, and you pretend that you want to pawn this gift from your ex-boyfriend."

"And we won't mention anything about Faith's murder," Erica said.

I followed the directions of my GPS to a rundown city street, littered with garbage and gang-sign graffiti. The windows to the shop had bars over them. We parked right in front, in a twenty-minute-free-parking zone, and I eyed the teens on the opposite corner with trepidation as we got out. We opened the door to the store, and an alarm buzzed loudly above our heads.

Inside was way different from what I expected to find. The store was neat and clean, and much larger than I thought it would be. Little neon signs announced the different products—*Watches*, *Gold*, *Musical Instruments* and much more. Stairs led to a second floor that looked like it was full of toys, bikes and collectibles.

A man in his forties looked up from arranging antique

watches; he wore a gray golf shirt with a large gold dollar sign logo. "Hello," he said, with a deep voice like a morning-radio DJ. "What can I help you with?"

"Hi," I said. "Are you Freddy?"

"Sure am," he said.

"Great," I said. "My friend Faith said you were the guy to see to get the most money for jewelry."

He gave me a sharp look. "Faith?"

"Yeah," I said. "She's in my . . . bowling league. As a sub," I added when he gave me an unbelieving look.

Erica dangled the necklace in front of him. "What can I get for this?"

The gold worked as a distraction. "Let's see what we have here," he said, taking the chain from her. "Nice." He nodded his approval.

"Her ex-boyfriend, the jerk, gave it to her, and now she wants to get rid of the bad juju," I said.

He ignored me and placed it on a small scale. "A little over two grams." He turned to me. "So, I assume you haven't heard the news about Faith?"

I frowned. "What news?"

He stared at me. "She's dead."

"What?" I asked, making my voice as stunned as I could. "What happened?"

"Don't know," he said. Something in his voice made me believe he was genuinely sad. "But she was murdered."

"Oh no!" I said. "I'm so sorry. Faith said you were great friends."

He lifted his shoulder in a *no big deal* shrug. "As good as you could get with a customer. She always brought me quality merchandise and didn't haggle much once we understood each other."

"It was more than that for her," I said. "Didn't she bring everything to you?"

He blew out a sigh. "Yeah. We became friends over the last couple of years and she brought all of her stuff to me. She used to shop it around but she figured out that I always gave top dollar, especially on the high-end items, so she didn't have to bother with those other guys anymore."

"Did she tell you where she got it?" Erica asked.

"Sure," he said. "She got a lot of gifts from men over the years and sold them for cash." He picked up the necklace. "Sorta like you're doing."

"How long has she been coming here?" Erica asked.

He narrowed his eyes at her. "Why are you asking?"

"I just want to make sure I should sell this to you," she said.

"I can give you seventy bucks," he said. "You won't do any better than that anywhere in Baltimore."

"I think you should take it," I said. "Faith told me that she didn't have a lot of friends, so this guy is special."

He cleared his throat. "I can go as high as seventy-five."

Erica pretended to consider.

I tried to sound super casual. "Did Faith ever bring a necklace made with wood and a little bit of gold?"

He scoffed. "Wood? Are you kidding? What hippie freak thought that was a good idea?"

I bristled but then thought better of it. "Someone who works with wood. It was supposed to be personal, not valuable."

"Ah," he said. "Wait. Was that you?"

"No!" I thought quickly. "Someone else on the bowling team."

"She wouldn't bring that to me," he said. "Only high-quality goods."

"Who would do something so terrible to Faith?" Erica asked, weaving the chain through her hands as if not wanting to let it go.

"Who knows?" he said. "The world's crazy." He looked out the window. "I told her once that it was time to settle down, and she said she wanted to live fast and die young so she could leave behind a beautiful corpse."

We stayed silent for a moment.

"I don't think she meant that though," he said.

"Do you remember the last thing she sold to you?" I asked.

"Yeah," he said. "It was an antique ring. Very nice."

"Did she say anything about who gave it to her?" Erica asked.

He shook his head. "Nah. It was a sale just like the others. I got a pretty penny for that one."

I turned to Erica. "So, ready to get rid of that necklace and close the chapter on that jerk?"

She closed her hand over the necklace. "I'm sorry," she said to Freddy. "I'm just not ready."

I rolled my eyes. "I could've predicted this."

"Thanks so much for your time," Erica said, and we went out the front door.

As soon as we were in the car, I brought up a new idea. "We haven't thought much about anyone outside of her 'dates.'"

"People she knew in real life?" Erica said. "She had to have some real friends, right?"

"Maybe Zane can check her calendar for anyone who wasn't one of her targets," I suggested.

She pulled out her phone. "I'll text him."

For some reason, Erica's social media campaign to make a video go viral last month came into my head. "What if . . ." I trailed off while I thought about what could go wrong.

"What?" Erica prompted.

"What if we started an online campaign with a photo of Faith and a kind of 'Do you know this woman?' question? And ask them to leave a comment if they knew her." I imagined all the false leads we'd get. But maybe we'd get real information that we had no idea was out there.

She thought about it for a moment. "Detective Lockett would not be pleased." Then she tilted her head. "But maybe if Reese implemented it . . ."

"Yes!" I readily agreed. "Then he can't blame us. We'll have to be devious about it." I mentally filed through our friends, their willingness to help us this way, and their access to Reese. Of course, she bothered almost everyone in town at some point or another. "Maybe we can have Iris mention it when Reese is eating at the diner? She could tell another customer in front of her that we're thinking of doing that and Reese will jump all over it before we can."

Erica smiled. "Sounds like a plan."

"Wait," I said. "She has to stress that we're planning to ask people to give us leads in the comments section and not email us directly, so it can start a conversation and maybe jog other people's memories."

"Good idea," Erica said. "That way, we can see what everyone's response is instead of them emailing her privately." She dialed the diner and had a short conversation with Iris.

"She said Reese is in there all the time," Erica said as she hung up. "And she's happy to do it. I promised we'd eat there soon."

We were both pretty quiet the rest of the way back. Erica went deep into her Halloween Festival spreadsheets, and I let her plan. I was about to drop her off at our house when I saw that we had guests.

Tommy's hearse was parked on the street, and Dylan was sitting on the porch stairs, with Quinn and Tommy beside him.

"Hey, guys," Erica said with a question in her voice.

"Hi," Quinn said.

Dylan looked miserably worried, chewing on the end of the string from his hoodie.

"Let's go in and have some hot cocoa," I suggested and walked up the stairs beside them.

They got to their feet as I unlocked the door and followed us into the kitchen. Quinn took a seat but Dylan and Tommy seemed too agitated to sit still.

"Seems like you have something to tell me," Erica said while I put the teakettle on to boil.

"I created the second Facebook account for my dad," he said, his voice bleak.

"Can you tell me why?" she asked gently.

"I knew . . . that woman wasn't who she said she was, but my dad was so gullible." The words burst out of him.

"So you did know Faith Monette," she said.

"Yes," he said. "But she called herself Faelynn Monet."

"How did you know she wasn't who she said she was?" Erica kept her voice gentle.

"My dad left his computer on with his Facebook account open and he had messages waiting from her. I read them. Anyone could tell she was trying to manipulate him. She said she couldn't meet him that night because her car broke down and she didn't have enough money to fix it."

"What did you do?"

"I cleared the window. Got rid of the whole conversation with her."

"Then what happened?"

"She wrote back, wondering why he didn't respond."

At Erica's nod, he continued. "So I wrote, as my dad, that I had been hacked and was starting a new account. And to ignore messages from his old account until he resolved it. She fell for it—probably thinks all old guys don't know what they're doing with a computer."

"Why did you start the secret account?" Erica asked.

"I don't know. I was going to prove to my dad that she was a liar and conman. Or conwoman. Whatever."

"Did he give her gifts?" I wanted to confirm that the information from Faith's records was accurate.

"Just some necklace that he made himself." His expression turned sad for a brief flash and then went back to bitter.

"What were you going to do next?" Erica asked.

"I was just trying to keep her attention on me and not my dad."

"We were all in on it," Quinn announced.

Tommy and Dylan looked at her, like she said something she shouldn't have.

"In on what?" Erica asked carefully, as if afraid they'd bolt.

"Nothing," they all said together.

Dylan stood up. "We have to go."

"Dylan," Erica said. "You can trust me."

He looked like he was getting teary-eyed. "I know."

I wasn't going to beat around the bush. "Dylan. I need to know. Did you or any of your friends kill Faith?"

He looked at me, stunned and hurt. "No," he said, his voice shaky.

Quinn's face had turned white. "How could—"

Tommy shook his head at me as they turned to go.

My apology got stuck in my throat. We watched them walk to the hearse and drive away.

"It's okay," Erica said. "Deep down, they understand."

I cleared my throat. "Understand what? That I accused them of murder?"

"That it makes sense for us to ask questions," she said. "Because they're still keeping something from us."

I stated the obvious. "Something big."

The next morning, Erica interrupted me filling my Flag Furls with milk chocolate ganache at the counter while Kona was on a grocery store run for more cream. I often made the red-white-and-blue spray-painted flags with a white chocolate shell and milk chocolate ganache inside, but this time, the whole thing was smooth milk chocolate. They were sure to sell out even faster than the others.

She watched me squeeze the ganache out of the pastry bag for a moment and then said, "Zane and I have eliminated some of the names on the list of men Faith dated and prioritized them. We should talk to Newell Woodfellow first."

"Newell?" I asked. "Did his mother hate him or something?"

Erica looked at me over her glasses. "I believe his full name is Newell Woodfellow the Third."

"Ah, that explains it," I said. "Poor guy. What do you think his nickname was in high school? Newt? Jewell? Fig Newton?"

"I wouldn't want to speculate," she said. "Perhaps you can ask him."

"Right," I said. "That'll get him on our side."

I pushed aside the completed tray and started working on the next one. "Why do you want to talk to him in particular?" I asked.

"He's by far the wealthiest person she dated," she explained. "First, we're researching local people she actually went out with more than a few times. Then we'll look into those who sent her money and gifts, but knew her only online. Newell is one of the biggest outliers of those she dated."

I raised my eyebrows. "Outliers? Someone named Newell is certainly an outlier wherever he goes."

She smiled and went back to her office, returning in a few minutes. "That's odd."

"What's odd?" I asked while refilling the plastic bag with the chocolate ganache.

"His personal secretary said he won't meet with us," she said.

"Really? Why?" I stopped. "Wait. He has a personal secretary?"

She shrugged. "She was very nice about it, but said he had no time to meet with us."

"Guess we have to track him down."

"He belongs to the Dulany Hills Country Club."

"Whoa," I said. "Country club *and* personal secretary? He's got mega bucks."

"Seems like it," she said. "They have their annual gala tomorrow. Want to go?"

"No!" I said. "We can't crash something like that. I'd stick out like a sore thumb."

"It's a Halloween party," she said. "You can wear a costume."

"I doubt very much the country club folks actually wear costumes. Unless they're those foofy masks like from Elizabethan times."

She paused to think. "You may have a point."

"Newt sounds like a pretty rich guy to fall for Faith's tricks," I said.

"Brains don't always go along with wealth," she said, and went back to her office.

I finished the second tray of Flag Furls and took off my gloves to pull up last year's gala photos on my laptop. Sure enough, no costumes. Just endless photos of mostly middle-aged to elderly couples, the women wearing dresses that had recently been on some designer's runway.

Then I remembered that I was hoping to go out with Bean after May's cat lottery party. Oh well. Dylan came first.

Erica came back to the kitchen and I spoke first. "I should go as the help."

She raised her eyebrows.

"Our torte supplier did their desserts last year," I said. "I'll see if she'll be there this year and offer to be a server." I pointed to a photo of a man in his sixties with a woman who looked like she was barely out of her twenties wearing a slinky silver dress that went to the floor and had a slit to her upper thigh. "You can get away with a dress like that but I can't."

Erica was almost a foot taller than me, and I tended to look like a fireplug when I wore anything shiny. Which hadn't happened since my high school prom.

"You'd look gorgeous in that," she said, ignoring my snort. "But splitting up is a good idea. So our intentions are not so obvious. Phoenix is a member, and I'm going to ask if I can attend with him and his partner," she said.

"Partner? I didn't know Phoenix was serious about anyone," I said, immediately curious about the kind of man Phoenix would fall for. "Do we know him?"

"I guess we'll find out," she said with a smile.

I met with Phoenix in the store kitchen, where we'd have some privacy. He was pleased that I'd pulled together my profit and loss statements, but wasn't happy that I didn't have my marketing plan with associated costs running up to the winter holiday season. He didn't seem to believe the *too busy with the Halloween Festival* excuse or the *I've been investigating a murder for a friend* excuse, but I let him stare at me in disapproval with barely an eye roll. "I'll have it next week."

"Fine," he said. "But why are you still investigating? Once again, I'm going to warn you that you should leave all of this skullduggery to the very competent police."

"We're just trying to help Dylan," I said.

"I understand," he said. "But there is no need. I know for a fact that the police are doing everything they can to find the real killer."

"How do you know?" I asked. "People get falsely arrested all the time. Can you imagine Dylan in a prison cell?"

"I understand," he repeated. "And I'll leave it at that." He slid copies of the papers we'd discussed into a folder and handed it to me. "On another note, I'll have one of my employees gather the numbers to figure out if merging finances will work. I'd like to set up a meeting with both you and Erica next week as well. I'd appreciate it if you could email me your marketing numbers before then."

"Okay," I said to get him off my back, but I wasn't sure how I could fit in the hours I'd need to think of a new and exciting marketing tactic along with cost projections.

Erica popped her head into the kitchen. "Phoenix. I'm so glad I caught you. Do you still belong to the Dulany Hills Country Club?"

"Yes," he said. "Why?"

"I need to get into your next big event," she said. "The Halloween gala tomorrow night."

He looked confused but said, "Sure."

"We just need to talk to a member who's on the guest list," Erica explained.

"How do you know who's on the guest list?" His face cleared. "Is this about your investigation?"

"Would that be a problem?" I asked.

"Not at all," he said, with an undercurrent of humor that I didn't understand. "Glad to help any way that I can."

"Oh good," Erica said. "Can you add me as your guest?"

"Sure. We can even pick you up."

"Thanks!" Erica said, and left, letting the door close behind her.

He turned to me. "You're not going?"

"I'll be there." I pretended to hold a tray on my hand. "As a server."

He smiled. "Undercover?"

"Kind of," I admitted. "So you're bringing someone? Other than Erica, I mean."

His smile turned into a grin. "Yep."

"Do I know him?" I asked, trying to figure out what was so humorous.

Phoenix laughed out loud. "I'm fairly confident you do."

His delight was infectious. "Is it serious?" I asked. "You seem so happy."

He nodded. "Very serious."

"Who is it?" I asked in a rather demanding tone.

"I'll let that be a surprise," he said with a chuckle.

11

Bean brought a bunch of meatball subs from Zelini's to the store for lunch. We sat on the back porch, and I had my mouth full of gooey deliciousness when Erica came out with her phone.

"Reese wrote an article that Chuck Sinsle was released on bail," she said.

I finished chewing. "Do you want to go and talk to him?"

"I don't know," she said. "Bobby made sure I knew the police are watching him. Twenty-four, seven."

"Shoot," I said. "Can we call him?"

"They might be monitoring his phone too," Bean said. "Just call the super and offer him fifty bucks to give Chuck a message. And the message is that you'll give Chuck fifty bucks to show up somewhere to meet."

"Why would Chuck meet with us?" Erica asked. "If he

talked to the super, he might know that you were responsible for him being caught with Faith's belongings."

My mind was stuck on the money. One hundred bucks? "That's a lot of money for just the chance at some information," I said. "Is that how all you reporters get your information?"

"You'd be surprised." He took out his phone and handed it to Erica. "Use this to call him." When she hesitated, he said, "Do it. It'll work."

Of course, Bean's idea worked like a charm. We were celebrating finishing the last major bit of the haunted house construction with an impromptu pizza party at the Boys and Girls Club when Bean got the message. Chuck had agreed to meet us in the food court of a mall on the other side of Frederick at noon the next day. Our Saturday was going to be crazy busy. It looked like we should add bribery to our investigation toolbox.

Bobby and Bean were supposed to be helping the Duncans, but, along with the teen volunteers, they seemed to be enjoying playing with the haunted house features more than anything. They especially liked trying to scare the heck out of each other.

Erica came in while we were sitting around the table in the quiet room, eating pizza and listening to the comic book kids razzing each other about how high they'd jumped when the mechanical spider had come at them from the corner. She dropped a kiss on Bobby's head and I was surprised and delighted with the absent-minded show of affection in front of everyone.

Bobby grabbed her hand as she pulled away and smiled.

She'd told me that they had agreed to disagree about her pursuing an investigation that he believed should be handled solely by the police, and not let it affect their relationship.

The teens quieted for a moment and then grabbed an entire pizza to take to the beanbag chairs in the corner.

"What can you tell us about Chuck?" I asked Bobby, quiet enough so none of the non-grown-ups could hear.

He shook his head. "Nothing."

"Come on," I said. "You arrested the guy."

"I have my orders."

"From Lockett," I said sourly. "Why can't you officially clear Dylan?"

"I'm not answering that," he said and took a huge bite of his pepperoni pizza. Then he mumbled nonsense to prove he couldn't speak with so much food in his mouth.

Bean laughed.

I waited for Bobby to swallow his food and asked, "Hey, what happened to Reese's Internet craziness?"

Our little ploy had worked and Reese had implemented our social media blitz idea right after breakfast. Her "Do You Know This Woman?" article, with a photo of Faith, was nearly word for word what Erica had said to Iris. The comments section already had dozens of replies.

Bobby's face darkened. "The chief paid her a visit, and she decided to abort that particular effort."

"But it seems to still be happening," I noted happily. That was the problem, and the benefit, of social media. Once something was out there, it was way out there. Even though Reese had taken the article off of her blog site, it had been duplicated on a dozen other sites, and was still spreading. People claiming to have known Faith were piling up in the comments sections of all the other websites that had reprinted her article, and Zane was having a hard time figuring out which leads were credible and which were from crackpots.

Bobby scowled even harder. "It's a damn pain. She could be warning off the actual killer."

"I heard she's very busy investigating a lot of false leads," I said.

"We can only wish her good luck on talking to the head of the CIA," Bobby said sarcastically, referring to only one of the crazy conspiracy theories people had floated in the comments.

Erica sat down and the conversation moved to opening night at the festival. It didn't take long for our little party to wrap up. We'd all spent so much time at the Boys and Girls Club working on this festival lately that if we could take a break, we did.

Bean walked me out to the parking lot, but before we reached my minivan, Leo drove up too fast on his motorcycle and stopped with a skid right in front of me.

Bean instinctively dragged me back with an arm around my waist.

"Leo!" I yelled. "What the hell?"

Leo cut the engine, swung his leg over and put himself right in Bean's face. "Did you take her to the murder site?" He was red with anger, a vein popping out of his forehead.

I pulled on Leo's arm, trying to move him back. "No," I told him emphatically. "What's going on with you?"

He looked at me like he didn't believe me. "Then why did Meg Johnson say she saw you at Green Meadows?"

That blabbermouth. She must have been the driver of the

minivan who paused to look at us that night. Did she have night vision goggles or something?

"That's not the murder site, just where the body was dumped." I tried to make it sound totally reasonable.

"What were you doing there?" His voice rose.

I ignored the question. He knew the answer. He just didn't like it. "Leo, what's wrong?"

Bean took a step closer. "Everything's okay, Leo."

"No. It's not." Leo turned toward Bean and pushed his chest with two hands, a furious expression on his face. "You're supposed to be protecting her and instead you're putting her in danger for your own selfish reasons." He pushed him back again, harder.

Bean put both hands up, not responding. "Leo, you need to calm down. She is fine. We didn't do anything dangerous."

"How do you know?" Leo yelled. "How do you know it's not dangerous until it's too late?"

I stepped in between them and grabbed his arm. It was hard as rock. "Leo. Look at me. I'm fine. What is this about?"

He wrenched his arm away and stared at me, breathing hard.

"Leo?"

Then he took a step backward, off balance.

"Worst day ever?" I asked him, my voice quavering. That was the expression we'd used on each other whenever something bad happened, ever since our parents had died—the absolute worst day of our lives. It was our code for making sure the other one was okay.

He turned around and limped fast toward his motorcycle, driving away in a roar.

..............

Erica came over to the counter the next morning as I was sending another text to Leo. I'd tried to catch him again right after daybreak, but he'd already left his apartment. Or maybe he'd never come home the night before.

"Zane's actually found someone worth talking to from Reese's social media campaign."

"You mean our social media campaign," I reminded her.

"Don't go spreading that around," she said. "Anyway, Zane contacted a man who says he was one of Faith's victims, and he responded."

"Really? What did he say?"

"He said his ex-wife might have been mad enough to kill Faith," she said. "They got divorced because Faith convinced him she needed thousands of dollars to leave her abusive husband. He wiped out his bank account, stole money from his employer, and gave the money to Faith. Then she dumped him. He got fired, and his wife divorced him over it all."

"And now he's throwing his ex-wife under the bus?" I said. "What a winner. Sounds like he has more of a motive than she does. I'm not so sure we should trust him."

"It's worth a visit," Erica said. "He gave us all of her information."

We decided to check out ex-wife Whitney before we met with Chuck. She was lucky to have escaped that dog, in my opinion. Of course, that was based on nothing except the knowledge that he'd cheated on her with Faith and then implicated her in a freakin' murder with no evidence.

Erica had called ahead to make sure Whitney was working. She'd certainly landed in a nice place. Zolo was an expensive women's clothing boutique that operated under the assumption that if you had to ask how much that scrap of material called a dress was, you couldn't afford it. And if you didn't wear a size zero or two, you shouldn't waste the salesperson's time.

Inside, only a few racks held clothes, in various shades of black, gray and white. "Did I just go color-blind?" I whispered to Erica, who ignored me.

Only one salesperson was there, and her discreet name tag said *Whitney* with *Manager* under it. She looked like a grown-up Barbie doll, minus the implausible curves, with blond hair, a perky nose and huge fake lashes. She gave us a discreet up-and-down review and said, "Welcome to Zolo. May I help you find anything in particular?"

While her tone was warm, her expression wondered, *And can you afford it?*

"Whitney," Erica said, her tone just as warm. "Just the person I'm looking for."

Whitney went still. She may have wanted to raise her eyebrows, but didn't. Maybe she'd had a recent Botox treatment or something.

Erica went for it. "We're wondering if you've heard about the death of Faith Monette."

Whitney gave one short bark of laughter. "Who *are* you?"

Erica introduced us as if this was a social visit, and then explained. "We'd like to talk to you about Faith Monette."

"Faith?" she said. "Why?"

"We heard that you knew her," Erica said. "Can you tell us about her?"

"How did you—?" She stopped and looked at both of us. "My idiot ex-husband sent you here, didn't he?".

Erica tried to be diplomatic. "He suggested you may have had a reason—"

"To kill her? He thinks I did it?" Whitney asked, and then gave a barking laugh again. "Aw, honey. That woman did me the hugest favor of my life."

"What do you mean?" I couldn't help but be suspicious.

"I married that lug right out of high school, and he turned into the biggest loser ever. If she hadn't scammed him, I'd still be working long hours in a job I hated while he bagged groceries and played video games all day."

"So you weren't angry with her," Erica asked.

"Oh, I was at first," she admitted. "Like, *Housewives of New Jersey* mad. I even went to her apartment to confront her. But then she calmed me down and told me not to blame Ed."

Erica and I both kept quiet, letting her talk.

"And she showed me what she did to all those men." She stopped talking for a moment, as if remembering that time. Then she blinked and seemed to come out of her reverie. "Okay, I know this is going to sound bad. But I was really angry, and not just at Ed for being an idiot. Yes, he cleaned out our account and stole money from his job to give her. But I was mostly mad at myself for staying in a bad marriage for so long. And a bad life."

"You could do more," Erica said, encouraging her to talk.

"Exactly." Whitney was happy that she understood. "Anyway, she taught me how to . . ."

"Be a catfish?" I asked.

"Exactly." She thrust her chin up as if proud. "And how to get men to give me money. And much more. If they liked me, it helped my self-esteem. A lot. I understood why she did it. So I tried it for a while. Just a little bit. But after I divorced that dud, I didn't find the need to mess with men anymore. I haven't looked back."

Erica smiled. "You're obviously doing great here. What's next?"

"This is just a stepping stone," she said. "Don't tell the owner but I've been taking classes on entrepreneurship and I'm saving up to buy a franchise. Not sure which one yet, but I'm going to be a business owner." She looked around the store. "And I have Faith to thank for it."

"You have yourself to thank for it," Erica said.

We'd all gotten off the point. "So you haven't seen Faith since then?"

"Oh no, I saw her," she said. "We used to have coffee once in a while, but then I realized that she was wasting her time, and life, on something so negative. I tried to tell her that she should try a different way that didn't hurt people. She said she had a new plan. She was going to get rich the old-fashioned way—"

"By inheriting it?" I asked.

"No." She looked at me like I was little crazy. "By marrying it."

Of course. "How was she going to make that happen?"

She shrugged. "No idea. I wished her good luck. I never saw her again."

"Why does your ex-husband think you're still mad?" I asked.

"He *wants* me to be mad," she explained, exasperated.

"He's living in some fantasy world where I'm still in love with him, and if I wasn't mad about Faith, I'd still be with him. But I have moved on. Like really moved on. I'm dating a great guy. I've got it all."

"Maybe he's still in love with you," Erica suggested. "Do you think he . . . ?"

Whitney knew what she meant. "Killed Faith?" She shook her head. "Not a chance. He wouldn't exert that much energy on anything."

"Do you think your husband implicated you as some weird attempt to get you back?" I asked.

"Who cares?" Whitney said.

I believed her. We got to the mall early for our meeting with Chuck, and watched all the families shopping together as well as the teens who had nothing better to do than hang at the mall. I'd spent a lot of time at the mall when I was a teen too.

Since I'd only seen Chuck passed out on the couch and wasn't sure I'd recognize him, we'd printed out his Facebook profile photo.

He showed up on time, but I had to look at his photo twice to make sure it was the same person. He looked like he hadn't shaved in days and wore a black leather "tough guy" jacket and sunglasses. When he took them off to look for us, he winced at the light coming through the glass ceiling. He saw Erica's wave and joined us at a table.

Up close, his eyes were red and puffy and the smell of alcohol seemed to emanate from his skin. Like he'd been on a bender the night before and his body was trying to get rid of the toxins.

"Hi, Chuck," Erica said. "I'm Erica and this is Michelle."

"Hey," he said. He turned a chair around and sat on it backward, full of aggression. "Where's the money?" He smoothed the hair out of his eyes with a gesture that seemed much younger than a twentysomething's.

She slid the cash over to him. "Thanks so much for your time."

He grabbed it and shoved it in his jacket pocket, seeming ready to bail at any moment. "What do you want?"

Over his shoulder, I noticed Junior coming down the corridor. Uh-oh. Chuck was being followed and no one on the West Riverdale police force would like us talking to him.

I stood up to block Junior's view. "Would you like to go into Kelly's Pub and get away from this crowd?" I asked. "Our treat."

"Sure." He pushed up from the chair. "I gotta eat."

"We're very sorry for your loss," Erica said as we walked through a pack of teen girls squealing about something on their cell phones to the restaurant at the other end of the food court. "It's hard to lose a friend in such a terrible way."

He grunted.

Really? A grunt? I glanced over at him and saw an expression of grief wipe away the tough-guy look for just a moment. Then he shook his head once as if getting rid of the bad feelings.

I looked over my shoulder as I went into the restaurant and saw Junior heading the wrong way.

I knew Erica was anxious to ask more questions, but she waited until we were seated. The restaurant was decorated like a stereotypical Irish pub, with photos of Ireland on the walls along with an *Every Day is St. Paddy's Day!* sign, and too many four-leaf clovers to count. Someone had tried for some originality by painting a mural on the wall but even that was pretty hokey, with castle ruins, rolling green hills and cows spotting the landscape, and a tiny leprechaun with a pot of gold in the corner.

When the waiter in a Kelly-green T-shirt came over to take our order, Erica asked for iced tea, probably hoping Chuck would follow suit, but he ordered a pint of Guinness. It was way early for me, but I ordered a pint of Harp so it didn't look like we were ganging up on him. I'd just have to nurse it.

The place was empty, and our drinks came right away. We ordered our food and Erica started. "The super said you and Faith were friends."

He snorted. "I bet he didn't have anything that nice to say about me."

She shrugged, waiting for him to answer.

"She used to come over and party," he admitted.

"Did you date?" she asked.

He snorted again so hard he choked a little. "Hell no. No way could I afford her."

"What do you mean?" I asked.

He stared at me, as if evaluating how much we knew.

"She only dated guys with money," he said. "And I didn't think of her that way." He paused, as if dredging up a memory. "Well, not since the beginning."

"Why not?"

He struggled to explain, as if figuring it out himself. "She knew how to keep things on a certain level, like a friend level, right away. Acting like, you know, a guy would."

Erica raised her eyebrows.

"Like putting her feet up on the table," he said. "And, I don't know, burping and shoving food in her mouth. She acted different around the guys she dated. More ladylike."

"Do you think she did that on purpose?"

"Sure," he said. "She was letting me know right away where I stood. It was cool."

"Did you know about her business?"

He stiffened.

"Talking to us can only help you," Erica said. "We know you didn't kill her."

Chuck looked like he wasn't sure he believed her. I wasn't sure myself if she'd meant it.

The waiter brought our food. Chicken Caesar salad for Erica and corned beef sandwiches and fries for both Chuck and me.

Chuck took a big bite and chewed before answering. "I couldn't miss what she was doing," he said. "'Cause those guys were at her place sometimes. At first, I thought . . ."

"What?" Erica asked, her fork holding a large chunk of lettuce in the air.

"That she was some kind of high-class hooker, you know?"

"But she wasn't," she said.

He shook his head. "Not at all. When I got to know her, she explained her whole setup to me. Genius, really."

"You mean the way she organized it all?" Erica seemed genuinely interested.

"Yeah," he said, getting enthused. "And how she played those guys. They were so easy to fool."

"Believing that she actually liked them?" I asked. I took a huge bite of the perfectly seasoned corned beef, gooey

Swiss cheese and wonderfully acidic sauerkraut. I was in heaven.

"Yeah." He curled his lip. "And sending her money and stuff. Idiots."

"I'm surprised they didn't get mad when they figured it out," Erica said, but he didn't seem to realize what she was fishing for.

"People are stupid," he said. "Most of them never did. And if they seemed suspicious, she always had a reason why she couldn't see them anymore. Like she was moving or too sick for a relationship. Or getting back together with her cop husband. That scared a bunch of them off."

"Did she talk about any of them in particular?" I asked. I took a sip of Harp, which went perfectly with my delicious salty sandwich, dripping with cheese.

"Mostly just this one really rich guy." He sipped his Guinness and wiped the foam off his lip. "He belonged to some country club and she dumped everyone else to focus on him."

"When was this?" Erica asked.

We were getting good at this tag-teaming.

"About a month ago," he said. "But he ended it."

"What happened?"

"They had a big fight," he said. "I could hear her yelling on the phone with him from my apartment. See, he was pretty old. He really dug her and had even changed his will to give her some money if he croaked or something. And then some really weird stuff started happening to him, like things going wrong in his car and at his house, and he accused her of causing them."

"Wow," I said. "And did she?"

"No!" He looked insulted. "She didn't want him dead. She wanted to live that country club life. *With* him," he emphasized.

"Do you remember his name?" Erica asked.

"It was weird. Like Newton Goodman or something like that."

"Newell Woodfellow?" Erica asked, surprised.

"Yeah," he said, turning cautious. "How'd you know?"

"He's kind of a big deal around here," I said, covering for her. "So they broke up?"

"Yeah," he said. "And she was really unhappy about it. Because she didn't know anything about those accidents and he didn't believe her. It kinda made her more, I don't know, determined to find someone else to marry and maybe not do this anymore."

Was that when she started dating Oscar? I thought about what it must be like, for him to be the focus of all of that manipulation.

"So she wasn't worried about anyone finding out that she played him and getting angry?" Erica asked.

He shrugged. "She never had a problem." Then he paused. "Except a few weeks ago, she said one of her exes might be following her. And to let her know if I saw anyone watching her apartment."

"And did you ever see anyone?"

He shook his head but looked away. "I'm not really outside much. But then she said she talked to the guy and took care of it."

"How?" I asked.

He shrugged. "She kinda implied that she kicked his butt.

She knew self-defense. She said she had to, with her line of work."

"Did she ever mention him following her again?"

"Nope." He ate his last bite of sandwich, while I debated finishing the sandwich or eating the fries. The sandwich won.

We'd been avoiding the elephant in the room. "So how did her belongings end up in your apartment?" I asked.

He swallowed as if finding it difficult, and looked down at the ground. "I was really drunk, and I was mad at my dad, who said he was cutting me off. Again. Faith sometimes helped me out and I always paid her back. When my parents came around. She said I was the only one in the world she loaned money to. But I guess she was in a bad mood or something, and she told me off. She had all this nice stuff and so much money . . ."

"And you cracked under all that pressure?" Erica asked.

"Yeah," he said, he shoulders slumping. "She went out on another date when I was thinking I could be homeless. And that was the same night . . ."

"The night she was killed," Erica said.

"Yeah," he said. "But I would never hurt her. As soon as I sobered up, I woulda given it back." He paused. "But then I heard what happened to her and I knew the police would think I did it. I didn't know what to do."

"Do you have any ideas about a possible suspect?" I asked.

"I don't know," he said. "But if any of those guys found out how they were played?" He shook his head. "Who knows what he'd do?"

12

"Newell Woodfellow broke up with her?" I asked. "It's a good thing we're going to the Halloween gala tonight. We can ask him about these accidents."

Erica stared out the window, her brain probably going over every facet of her investigation project plan and this new information about Newell. "Yes," she said absentmindedly. "I'm just wondering why someone like him dated her, and what possible reason he could have to kill her."

"To keep his money?" I asked. "That seems to be what a lot of rich people like to do."

"But they weren't married. If what Chuck said was true, and he really did change his will, he could change it back. Perhaps it's something to do with his reputation," she suggested. She pulled out her laptop and I lost her to her spreadsheets.

I let my mind consider other possibilities. "Maybe she was pregnant with his baby!"

She laughed. "I think the police would have figured that out. And then there'd be DNA evidence."

We were approaching our town. "Are you going to the store or home?"

"You can drop me off at the store," Erica said. "I have a few things to work on but I'll be home in time to change before Phoenix picks me up at seven."

"I have to be at the country club at six," I said. "In all my catering waitstaff glory." Of course, I'd be going in the back door.

Erica frowned. "You can't take the minivan."

"Oh yeah." I was supposed to be undercover, and my car was wrapped with an advertisement for my chocolates.

"My car should make it, but I know you don't want to push it. We can stop at the charging station after the gala or maybe you can switch cars with Bean at May's party."

She knew I had "range anxiety" when her electric car's charge read less than twenty miles in the metaphorical gas tank.

"Bean's going to May's?" I asked. "I didn't know that." I couldn't imagine that he could fit a cat into his life. He barely had time for me. "I have to pick up chocolate to take to the party." The fact that my hostess gifts were always chocolate just might be the reason I was invited to any parties at all.

I dashed into the store while Erica followed more leisurely. Kona was chatting with ladies who had stopped over for truffles, tea and gossip after their weekly bridge tournament in the community center, and Kayla was gift-wrapping a huge coffee-table book for an older couple.

Kona called out, "Hello and good-bye!" as I rushed by the counter. I pulled a pre-chosen "traditional" box from the cooler in the kitchen and went out the back door, where my minivan was parked.

May had a delightful little house not too far from Main Street, and I arrived only a few minutes late. I'd been there before, surprised that she'd kept her décor free of anything remotely related to flowers, other than the florist-themed gifts in her kitchen—the mechanical flower that danced to music, a photo of flowers with *Be Calm and Smell the Flowers* on it, and a little sign that had a small, medium and large bouquet of roses with *How Mad Is She?* written beside it.

She said she relaxed better in a simply decorated home. Her walls were painted cream, with very few items hanging on them, and her furniture was modern with clean lines.

For the party, she'd brought flowers from her store and had decorated in an adorable winning-lottery-ticket theme, with enlarged lottery tickets and Maryland Lottery checks taped to the walls. The checks were made out to *Winner of Free Kitty* and with *A lifetime of happiness* on the line where the dollar amount was normally written.

"Welcome, welcome," May said. "I'm so glad you could make it—especially since you brought chocolates." She hugged me and happily took the box. "I'll put this on the dessert table. But I'm hiding it in the back." She laughed. "Drinks are in the kitchen and food is on the dining room table."

Truffles immediately came over to me, winding his way through the crowd and mewing. I sat on a beige ottoman and let him climb on me, petting his soft fur. "I'll miss you most of all, Scarecrow," I whispered, unexpectedly fighting back tears.

Bean must have seen me arrive, because he handed me a soda and sat on the chair opposite me. "You okay?"

"Yeah." I drew it out, my disappointment most likely written on my face.

He wore an unbuttoned green flannel shirt over a T-shirt and khakis, and his brown eyes were sympathetic. He held out his plate piled with appetizers. "Mozzarella sticks? Mr. Zelini brought them."

"My favorite," I said. Truffles jumped to the floor and then crawled up my leg again, his tiny claws digging in. He sniffed the food before taking off to chase after Nibs.

"How'd it go at the mall?" he asked.

The background noise of the party made it hard for anyone to overhear us, but I decided to talk in code anyway. "Interesting," I said. "He knew her pretty well, including her whole operation."

"Got some names to go after?" he asked.

"Aren't you in the middle of your own deal?" I asked. He was investigating something to do with prison guards. As usual, he didn't discuss it with anyone except his editor, but I'd overheard a conversation about it.

"I can do two things at once," he said. "But I may have to cancel our date night tomorrow. I have an appointment to interview a Baltimore cop."

I shrugged off my disappointment. "No problem."

"You should come and check out the progress on the house," he said with enthusiasm. He'd painted his office and the bedroom and more furniture had been delivered.

My pulse quickened at the mention of his bedroom. "Sounds like everything's on track." I was proud of my nonchalant tone.

He gave me a lazy smile. "You'll have to come over and celebrate."

I blushed. "Absolutely."

He held my gaze for a moment and then looked away, pushing out a breath as if he'd held it too long. Whoa.

Just then May clapped her hands. "Can I have everyone's attention? It's time for what you've all been waiting for." She waited until all of her guests had gathered in the living and dining rooms and quieted down.

Truffles slid his way back to me and crawled up to cuddle in my lap, as if understanding that something momentous in his little life was about to happen. I was surprised to see that my hands shook as I petted him.

I shouldn't be worried. May had carefully vetted everyone on the list, and Truffles would be well cared for. Maybe I could drop by and visit him. I hadn't asked for any details of who was on her list, but now I wished I had.

"Last chance to put your name in!" May had asked everyone to write their name on a small piece of paper and place it in a bowl. "I'm going to pick names out of the hat, I mean, bowl, and if your name is called, you get to pick your kitten."

Iris called out from near the kitchen, "Yun better pick ma name first!" and the crowd laughed.

"Drumroll, please," May said with a smile, and her guests obliged, tapping on whatever surface was close to them. She put her hand in the bowl, moved it around dramatically, then pulled out and unrolled the tiny paper. "And the first name is . . . Benjamin Russell!"

Almost everyone cheered good-naturedly, while a few people said, "Aw."

I blinked, not sure I'd heard correctly. I turned to look at him, my mouth open.

He stood up, his eyes on me. "I pick Truffles."

"I can't believe you were first," I said. I had given up trying to hold Truffles in my lap and had put him back into the cat carrier that May had provided for each new owner. The little brat was sticking his tiny paw through any hole close to the latch, attempting to escape so he could explore this new world of Bean's car. I was tagging along on his trip to the pet store before trading cars with him for the country club.

May had told Bean, "This lil' bugger takes after her momma," when she'd patted him good-bye. There may have been a little relief on her face.

Bean looked a little sheepish.

"What?" I asked.

"Don't tell anyone," he said. "Especially Iris."

Iris had been deeply unhappy about not getting a kitten and let everyone know it. None of the new owners should be eating at the diner anytime soon.

Bean went on. "May and I kinda had an arrangement."

"Really?"

"She knew how attached you are to Truffles, even though you can't keep him yourself. I wanted to make sure I got him so you could still come to see him. But neither one of us wanted to *cheat* cheat. So I suggested, hypothetically, that if I were to roll my name up into a tiny ball she just might be able to reach around and pick it out first."

For the second time that day, I was dumbfounded. "I love you guys," I blurted out, and then was horrified. "I mean, you know what I mean. It's just such a nice thing for you to do. Both of you. For me." *Stop talking right this instant*, I told myself.

His head had whipped around to stare at me, and I couldn't for the life of me figure out what he was thinking. "Everyone loves you," he said simply, and turned to watch the road.

I started sweating and desperately searched for a new subject. "May said Coco was getting spayed on Monday, so I guess she won't be showing up on my porch again for at least a week."

He winced at the word "spayed."

"What?" I said. "You're taking Truffles in soon, right?"

"Let's just call it 'the procedure,'" he said.

I snickered. "We should stop at the Pampered Pet Store. They have May's list of recommendations for food and toys and stuff. Knowing her, she probably has a cat bed made out of mink on there."

He smiled, giving the little joke far more than it deserved. "From what I remember from having cats growing up, they don't need much more than food, water and a paper bag."

"Right," I said. "Let's see how many toys you'll have when we leave."

We got out of the Pampered Pet with only one bag of cat toys, but also food, bowls, an elaborate "cat condo" with a scratching post, and most important, an automatic litter box.

"What are you going to do when you travel?" I asked.

Bean had visited countries in the most remote parts of the world, sometimes for months at a time.

"I'm cutting way back on that," he said. "And between you, me and Erica, he'll be taken care of."

I smiled at the idea that he thought we'd be connected in the future.

I helped him put all cat-related items in the now-empty room that was destined to be a home gym, and watched Truffles ignore it all to go straight for the closed door when we opened the carrier.

"Not happening, cat," Bean said, amused. Truffles stared right at him as if challenging his authority. Then he walked over to meow and wind around Bean's ankles, choosing diplomacy, and probably cunning, over outright defiance.

Bean looked adorably baffled when Truffles ignored even a mouse toy filled with catnip to explore the room for alternate escape routes.

"You're going to have your work cut out for you," I told him. "Can you hold on to him while I get out the door? I have to go serve some rich folks their appetizers."

I wanted to dislike the members of the Dulany Hills Country Club, but everyone I served was delightful, thanking me for their appetizers and seeming to have a wonderful time at the cocktail party, as if hanging out with a bunch of old friends. Not everyone was dressed to the nines. Plenty were in what I'd consider business casual, with a few men in golf shirts, their discarded sports jackets hanging on chairs. Maybe rich people weren't so bad.

I returned from the kitchen with a tray of bacon-wrapped

scallops and saw Phoenix and Erica handing their coats to the coat-check clerk. A little crowd had gathered and even though I stood on my tiptoes, I couldn't see Phoenix's date.

Then the crowd parted and I saw him. I couldn't have been more stunned.

Detective Lockett.

His amused eyes took in my black vest and white shirt and shocked expression.

I ran through our short history and the clues clicked into place. Detective Lockett and Phoenix were a couple. I smiled and walked over to him. "Bacon-wrapped scallop?" I offered.

He shook his head at me with a mixture of annoyance and entertainment. "What are you up to?"

Phoenix put his hand on his arm, wearing a ring that matched Lockett's. "Be nice to the staff, Roger." His eyes laughed at me, delighted with his surprise.

It was hard for me to think of him as Roger.

"Nice ring," I said.

He started to say something but was interrupted by a man with a Southern accent. "Detective!"

"We'll talk later," Lockett said, and turned away.

Erica had taken the opportunity to zero in on Newell while the detective was distracted. She'd sent me his photo from the Board Members page of the country club website, and he looked exactly like I'd expected—a well-kept man in his sixties wearing a conservative suit and red tie. He had arrived alone and taken a seat at the corner of the ornate wooden bar. He had plenty of company as members greeted him while ordering drinks and then moved out of the way for others getting their drinks. A good location for not getting stuck talking to anyone for very long.

Erica must have talked Phoenix into introducing her to Newell. They were discreet about their goal, but if anyone was watching like me, they'd see the pair making a slow but inexorable journey to Newell's end of the bar. It might have taken a shorter amount of time, but Phoenix seemed to know just about everyone along the way, pausing to say hello and introduce Erica.

I desperately wanted to watch, and could busy myself with cleaning up discarded glasses in the corner only so long. Finally, after making it through the phalanx of Phoenix fans, they were standing right beside Newell Woodfellow the Third. Luckily, Lockett was distracted by his own conversation with the Southern man, who gestured a lot with his hands.

The room for the cocktail party portion of the evening was elegant but small for so many guests, and I couldn't hear anything across the room. But I was watching when Erica turned to chat with Newell as they ordered drinks.

An elderly woman in a gray suit with green trim grabbed my sleeve when I attempted to move closer. "Could you be a dear and get a pillow from the library? I'm afraid this old back just can't handle these chairs anymore." She looked up at me, smiling with big cheeks like a chipmunk. "Not one of the frilly ones. Those little knobbies are even worse than nothing. One of the smooth satin ones."

"Of course," I said. I stopped in the kitchen to ask which of the many doors led to the library, then stepped into the dim light of a lavish room with books from floor to ceiling—Erica's idea of heaven—and grabbed the first non-knobby pillow I could find.

"You're new here," a man's voice said from near the fireplace as I turned to rush back.

I gasped. "Sorry to disturb you. I didn't know anyone was in here." It didn't help that he looked a little bit devilish with the way the fire played over his face, shadowing half of it.

He stood up and took a step toward me. "But you look very familiar," he said, his voice both playful and curious, as if we were in a game. "Where do I know you from?"

"I don't know." It came out a little defensively as I edged toward the door. "I have to take this back."

"I never forget a face," he said. He tapped his finger on his chin in an impish manner. "Let me think."

"Can I get you something?" I asked, and took a step backward.

"Not at this moment." He kept his eyes on me as I rushed back to the room where the cocktail party was being held. I delivered the pillow, following the woman's directions to place it behind her lower back, and moved to the corner to watch Erica operate.

The man from the library appeared beside me and I jumped. "You're that chocolatier who solves mysteries!" He looked around the room in time to see the expression on Newell's face harden, which didn't bode well for us getting any information. Newell got to his feet with a scowl and headed for the farthest door from us.

"You're asking Newell about Faith?" Library Man asked with a shocked expression. He was short, just a couple of inches taller than me. His face was thin, and his hair was graying at the temples. "But why?"

"What?" I managed after my heart calmed down. "I don't know what you're talking about."

Erica spoke to Phoenix before heading over to me.

I took a few steps away from the man to meet her. "What happened?" I asked quietly.

"As soon as I mentioned Faith, he got extremely angry and walked out the door." Erica seemed surprised that she'd caused such a response.

"You are so wrong." The man from the library had stayed right on my heels.

"Who are you?" I asked.

"Ullman Childers." He held out his hand. "Pleased to make your acquaintance."

I shook his hand, even though his greeting was said in a mocking tone. Why did all these rich people have odd names?

Ullman Childers looked at Lockett, who was staring at us with narrowed eyes. "Let's go somewhere quiet, so I can explain."

# 13

Minutes later we were housed in a small meeting room of the club, surrounded by mahogany walls and flowered overstuffed chairs mixed with ancient leather couches that were as soft as butter. I expected Lockett to burst in at any moment. Maybe Phoenix was keeping him away.

"What can you tell us about Newell?" Erica asked. She looked perfectly at ease in her black cocktail dress and tasteful gold jewelry, her long legs tucked against the chair like a perfect lady.

"He's a dear friend," Ullman said. "But he can be a bit stodgy, which happens to people who are born with as much money as he was."

"You weren't?" I asked.

"Born with a silver spoon in my mouth?" he asked. "Oh heavens, no." He leaned toward us as if letting us in on a delicious secret. "I have far fewer zeroes in my bank account than all of these people, but I'm valuable in a whole other way."

"And what way is that?" Erica asked.

"I am a fund-raising genius," he said. "And that's me being modest. All of these people here have their pet charities—all very important and meaningful organizations in their own way—and I help them raise tons of money for them."

"How?" I asked.

"I'm a charming bastard," he said simply, as if that explained it. "I used to be a stockbroker. It's the same basic steps to get people to part with their money."

Erica changed gears. "How do you know Newell wasn't involved?"

"He was head over heels in love with her," he said. "He'd never hurt her."

Erica shifted in her leather chair. My face might have shown my skepticism too because Ullman gave an impatient sigh. "He doesn't have it in him," he said. "He's simply incapable of violence."

"What does that mean?" I asked.

"People like him don't really live, if they're not careful. They just cling to what they have. Being conservative in everything they do. After his second even-more-boring-than-he-was wife filed for divorce, I encouraged, dared him even, to date outside his very insular circle. I wanted to push him out of his comfort zone."

"And he met Faith," I said.

"Yes," he said. "She was so delightfully—how should I say it?—*not* conservative. Young. Adventurous. A breath of fresh air. Or so I thought."

"What do you mean?" I asked.

"I noticed pretty early that she was an operator," Ullman said. "It takes one to know one."

Erica raised her eyebrows. "Oh?"

"Asking the man to donate to some horse charity that seemed pretty irregular," he said in a dismissive tone. "Getting him to pay for her car repairs. It was rather distasteful."

"Did you tell Newell what you thought of her?" I asked.

"Of course," he said.

"And what did he say?"

"By then it was too late," Ullman said. "He was completely enamored of her. He had an excuse for everything she did."

"That must have been upsetting for you," Erica said, "to see your friend taken in like that."

His expression turned wary. "Dear girl, I had nothing to do with her murder."

"Of course not," Erica said. "He eventually saw the light, right?"

"Yes," he said. "And none too soon." He stopped, obviously hiding something.

"How did that happen?" I asked.

He pursed his lips. "Okay. Since Newell will most likely spill the beans as soon as Phoenix's beau gets to him, I'll confess."

"What?" I prompted him.

"When I found out that ninny had actually *changed his will* to include her, and then *told her about it*, I hired a private investigator." He raised his chin as if proving that he was proud of his actions.

"What did the private investigator find?" Erica asked.

I bet she wanted to get a look at *that* report.

"That she was a scam artist," he said. "Just like I suspected."

"What did Newell say to that?"

"At first he didn't believe the report on her criminal past," he said, "but then he encountered little mishaps and came to believe he might be in real danger. From her."

I sat up straight. Chuck had mentioned that Mr. Rich Man had dumped Faith because of "accidents." "What kind of mishaps?"

"A railing on the deck of Newell's house was tampered with, and one of his employees was injured. The temperature of his water heater was turned way up. Then the brake line of his collectible Porsche was cut," he said, turning angry. "Right after Newell changed his will? They couldn't all be coincidences."

"His brake line was cut?" I asked. "What happened?"

"Nothing, but only because he saw the brake fluid on the ground before he drove it," Ullman said, his voice indignant. "He could have been killed."

"And that's when Newell broke up with her?" Erica asked.

"Yes," Ullmann said. "But just in case he wavered that time, I was forced to apply some social pressure."

"What do you mean?"

"He still didn't believe his little girlfriend was capable of such things, but then I told all of our friends how utterly stupid he was being, and with everyone, including his rather demanding family, clamoring for him to get rid of her, he finally called it quits."

We stayed quiet for a moment.

"Are you still friends?" I asked.

"No, not at all like before," he said in a somber tone. "But at least Newell is still alive."

I was up early the next morning. I planned to spend the entire time before our late Sunday opening waiting for Leo. If he didn't show up in time, Erica would open up for me and call Kayla in for backup.

What were all these early-morning motorcycle rides about? Was Leo running from demons or riding toward something better?

I parked in front of his apartment building in the shade of a huge elm tree that would hide my chocolate-photo-covered minivan until he was too close to drive away. I still wasn't quite sure what I was going to say to him. Leo had experienced so much loss in his life. First our parents and then his fellow soldiers. Even his leg. It was no wonder he'd experienced PTSD. But he'd been doing so much better. He shouldn't have to go through that pain again.

He pulled up just as I was about to call Erica and let her know I'd be late. I waited for him to park in his assigned spot in the garage and take off his helmet before approaching him.

"Good morning!" I said cheerfully and handed him a coffee the way he liked it, with a lot of cream and sugar.

He smiled tightly, knowing it wasn't a social call, and took the now-not-so-hot coffee. I noticed that his face looked leaner, as if he'd lost weight in the past week.

"You working out?" I asked.

He shook his head and took a sip, not looking me in the eye.

"Not eating?" I asked.

He shrugged. "Not hungry."

"Leo," I said. "You know you have to keep your diet and sleeping schedule and everything consistent."

"Right," he said. "Like you take such good care of yourself."

"This isn't about me." I'd practiced that line. "I'm worried about you."

He looked incredulous. "If you were worried about me, you'd stop this nonsense."

I bristled at his manipulation, but made myself stay on track. "It's not your job to take care of me anymore," I said. "You have to take care of yourself. How are you doing on that?"

And with that question, his belligerence left him. He sat down heavily on the concrete wall leading to his steps. His stooped shoulders telegraphed defeat.

"Leo?" I asked, wanting to cry.

He whispered, "I can't . . ."

I sat down beside him and rubbed his back. "What is happening?"

"I don't know." His face was so lost, I got scared.

I wrapped my arms around him and hung on tight, tears coming to my own eyes. "Can I ask you some questions?"

He nodded once stiffly.

"Are you still seeing your therapist?"

A nod.

"Are you still taking your meds?"

Another nod.

An intense wave of relief washed over me. If he was doing both of those, he could weather this storm.

I blinked away my tears. "Worst day ever?"

He took a deep breath and the tension in his body relaxed just a little, and he shook his head.

Nothing was solved with Leo, other than me letting him know several times that I loved him no matter what. We didn't discuss the whole him-being-overprotective thing, and I really hoped that was behind us.

Lockett stopped by the store after our lunch rush. "So you talked to Mr. Childers last night."

I wasn't up to sparring with the police, especially after such an emotional scene with my brother.

"What are you talking about?" I tried to look innocent. "Coffee?"

"Sure," he said, sliding into a stool at the counter. "You look tired."

I shook my head, not rising to the bait. "Thanks for the compliment."

He waited a moment. "You don't look so bad." His voice was gruff.

I sighed. "I'm fine. I just had a difficult conversation with Leo."

"I get it," he said. "So I won't yell at you."

"You promise?" I asked.

He raised his eyebrows in a *don't push it* way before admitting, "Mr. Woodfellow was on our radar too. We had an appointment to talk to him this morning, and he said Erica had ambushed him at the country club last night. He's not pleased that a fellow country club member betrayed him."

"First of all," I inserted, "he gave you an appointment? He totally blew us off."

Lockett's jaw tightened. "I guess it's more difficult to blow off an officer of the law."

Oh yeah, there was that. "Second of all, he really used the word 'betrayed'?" I asked. "Is he going to challenge Phoenix to a duel?"

Lockett smiled. "I believe there's an unwritten code, or perhaps even a written one, that Phoenix broke."

"Did Newell confess?" I asked. "Did he do it?"

"Because of Erica's little stunt, Mr. Woodfellow had his attorney with him," he said.

"So he's guilty?" I asked.

"No," he said. "Just careful. He actually has an alibi. He was at a fund-raiser for the next congresswoman for Frederick."

I opened my mouth, about to say, "But—" except he cut me off.

"There are photographs in the paper," he said.

I opened my mouth again, ready to tell him that maybe he should look into Newell's way too involved friend.

"And his buddy, your new best friend, Mr. Childers, was at the event as well."

I scowled. "Are you psychic?"

"No," he said. "But much to my dismay, I'm beginning to understand how you think."

"What about all of those accidents Newell had?" I asked. "They have to mean something."

"Now that's still a mystery," he said. "He never reported them, but since they may be connected to this murder, we're looking into them. Unfortunately, any evidence is probably long gone."

"Do you think Faith was behind them?" I asked.

"I have no idea," he said. "Unless she knows how to cut a brake line and break into a house to turn the temperature up on a water heater."

"I wouldn't put it past her," I said.

He raised his eyebrows. "Anything you'd like to share?"

I ignored his question. "Ooh, are we becoming work buddies, like, colleagues?"

"Don't push it," he said.

"So, rings," I said. "That sounds serious."

"Yes," he said, his face warning me not to go there.

I'd have to find out how serious from Phoenix.

"Are you going to ask Reese about her progress?" I regretted it as soon as the words left my mouth. Was I feeling competitive with that dingbat?

He sighed. "Not that you'll listen, but this murder was particularly brutal. You all should stop what you're doing, Reese included. The victim was beaten with a baseball bat, even after she was dead. Whoever did this is a maniac."

After Lockett finished his coffee and Wild Huckleberry Milks and left, I realized that he hadn't mentioned Chuck, which meant he probably didn't know that we'd talked to him. That was good, because we had new questions for Chuck.

I went to the office to call Bean, who was waiting for a phone call from his contact in Baltimore. "Can you use your burner phone to get a message to Chuck?" As a journalist, he often used prepaid, untraceable cell phones with his sources.

"Sure." He sounded amused that I was using the phrase "burner phone." It did make me feel kinda cool.

"Can you ask him to meet us at the same place for a meal this week?" I asked.

"Will do," he said.

"But don't offer fifty bucks this time," I said. "Maybe he'll do it for a free lunch."

"You know what they say," he started.

"I know, there's no such thing," I said. "How's Truffles?"

"A handful," he said. "One: he never sleeps. And I'm not sure how long I can keep him as an indoor cat. He's always trying to get out. It's a good thing he's cute."

"Aw," I said.

"Colleen brought the kids over earlier," he said. "They all had a great time but Truffles is exhausted."

"I'll bet," I said. His sister Colleen's twins were adorable but could certainly tire out a tiny kitty.

"I gave Erica a key for you," he said, his voice casual. "I was hoping you could check on him tonight if I end up staying later than I planned."

"Sure," I said, looking forward to seeing that little monster again.

We said our good-byes and Erica came in when I was contemplating if "giving me a key" meant more than checking on Truffles. Erica had given Bean a key to our house as soon as he'd come back into town but that wasn't the same thing at all.

"What did Lockett want?" she asked.

"Both Newell and Ullman have alibis," I said, sounding a little bitter.

"That was fast," she said.

"Do we have any more information on the people she knew that she didn't date?" I asked. "What about her family?"

Erica went into her thoughtful mode. "Maybe we can ask Chuck about that."

I nodded and looked over my own notes. "I still think we should talk to that guy who had a crush on her in high school."

Erica looked up from the list. "Wade Overton?"

"Yes," I said. "Did Zane find out any information on him?"

She clicked a few times on her computer. "He's a mechanic in Hagerstown. He's not on any social media."

"Not even Facebook?" I asked.

She shook her head.

"That's all Zane gave you?" He was usually more thorough.

"He had a lot of people to go through," Erica reminded me. "Maybe you can take my car in for a checkup and ask Wade some questions."

"Good idea," I said.

I waited until closing time to approach Erica. "Did Bean give you a key so I could check on Truffles?"

"Yes," she said. She pulled it out of her pocket, and it was on the most basic key ring. It looked less like a *want to live with me?* key ring, and more like a casual, neighborly *can you bring my mail in?* key ring. I was definitely not reading anything into it.

"I'm going to stop at Bean's on the way home tonight,"

I said. With no Sunday-night date and no Halloween Festival prep scheduled, I didn't know what to do with myself.

"I'll go with you," she said. "I want to see the little guy. I'll bet he's grown."

"It's been less than a week since you saw him," I pointed out.

"You're right," she said. "But it's been a very long week."

It took only a few minutes to drive over to Bean's house. He'd left a few lights on and the house looked welcoming. He'd carved a jack-o'-lantern out of an enormous pumpkin and placed it in the corner of the porch under an elaborate spiderweb.

We let ourselves in and Truffles popped his head up from the couch, stretched and started mewing to be picked up. Who could resist?

We gave him new food and water and spent a half hour playing with him until we all ended up on the couch. Once he settled in between us, Erica hypnotically petted him until he fell back asleep. We carefully got up from the couch and tiptoed out, the sight of the sleeping cutie-pie making us smile.

## 14

The next day was not my normal Monday. My best client, a boutique hotel in Washington, DC, that catered to the political elite, had decided to include a trio of cheese and chocolate pairings as a unique dessert option. They planned to pair my Fleur de Sel Caramels with an aged Bijou goat cheese; my spicy Mayan Warriors with Spanish Manchego; and Royal Blue Stilton with my Extra Dark Mochas. I brought both Kona and Kayla in early to work on these special orders, and didn't have time for any new truffle inventions.

We were almost done by the time Kona had to open up the store, so Kayla and I finished. It felt good to push everything else aside and focus on the fun part of my mission in life. Making little bits of happiness for other people. I played a game that I hadn't thought about in quite a while: imagining who might be on the other end, opening up the box, but this time I substituted taking a bite from an elegant dessert dish. Would it be a businesswoman taking a client out to dinner in the fancy hotel restaurant? Maybe she'd be anxious about making a deal, but taking a bite of a truffle would make her stop for a moment and relax, just to enjoy her indulgence. Maybe she and the client would make a connection over their love of chocolate, and she'd win that contract.

Perhaps it would be a child enjoying a Halloween treat with his grandmother, a treat that tasted so much better than everything else in his loot bag. Or a middle-aged man, on his first date since his wife unexpectedly divorced him. Maybe they too would bond over a love of my chocolates.

I returned to the real world from my Candyland daydream with a sigh. I walked to the front of the store, and all conversation died. Kona looked at me with anxious eyes from behind the counter. She jerked her head toward the back, and I went straight to Erica's office without talking to anyone. Erica looked up from her computer, distraught.

"Reese?" I asked.

She nodded. Front and center was one of the photos that poor excuse for a journalist had taken when Dylan was brought in for questioning. Erica and I were holding up our hands in response to her obnoxious flash, but it looked like we were trying to duck and run.

The headline screamed, *Detective Duo Out for Blood*.

"That freakin' . . ." I couldn't say what I wanted to call her out loud.

I read on. *By day, you'll find West Riverdale citizens Erica Russell and Michelle Serrano running their Main*

*Street store, Chocolates and Chapters. By night, you'll find them volunteering at the West Riverdale Boys and Girls Club, preparing for the annual Halloween Festival. But what many citizens don't realize is that behind this community-oriented facade lies a manic desire to act as suburban vigilantes to bring down the criminals behind the spate of recent murders in our town. To get in the way of our excellent state and town police professionals . . .*

I groaned and put my head down on the desk, exhausted by the spite behind her words. When would she stop? "I can't finish it. Just give me the highlights. Or low points. Whatever."

Even normally cool and composed Erica seemed flustered. "Basically, she accused us of having giant egos and using our investigation to make sure our friends Dylan and Oscar, the guilty parties, are cleared. That we're searching desperately to find innocent people to accuse. And that everyone should avoid us, so we don't cast our nasty aspersions on them."

"She used the word 'aspersions'?" I asked.

Erica nodded. "And that we are enlisting the comic book club in our efforts."

"Nice," I said. "So anyone who's following the news coverage about Faith's murder can see that we're asking questions now. What does your Geek Team think of all this?"

"I've only heard from Tommy, who told me to ignore it," she said.

Then I figured it out. "She's trying to sabotage us," I said with an *aha!* tone to my voice.

Erica knew what I was talking about right away. "Reese? Could be," she admitted. "But why?"

"Maybe she realized we were figuring things out before her," I said. "And maybe she's tired of being the laughing-stock of the whole town." I didn't even want to bring up Reese's sense of rivalry left over from our high school basketball team days.

Reese needn't have bothered. We didn't seem to be making much progress. Unless she knew something that we didn't.

Erica and I had planned to spend the day in the back, away from curious stares. After we finished the order for the hotel, I worked with new milk chocolate recipes, trying to make up for my heavily dark-chocolate schedule from the week before, and then I got antsy.

"Forget Reese," I told Erica when I found her hiding in the office. "It's time to see Wade for a tune-up. We have to make progress. Can I take your car?" My chocolate-themed van would get too much attention.

She looked up from her computer. "Are you sure?"

"Absolutely," I said. "Let's hope that the people in Hagerstown have better things to do than read her nonsense."

I hadn't been to Hagerstown for years, and wondered why as I drove through the beautiful hills and came into the center of town. I had a flashback to my father telling me all about the Stonehenge limestone that was mined there and used to make many of its older buildings. At the time, I'd gotten confused about the real Stonehenge in England, and demanded to go see it. Luckily, he'd set me straight before we made the road trip.

Erica called as I drove into town, making sure I stayed

under the speed limit. "I found out why Reese wrote that article."

"Why? Besides being a horrible person."

"Iris was telling someone at the diner how she tricked Reese into starting that social media campaign and that it was our idea," she said. "She didn't know Reese had come in while she was on a smoking break and was in one of the booths. Reese heard everything and stormed out."

"Oh great," I said. "She's going to think of us as her enemies even more." She might be an idiot, but her website gave her a big bullhorn in our area.

I walked into the garage area of a large car repair station on the north side of the town, ignoring the small lobby where customers were supposed to sign away their firstborn to pay for car repairs. The smell of oil and burning metal assaulted my nose. The first mechanic I stumbled across had *Wade* stenciled across the pocket of his gray mechanic jumpsuit, which was covered with oil splotches. We'd found Wade's photo on an online yearbook site, but unfortunately, he didn't look anything like his high school photo. I knew people changed, but I doubt he could change from a blond-haired man with a round face who looked like he came from Iowa to this man with olive skin and black hair.

"Are you Wade Overton?" I asked.

The man looked puzzled. "No?" he said with a Spanish accent.

I pointed to his name on his pocket, and he laughed. "Wrong uniform." He looked around and yelled, "Wade!" with his hands making a trumpet around his mouth.

A man standing under a raised car stuck his head out around the tire. "Yeah?"

Fake Wade stuck his thumb out to point to me. "Someone's here to see you."

Real Wade, who looked only slightly older than his teenage photo, pulled a rag from his back pocket and wiped his hands while he walked over. "Can I help you?" He must have been over six feet tall, towering above me.

"Hi!" I went right into ditzy mode. "My friend said you were the best mechanic in Maryland, so I'm hoping you can work on my car?" Ditzy Michelle ended a lot of her sentences with a question mark.

"What kind of car?" he asked.

"A Nissan," I said. "I think the dealership messed something up so I wanted to ask you some questions before you actually work on it."

He looked at me like he thought I was crazy but he'd humor me. "Sure."

"I know, like, interviewing your mechanic is unusual, but they had to fix it, like, three times and now I'm kinda nervous." I might be overdoing it. "First, my friend Faith recommended you but I wanted to find out how you knew her? Like, she's not getting paid to tell people about you, is she?"

He blinked. "Faith?"

"Faith Monette?" I said. "She said she went to high school with you? And that you were a really good mechanic."

"Yeah," he said. "We both went to Buckey High." He paused, looking a little suspicious. "How do you know her?"

"She's, like, my neighbor, and she saw me having trouble with my car a while ago and said I should bring it to you."

"She said I was a good mechanic?" He smiled a little, as if her opinion mattered.

"Oh yeah," I said. "So, you didn't, like, give her money to tell people that, did you?"

"No. That's not something mechanics do." He said it slowly, as if talking to an idiot.

"Oh good," I said. "Isn't it terrible what happened to her?" I carefully watched his face.

Now he just looked confused. "Something happened to her?"

I brought my hand to my mouth. "Didn't you hear? She was murdered!"

He looked stunned. "What?"

I took a step toward him and grabbed his hand. "I'm sorry that I sprung it on you like that, but it's been all over the news."

He stared at me.

"Did you know her well?" I asked, covering his hand with mine in a little hand sandwich. I hoped it was soothing rather than strange.

"We went to high school together but . . ." He gave a *not really* shrug. "She was in here a few months ago, and I recognized her right away."

"Oh," I said in my most understanding tone. "You were friends way back in school."

He shook his head. "Oh no. She was real popular, and I was just . . . you know."

"Oh," I needed more platitudes in my questioning arsenal. "I think she mentioned a reunion or something."

He nodded. "I was hoping—" He stopped, clearly embarrassed.

"Yes?"

"It's stupid," he said. "But I thought if I bought her a drink at the reunion, that maybe she'd go out with me or some-thing."

"That's so romantic," I said.

"Yeah, well. She probably has—had—a lot of men who wanted to date her," he said.

He had no idea.

"But she told you I was a good mechanic?" His tone was probably more wistful than he intended.

"Best in Maryland," I said. "She also said you gave her the friends-and-family discount." I was totally fishing at that point.

He looked over his shoulder. "I kinda made that up," he said. "Don't tell my boss."

From what I'd learned about Faith, she'd probably asked for a discount, based on nothing but being a fellow alumni. "Oh," I said in a disappointed tone. "I won't. You know, I'm surprised you didn't connect on Facebook with her before this."

He shook his head. "I'm not into computers. Plus, that whole thing seems to be a bunch of showing off."

Which is why we didn't find him on any social media. "I thought I was the only one who thought that!"

"So what's wrong with your car?" he asked.

As soon as Wade saw that I was driving a Nissan Leaf, he'd apologized and told me that only the dealer could work on those cars. He'd watched me drive away, and I couldn't read the expression on his face.

I was about to park back at the store when Bean called me, his voice urgent. "Can you take a break and help me?"

"Sure," I said.

"The kids let Truffles out and he's in a tree in the back-yard," he said. "He'll probably come down for you."

"I'll be right there," I said, and drove just a little too fast to his house.

I went around the back and Colleen's two-year-old twins ran right up to me. "Auntie Schmell," they said together. Then they pointed and talked to me in a mixture of English and toddler speak. All I could hear was "kitty," several times, but I got the gist from their expressions that it wasn't their fault. No matter what anyone said.

"It's okay," I said. "I'll get him down."

Bean stood at the bottom of a large oak tree, and I could see Truffles was busy exploring a wide branch. "Boys," Bean said as they fluttered around me, pointing and explaining. "I bet you could see the cat better from the porch."

They stared at the porch as if evaluating it, then at each other, and they ran, stomping up the two steps and watching us over the railing. Luckily, a box of large building blocks grabbed their attention and they plopped down and started playing.

"Truffles," I called.

He looked down at me and was immediately distracted by a moving leaf.

"Truffles," I said in a singsong voice. "Come on down for a treat."

He stopped swatting at the leaf to meow piteously.

I talked out of the corner of my mouth. "You still have treats, don't you?"

"Of course," Bean said. "What do you think about a ladder?"

"Let's wait a minute," I said and then turned my attention back to Truffles. "You can come down," I said. "You can do it."

Truffles tumbled a little down to a branch closer to the ground, his short fall making me inhale sharply. "It's okay," I said.

His success must have made him more confident, because he hopped down the next two branches quickly. The closest branch to me was still pretty high up. "Let's go," I told him. "Time for a nap."

He started and stopped several times, and I said to Bean, "Maybe we do need that ladder," just as Truffles tentatively took a few steps toward me, head down, and slipped. His nails were not made for coming down headfirst, and I suspected he was too young to figure out how to back down.

"On its way," he said and went to his garage.

"Just wait a minute," I told the kitten.

The twins got very excited to see their uncle bringing out the ladder and dashed toward me, sending Truffles back up a few branches.

"The ladder is for grown-ups, right, boys?" I asked. "You should build a ladder with your blocks." They went back to the porch but sat down on the steps to watch the excitement.

"Want me to go up?" he asked.

"Let me try first," I said, and climbed the ladder while Bean held it stable.

Truffles meowed a few times, and then hopped toward the bottom branch again.

"Time to move," I said, reaching up as high as I could.

The kitten complained a few more times and then reached his paw out to me. I stood on my tiptoes on the highest rung that I could and then hopped a little to grab Truffles by his scruff.

"Yay!" the boys cheered. "Auntie Schmell is a hero!"

I climbed back down, not letting go of Truffles until he was safely inside the house. Bean's relief was obvious. I even felt a little like a hero.

"Knock, knock." West Riverdale's chief of police, Eric Noonan, stood in the doorway of Chocolates and Chapters' kitchen, his shock of gray hair standing more on end than it usually did. He was not happy about another homicide in his small town.

"Hello, Chief," I said cautiously. His visits never came with good news.

"Michelle," he started right away, "I've known you a long time. You must stop this nonsense."

"Do you really believe anything Reese puts in the rag she calls a newspaper?" I asked, but he knew I was trying to get around him.

"I've heard from other sources, as you well know," he said. "We're dealing with one angry killer."

"Do you still think Dylan had anything to do with her murder?" I challenged him.

He didn't answer for a moment. "That's not the point."

"That's exactly the point for us," I said. "If we *were* actually investigating something, then we'd stop once he was cleared." I gave him my best pointed stare. "When is that going to happen?"

"I don't know," the chief admitted. "But you still need to stop."

. . . . . . . . . . . . . .

Working at the Boys and Girls Club that evening didn't give us much respite from Reese's negative publicity. Yvonne, Steve and Jolene were totally on our side, but a few of our teen volunteers didn't show up.

"How's Dylan?" I asked Quinn.

"He's okay," she said. "Tired of being cooped up." She paused. "The other kids want me to apologize. They all wanted to come, but their parents kept them away."

I ended up working angry while stacking tables and chairs, and came away with a strained shoulder. Erica insisted I take a break in the quiet room with an ice pack.

I tried Star, and after two rings it went to message. Uh-oh. One ring meant her phone was turned off. Two rings meant she'd rejected my call. Which meant she didn't want to talk to me. Which meant that Leo might have done something stupid.

I left her a message anyway. "Hi, Star. I'm sorry to bother you." I paused, not knowing exactly what to say. "Could you return this call?"

It took her fifteen minutes, but she called me back. I jumped and hit the Accept button before she could change her mind and hang up. "Star, thanks so much for getting back to me."

"I don't know where your brother is," she said in a flat tone. "He isn't returning my calls."

This was bad. "I'm so sorry. All I can say is he's really messed up and I don't know what to do. I know he loves you, so none of this makes sense."

She didn't say anything.

"Thanks for letting me know," I said. "I think he's having some . . . issues."

"Ya think?" she said.

"Did he ever tell you about . . . them?" I left the question open.

"Of course," she said. "And he said he was able to cope with those issues. But if he's gonna be such a wuss, he and his issues can kiss my ass."

I couldn't help but laugh, even in my worried state. We said our good-byes and I called Bean. He also didn't answer—where was everybody today?—so I sent him a text asking if he knew where Leo was.

Erica opened the door to the haunted house break room while I was emptying the ice pack to put it back on the first-aid shelf.

"I'm really sorry," she said, her face white with apprehension. "Something happened to your minivan."

"What?" I asked as I followed her in a dead run toward an exit.

"Someone hit it," she said, "with a baseball bat."

15

It was worse than just a baseball bat. Someone had slashed *Stop Now* in white spray paint across my beautiful truffle photos. I nearly cried. Okay, I did cry. I was so proud of this van, which advertised my business and transported my products to my customers.

Erica grabbed my shaking hands and looked me in the eyes. "It's okay," she said.

When I nodded, still sniffling, she walked me to the retaining wall with the *West Riverdale Boys and Girls Club* sign on it, and made me sit down. Probably to make sure I didn't faint. She called 911, and within minutes, Junior arrived in the West Riverdale police car, sirens wailing and red lights flashing.

We'd been smart enough not to touch anything. With the painted threat, the crime scene techs were sure to be here soon to take fingerprints, at a minimum.

Erica handled Junior's questions, but really the scene in front of me had all the answers. The baseball bat, which had been jammed into the windshield, was a horrible message in itself, without the threatening words.

The van was right under a streetlight. Whoever did it took a real risk of being caught. Were we that close to finding something out about the case that someone felt the need to scare us off? If the killer did this, how many bats did he carry around?

I thought about my own softball bag that I kept in my car all of softball season. I owned four bats myself.

Then Bobby arrived in his own car, trying to be all professional, but I could tell he was worried and ramping up to give us a hard time about our investigation.

"This is Reese's fault," I said to him from my seat on the wall.

He stared at me, with Junior nervously eyeing him, waiting for direction.

"She wrote that article," I said, "to instigate something like this to happen." I needed a place for my growing anger to go, and Reese was an easy target. "I want you to arrest her for it." Which made complete sense to me.

Bobby paused, choosing his words carefully. "On what grounds?"

"Isn't there some crime for inciting riots?" I asked. "Or hate crimes or something? She incited this hate crime."

Erica took a step toward me. "Michelle," she said in her *why don't we all calm down* voice.

"No." I stood up, as tall as my short body would go. "Officer Robert Simkin. I demand that you arrest Reese Everhard for inciting this criminal act."

. . . . . . . . . . . . . .

An hour later, I'd cooled off a bit. Bobby and Erica had blathered on about "freedom of speech" or some such nonsense, but all I could hear was the white rage in my head.

Then Tommy pulled up in his tricked-out hearse, with Quinn in the front seat and that silly life-sized skeleton waving from the backseat. "Need a ride?" he asked, with a sideways look at Lieutenant Bobby. Quinn must have called Tommy, and they'd decided to rescue me.

"She doesn't," Bobby said at the same time I said, "I'd love one."

I ran around to the other side, so I wouldn't have to push the skeleton aside. "Am I done here?" I asked Bobby.

He nodded, not looking very happy about it. He probably wasn't happy about any of it, including taking my poor car in for evidence.

I had to push aside a few action figures and a large stuffed tube with eyes. "What is this?" I held it up so Tommy could see it in the rearview mirror.

He smiled. "Mad cow disease. You have Ebola and flesh-eating Streptococcus back there too."

He focused on driving away, and I decided not to look too closely at the assorted plush toys around me. "Good thing I had my shots."

"Scarier than a jack-o'-lantern," he said.

Quinn turned around from the front passenger seat. "Are you okay?"

I nodded. "Thanks for getting me out of there."

"NP," Tommy said, the text shortcut for "no problem," although I'd never heard it spoken aloud.

"Do the police have any idea who did that?" Quinn asked.

"Nope." I felt my anger flame back up again and forced myself to calm down. "Could be someone connected to the murder, or anyone who read that article and decided to be a real jerk."

Tommy took a turn off of the road that I didn't expect. "You're not going down Main Street?" I asked.

"Nope," he said. "Got a shortcut."

Who needed a shortcut in such a small town? But I stayed quiet.

We ended up on a dirt road that cut between the houses across the street from me and the farm on the other side. The hearse wasn't made to handle bad roads and the ride became extremely bumpy.

We came out a little bit past our house, where the hill that I cursed every time I ran began. Our outside lights were on timers and they were blazing.

And then we all noticed the black car stopped on the hill, on the side of the road. With a clear view of our house.

"Stop," I said urgently. "Quinn, take a photo of that license plate."

Teens were way faster at opening apps than I could be.

"Tommy," I said. "Pull a little closer."

Quinn opened her window and hung out to take a picture. The flash that seemed as bright as lightning alerted the driver, and he squealed out, past my house and toward town, as fast as a race car.

"Follow him," I demanded, adrenaline flying through my body. I wanted to catch this guy.

Tommy was already chasing after him, the huge hearse moving faster than I thought it could go.

Quinn scrunched down in her seat and covered her face with her hands, and I realized this was a bad idea. These were kids, for heaven's sake.

"Slow down," I told Tommy. "It isn't safe."

"But," Tommy protested, taking the next turn in a screech, "maybe it's him. The killer."

"Forget it," I said. "Quinn took a picture. We got him."

It helped that when we reached the top of the next hill, the black car was gone. Tommy slowed down and pulled over. He looked over at Quinn. "You okay?"

She unraveled her body from the fetal position and nodded. "That was so cool!" Her shaking hands didn't go with her words, but we let it go.

"Quinn," I said, "can you email that to me right away? I'll send it to Detective Lockett."

She nodded, wide-eyed.

"It's a good thing you took that shortcut, Tommy." My voice was as shaky as Quinn's. "Or we might not have known he was there."

It took quite a while for all of us to settle down. Tommy had walked me inside and insisted on looking around for intruders before leaving to take Quinn home. He even waited at the front door to make sure I turned the security system back on. I was shaken up enough to not question it.

I left a message with my insurance company and also with the company who did the original artwork, hoping my insurance would pay for a good deal of the repair. And then I went online to rent another minivan.

Erica arrived, and I told her about the car watching our house.

"Send me the photo," she said, and opened her laptop on the kitchen table. She blew it up and we could the see the four rings of the Audi logo as clear as day. But the license plate was a highlighted blur.

"What happened?" I asked.

She frowned. "He must be using a reflective cover to avoid those cameras that take pictures of speeding drivers."

"So a dead end?" I asked, totally exasperated.

Just then Bean texted me back that he hadn't heard from Leo either. I was so high-strung I wouldn't be good at talking to my brother even if I could track him down. Besides, this nasty business just confirmed that he was right. I didn't want to cause Leo any more stress, and I couldn't deal with a lecture from him.

A few minutes later, Bean called. "What happened to your car?"

"Who told you?" I asked.

"Never mind that," he said. "Why didn't you or Erica let me know?"

"It just happened," I said, feeling defensive. "We were going to tell you."

He was silent for a minute. "Okay," he said. "Just . . . take care of yourself."

I softened my tone as well. "Of course. You too." Then I told him about the car waiting outside our house.

"You were in a car chase in a hearse?" He sounded amused and worried at the same time.

"I know," I said. "Sounds like bad TV."

"I can totally picture it," he said. "Just think about what Tommy's Facebook post is going to be tonight."

I laughed, sure that Tommy would be the hero of the day once word got out, but hoped both he and Quinn had better sense than to post anything about this online.

Lockett and Bobby arrived at our house, after doing whatever police do with a scene like the rampage on my minivan. "So who'd you piss off this time?" Lockett asked, his face grim, as I led them to the kitchen.

"The list is endless," I said, my joke falling flat.

"We're actually at a loss," Erica admitted. "There are just too many people who had an ax to grind with Faith, and we're not any closer to finding out anything important."

The clever girl never used the word "investigation," but Lockett didn't quibble.

"I should tell you that someone was watching the house when I got back," I told Lockett.

"What do you mean?" he demanded.

I explained Tommy's shortcut and the black car waiting and our following until it took off. I left out the excessive speed of the chase.

But Lockett wasn't fooled. He turned bright red.

To distract him, Erica pulled up her notes on her computer and let him know everyone we had talked to, along with our disappointing results.

I had a hard time paying attention, wondering if whoever had attacked my car was someone I had talked to, or someone who had read Reese's article and just wanted to scare us off before we figured him, or her, out. Was there any chance the same person was watching our house?

"We'll follow up on everyone on your list, to find out

where they were tonight and the night of Faith's murder," Lockett said when Erica was finished.

"Do you think this was because of that article?" I asked.

"We won't know until we find out who did it," he said. "Whoever it was might have followed you or maybe they knew you'd be at the Boys and Girls Club this evening. A lot of people know when the festival is going to open, and that you're both involved."

Erica walked them out. I was too exhausted to listen to him tell us again to stay away from his investigation, even if it really did seem like it would be for our own good.

The next morning was gloomy, matching my mood, with rain clouds looming. I was surprised to see Dylan waiting for me on the back porch to the shop. He got to his feet while I parked.

"Hey," I said. "How are you holding up?"

"I'm fine," he said, his haunted eyes telling a different story. "I heard what happened last night and I wanted to apologize for getting you guys into this mess."

"That is not your fault," I told him.

"But your car," he started.

"Again, none of that is your fault," I insisted. "The police aren't even sure it's connected."

"Right," he said with sarcasm.

"You here to work?" I asked, trying to change the subject and get the guilty look off of his face.

"Yeah," he said. "My dad said I can either work here or go to school. Guess what I picked?"

"Yay for us!" I said. "There are boxes of books calling your name from the storage room."

Phoenix stopped by and I groaned inwardly. I hadn't done a thing about my marketing plan, let alone figuring out costs, and I knew he wanted to set up the meeting about possibly merging Erica's and my finances. Outwardly, I said, "Good morning!" a little too cheerily, as if to combat the weirdness in my head. "Cappuccino?"

"You know it. How are you holding up?" he said with sincere sympathy.

"We're okay."

"Let me know if there's anything I can do." It didn't sound like a platitude coming from Phoenix.

"I will," I said. "Thanks."

"I was thinking that perhaps we should put off any meeting about possible merger plans until after the festival."

I swung my head to look at him. "Did Erica suggest that?"

"No," he said, puzzled. "It just seems like the two of you have a lot going on right now and this can wait."

I couldn't believe Erica and I hadn't talked about it yet. "No, go ahead," I said, feeling very adult. "We should figure it all out sooner rather than later."

"I hoped you'd say that." He pulled out two folders. One labeled *Erica* and one labeled *Michelle*. He handed me mine. "In here is everything you need to consider before making your decision."

"Everything?" I asked. I riffled through the papers without really focusing on them.

"Including legal papers to create the partnership in the back." He watched my reaction.

"Whoa," I said.

"It's a big step," he said. "I know you'll make the right decision for both of you. Would you like to give Erica her copies?"

I nodded and rushed back to talk to Erica as soon as he left. "Phoenix was here."

"Uh-huh," she said, paying more attention to her computer than to me.

"He suggested that we put off the discussion about merging our finances until after the festival," I said.

"Okay." She typed a few words and squinted at the screen. "Whatever makes sense."

"So what do you think about the idea?" I asked.

She must have heard something in my voice because she looked up. "I don't know yet," she said. "We have to see if it makes sense financially."

"So, you'd be okay with merging if Phoenix showed us it would save money?" It came out more confrontational than I intended.

"Sure," she said. "Are you okay?"

I blinked at her. "But you've been in business for, like, ever, and I've been around only a couple of years."

She tilted her head as if trying to figure out what I meant. "We're partners." She paused. "And best friends. Nothing can affect that."

I blew out a breath, suddenly having to blink back tears. "But don't you worry that it would change things?"

"No," she said. "It's just numbers. And probably a legal document."

"But . . ."

"Are *you* worried that it'll change things?" she asked.

I took a moment to answer. "Yes."

Her eyebrows lifted. "Then we won't do it," she said. "But let's see Phoenix's recommendations and decide then."

I handed her the folder. "Phoenix said this is everything we need."

She put it to one side. "Great. Let's look at them on our own and discuss it when things aren't so crazy."

I nodded and changed the subject. "How's Dylan?"

She paused. "I'm not sure."

"Did you ask him anything?"

She shook her head. "No. He's here for a reprieve. Not a bunch of questions."


The next day, we met Chuck at noon at the mall, this time inside Kelly's Pub. Erica had driven me to the next town to pick up my rental minivan, which wasn't anywhere near as cool as mine. I had to reject the one that stunk of cigarette smoke, but after driving this one a few miles, it started to smell a little like wet dog.

Once again, Chuck reeked of alcohol. I suffered for our investigation and had another Harp to match his Guinness. My mouth watered at the memory of the corned beef sandwich, and I kept looking over my shoulder after we ordered to see if our waiter was returning with our food yet.

Erica asked Chuck if the police had told him anything yet.

"Not a chance," he said with bitterness. "But they're not following me anymore." He wore his black leather jacket but had lost his tough-guy sneer.

"We had a few questions that only a true friend of Faith's could answer," Erica said. "And it seemed like she didn't have many of those. Did you ever meet her other friends?"

"No," he said. "She kept most people at a distance."

"So you were her only real friend?"

He paused, looking like he was trying to get his hungover brain synapses to fire. "I guess so. She made some other friends, like this one lady, but they didn't stick around very long."

"So no other friends?" I asked. "That she didn't meet online?"

"Not really. Maybe her pawnshop guy."

"We met him," I said. "He seemed like a good guy. He really misses her."

Erica let him take a sip and then asked, "Did she like any of the guys she dated?"

"Sure," he said. "She wasn't a monster. But she was real practical. She needed someone who could take care of her. But she didn't date guys she didn't like. For very long, anyway." He waved his hand around. "Maybe because there were just so many out there."

Erica nodded. "Did she ever fall in love?"

He thought for a minute. "She got really excited about one guy that she didn't meet online. He didn't know about, you know, her business, and she liked that he thought of her as innocent or something."

Just then, our waiter brought our food. Now I was more impatient for information and not the food.

"Did she *say* she was in love?" I asked as soon as the waiter left.

"Not in so many words. She said he made her happy, just

hanging out with him. She could relax around him, instead of having to fake it like with that rich guy at the country club."

"Do you remember his name?" Erica took a sip of iced tea, acting casual, but her intent look gave her away.

He shook his head.

"Do you remember anything about him?"

"Only that she was really mad when she found out he didn't have as much money as he said he did," he said. "He lied to her about owning the place where he worked."

"What did he do?" I asked.

"I don't know," he said, clearly wishing he could help us. "I think it was some kind of small business, maybe a blue-collar job?"

That narrowed it down.

"Why did they break up?" I asked.

"It was kind of a combination of things. The rich guy got serious about her at the same time she found out the other guy lied about owning that company. She can't—couldn't—abide lying." Then he seemed to realize what he said. "Ironic, isn't it?"

"Did she have any family that she was close to?"

"She told me she had a brother who was married to a horrible woman who kept them apart." He took a bite and chewed, wiping his mouth with his other hand. "But another time she said they were estranged, on account of her dad's abuse."

"Abuse?" Erica said.

"Yeah," he said. "But to tell you the truth, I wasn't sure if it was real or not. Whenever she drank a lot, she made up a bunch of stuff. And one time she said her dad used to hit her."

"Did you think it really happened?" I asked, appalled.

He shrugged. "I know it sounds bad, but you could never really be sure with her."

We waited.

"But if it was true," he said. "It would explain a lot."

"Like what?" Erica asked.

He shrugged. "Like how messed up about men she was. And, you know, why she cried for days when her dad died."

"Days?" I asked. It didn't fit with the mean girl we'd heard about.

"She was a weird chick," he said. "But I still miss her. She was a lot of fun."

After Chuck left, Erica called Bobby to ask him about Faith's brother. After some persuasion, he told her that Vaughn Monette had identified Faith's body, which hadn't been easy. She'd been so badly beaten up that the only way he knew for sure was a small tattoo of angel wings on her hip.

Bobby had probably told Erica that last bit to scare us.

"Another road trip?" I asked after Erica called Zane to look up Vaughn's address in Frederick for us.

We decided to surprise Faith's brother, and drove straight from the Irish restaurant to his home. We found a woman in her early thirties planting bulbs in the flower bed out front.

We debated waiting for a man to arrive on the scene, but after the third time the woman looked over at our car, we decided we'd better talk to her before she called the police on us. It was the kind of neighborhood where people didn't hang out in cars. I was surprised she hadn't called 911 already.

"No comment," she said as we walked up.

"Oh, we're not with the press," I rushed to say.

She pointed to a tiny No Soliciting sign at the end of her walkway. "I'm not buying anything."

"We're looking for Vaughn Monette," Erica said.

"I'm his wife, Nancy," she said. "What do you want?"

"We're looking into his sister Faith's death," Erica said. "We're hoping you can shed some light on what she was like."

"Are you with the police?" She stood and began taking off her gardening gloves, pulling one finger at a time.

"We're here because a young boy has been falsely accused and we're trying to clear his name," I said.

She stared at the row of bulbs she was working on, as if daring them to not be in a straight line, and then turned her glare on us. "You think you can implicate my husband?"

"No!" Erica said. "Not at all. We're just trying to find out all we can about her from the people who knew her best. We understand that your husband has an airtight alibi and has no motive."

Either she got that information from Bobby and didn't tell me or she was getting good at making up stuff so we could get our questions answered.

Nancy blew out a breath. "You sure sound like those police."

"I'm a bookstore owner and Michelle sells chocolates."

Part of me bristled at the dismissive tone in Erica's voice even though I knew she was trying to let Nancy know we weren't a threat.

"I'm just surprised it didn't happen earlier," Nancy said, with anger in her voice.

I caught my breath.

"Oh," Erica said. "Because of how she . . . made money?"

"You mean conning men into falling in love with her and then bleeding them dry until she tossed them aside like garbage?" Nancy said in a cynical bray. "Yes, that's why. Maybe she was killed because she was a manipulative sociopath who only thought of people as targets to get something out of."

"That's what we keep hearing," Erica said. "Was she like that her whole life?"

"Sure was," Nancy said. "She had their parents convinced she was an angel and blamed Vaughn for anything bad she did. With those big brown eyes, she had them totally fooled."

She looked at the house across the street, and I turned in time to see a curtain twitch.

Nancy turned away, making it difficult for her neighbor to see her face. "I told Vaughn it started because she was born premature and wasn't expected to live," she said. "And the entire family called her a miracle child her whole life. I took just one psych class in college and learned enough to know that she had full-blown Narcissistic Personality Disorder."

I could think of a few people who probably had that.

"By the time they figured it out, it was too late," she said. "They sent her to shrinks and everything, but that woman thought she was the center of the world and that everyone owed her. Finally her parents just moved far away from her."

"What did she think about that?"

"She didn't care one wit," she said dismissively. "Just kept sending them letters asking for money. I believe it's why they died so young. Wondering what they did to deserve a child like her."

"Can you tell me what her relationship was like with your husband?"

She jutted her jaw out. "He's too much like his parents. He'd tell her to leave him alone but he still let her in once in a while, hoping she'd somehow grown up." She snorted. "I kept telling him she was a complete narcissist and would never 'grow up.'"

"Did she come around a lot?"

"Not often, and only when she wanted something." She gave a satisfied smirk. "But not anymore."

16

Whoa. What did that mean?

"When was the last time you saw her?" I asked, treading lightly.

"Two weeks ago," she said. "She actually knocked on our door and said she was here to take 'her niece,' *my* daughter, out for a mani-pedi, like she had any right to do that." Her face flushed deep red at the memory. "She said my husband had told her it was okay, but I know for a fact he would never approve such a thing. So I shut the door in her face."

"And then what happened?"

Nancy looked away as if she didn't want to tell us the rest. "She knew what was good for her and she went away."

"Are you sure that's all?" Erica asked.

"Yes," she said. "I have to go pick up my daughter now, so it's time for you to go."

"Thanks so much for your time," I said. "Just one more question. I'm sure it's not true, but Faith told someone that she'd been beaten by her father. Did you ever hear anything like that?"

Nancy's face went white and then red in such potent rage that I involuntarily took a step back.

"That. Is. Impossible." Her voice was deep and forceful.

"You sound sure," I said carefully.

"I am," she said. "I knew their parents very well. They were the nicest, kindest . . ." Her voice trailed off and her anger vanished, replaced by a deep sadness. "I can't believe Faith would say something like that. But I guess even now she has the power to horrify me."

I couldn't think of anything to add. Erica handed her a card and we headed to the car. I noticed a curtain move again across the street, as if someone had shifted behind it. Maybe a nosy neighbor would give us more. I looked back to see Nancy watching us. It would have to be another time.

Kona handed me the store phone as soon as I got back. "It's Bean's biggest fan," she said, her brown eyes laughing at me.

When I raised my eyebrows, she filled me in on the joke. "Honor Tambor."

I held back a groan. She'd already sent us pages of information on her classmates, mostly outlining insults from a decade ago. I answered, "Michelle Serrano," in my cheery voice.

"Hey, Michelle. This is Honor," she said. "I really hate to let you know this, but the cat is out of the bag."

"What do you mean?"

"I kinda told my best friend from high school about the plan for Benjamin, and you, to come to the reunion and she told a few people and now everyone knows," she said, not sounding all that sorry. "Someone even put it on the special Facebook event page."

I gritted my teeth. "Okay, then," I said. "That'll make our, I mean, his job harder, but we'll give it a try."

"Um," she said, "and someone posted Benjamin is probably investigating Faith's murder."

I took a deep breath. So much for going undercover. How would we question people when they knew exactly what we were up to?

"He's not," I said. "Except as it relates to the reunion."

"I told them that, but you how people are."

Yes, I did.

"They're all excited to meet Benjamin," she rushed to say. "I mean, both of you." As if that would make me feel better.

"Thanks for letting me know," I told her.

"See you soon!" she said.

Kona had been listening to my side of the conversation. "Trouble with Bean's fan club?"

"Yeah," I said. "The president can't stop gossiping to save her life."

The next two days flew by as we prepared for the festival opening. I couldn't believe I was actually looking forward to a high school reunion. It wasn't even my school. But

I was wearing my special-event dress that gathered in a high waist and then fell into a frothy blue and green skirt, and Erica had loaned me her dark blue pashmina, which made me feel elegant when I wrapped it around my shoulders. Bean had on his dark gray suit with a white shirt, and we both looked dashing, as Erica had said when he picked me up.

"Dashing?" I'd made fun of her, even though I actually did feel a little dashing. Of course, wearing anything that wasn't chocolate-stained was a step up for me.

I'd given Bean the rundown on the bullying information Honor had sent over. She'd included a copy of the yearbook, and I looked at any name I knew with interest. I knew some people never really left high school, but I couldn't imagine that someone would kill because of a long-ago stolen boyfriend, ostracizing, or being the victim of a food fight. Zane and Erica had gone over the attendee list and no one had a high enough murder quotient to pay special attention to, but we'd do our best.

We were almost at the hotel that the Buckey Central High School class of 2006 had rented for the event. "I was looking forward to going undercover," I complained to Bean.

"I'm sure you were," he said. "Who were you going to be?"

"What do you mean?"

"You know. Cheerleader? Jock? Science kid?"

I snorted.

"You could've pulled off any of them," he said, parking in the lot in front of the hotel.

"Right," I said. "So what are we looking for here? No one's going to come out and say, 'I hated Faith Monette enough to kill her.'"

"You'd be surprised," he said as we got out of the car. "Just buy people a few drinks and then create a little competition centered around who knew more about Faith, and they'll start spilling all kinds of information."

"Maybe I should watch you, the master," I teased.

He smiled and grabbed my hand. "This could actually be a good time. All the fun of a reunion without the pressure to appear successful."

"Like you'd have to worry about that."

"Plus, I already have a date." He pulled me close and kissed me, causing my head to spin.

I tried to steady myself. "So you don't have to pick anyone up." I sounded a little breathless.

"Exactly." He opened the door to the hotel. "Just fun and games tonight."

"Except for that pesky murder investigation," I reminded him. And myself.

We looked at the sign in the hotel lobby and headed for the Regency Ballroom.

"I say we party first and question murder suspects later, when they're soused," Bean said.

"Soused?" I asked. "Is that what they teach you in Journalism 101?"

"Exactly," he said. "Wait and see."

Honor greeted us as soon as we entered the lobby. "Benjamin!" She took in our clasped hands and her mouth fell open. I thought that only happened in cartoons. "Oh," she said, her disappointment shining through. "You get a bag." She tried to sound enthusiastic but her tone was flat.

He let go of my hand to take it. "Thank you for allowing us to attend. We thought it would be a good idea to sit back and observe at first to get the lay of the land before we start asking questions. Do you think that's a good plan?"

She positively glowed. "Absolutely."

Bean pointed. "Reunion this way?"

Honor gave a little game-show wave. "Right down the hall."

We walked toward the open doors of a ballroom where Gwen Stefani's "Rich Girl" was blasting. I hadn't thought about what to expect, but this room wasn't it. At our high school reunions, we were lucky to have a few streamers taped up in the school gym, but this looked like a cocktail reception for a wedding, with flowers on every table and wandering waiters offering appetizers. I grabbed beef taquitos from a passing tray.

When I got closer, I noticed the little cards on the tables saying the flowers were donated by an alumnus. I wondered if the hotel owner was an alum as well. Something made me look up. A net full of red and gray balloons was hanging from the ceiling, ready to drop whenever scheduled.

I put my clutch down on a table and opened the bag Honor had given me. Inside was a small program of attendees as well as handouts and giveaways from local businesses. I showed them to Bean. "She got companies to sponsor this thing?"

"Looks like it," he said and pointed to the dance floor. "Come on. Fun first. Let's blend in."

We joined several couples under the disco lights, and I felt a momentary panic. I hadn't danced in years. But then Bean smiled and started stepping in an unexpectedly smooth move, and I joined in.

He was just the right kind of dancer, comfortable without taking it too seriously, and I found myself trying a little harder than my normal technique of moving my feet and arms around in a dancelike movement without actually committing to dancing.

After "Don't Phunk with My Heart" and "Feel Good Inc," the slow songs started. Bean held his arms out and I moved close for Green Day's "Wake Me Up When September Ends."

"If we were in high school," Bean whispered in my ear, "I'd be trying to look down your top."

"If we were in high school," I murmured back, "I'd be smacking you."

He laughed, and I could feel the rumble in his chest. I looked up at him and his laughter died. Something hot sparked between us, and I took a step back. He shook his head as if to clear it. "Ready for a drink?"

We headed for the open bar. While we waited our turn, a slide show started with photos from this crowd's high school years, interspersed with attendees' answers to the survey questions.

Honor joined us in line to hand us our name tags. I fought back an urge to cross out the "jamin" and add an "a" to Benjamin to make it say "Bean." "You have to meet Faith's best friend from high school." She looked around and spotted her sitting at a table with a small group.

Honor was definitely blowing our cover. I sighed. It was time to get to work.

Two hours later, I had to admit that Bean was right. Getting the sources soused and challenging them to perform information duels, metaphorically of course, worked. We focused our questions on reunions in general and how much they kept up on social media.

An In Memoriam page of the slide show was on repeat, with Faith's high school photo and thoughtful comments from her fellow students. I must have seen the phrase, *A bright light is among the stars* about a hundred times. Each time the slide came around, we were able to point to it and bring up the unfortunate tragedy to affect their classmate.

At first, they all had only nice things to say about Faith, but as time wore on, they started revealing more and more about the darker side of this popular mean girl. Everyone seemed willing to share at least one story of her being hell-bent on causing misery to another student. Even her best friend said she was afraid of Faith sometimes; that if you weren't part of her posse you were fair game for all forms of abuse.

After a completely wrenching tale from a man about Faith convincing him to invite her to prom in an elaborate production that involved playing his saxophone outside her window and having the whole thing, including a rude rejection, filmed and passed around, I had to take a break.

The fact that the man went on to Juilliard and was part of fabulous jazz band in DC and was so cute and cool that a lot of the women were making googly eyes at him didn't make me feel any better. Okay, maybe a little.

Honor walked by, her face flushed with whatever was in her martini glass, and perhaps the fun of revisiting her high school glory days. She also may have been acting on her leftover crush, hanging on to the captain of the swim team, who still had his V-shaped physique from his days on the pool deck. She'd mentioned that a lot of attendees were staying at the hotel so they could drink and not drive. I wondered if that would lead to some unintended, or intended, endings to the evening.

The most interesting piece of information we gathered was that no one had seen or talked to Faith since she went off to college ten years before. She'd dropped all contact with everyone. Even her so-called best friends hadn't thought much about her since she left town ten years earlier.

The music was cut off and the DJ made a garbled announcement. "Will the owner of a blue Honda Accord with license plate (something, something) come to the registration table?"

Bean and I had been talking to two of the high school's smartest women, one of whom had passed the state bar exam on the first try. He turned his head to focus on the DJ's words and met my eyes. "Excuse me," he said to the women and we headed to the door. He must have been able to decipher the gobbledygook.

"Yours?" I asked on the way.

"Sounds like it," he said.

Two hotel security guards waited at the registration desk.

"I'm pretty sure the Honda belongs to me," Bean said.

"Sorry to hear that," one of the guards said. "A hotel guest noticed that your tires have been slashed."

"What?" I was stunned.

"Got any enemies?" the other asked.

Bean stopped still. "I'm an investigative journalist," he said, as if that explained it. "Have the local police been called?"

"Yes, sir," the security guy said, sounding a little suspicious.

Bean turned to me. "I'm calling Bobby. Do you want to continue in there or come with me?"

"Go with you, for sure," I said.

"Right this way," a guard said, as if we didn't know where Bean's car was parked. "Any idea who coulda done this?" he asked as we followed him.

"No, sir," Bean said.

I almost snorted, but I was too scared. Luckily, the guard didn't ask if I could think of anyone. My guess was that someone in that ballroom was angry about our questions, and that was scary. I filed through everyone we had talked to. No one stood out.

Then I wondered if Bean had considered that it might be someone from the story he was working on. Had we been followed from West Riverdale?

We were some couple, weren't we?

The cool night air whooshed over us as we went out the doors. Bean's car was outside the light shining from the front of the building, and the closest street light in the parking lot was out.

The guard turned on his flashlight and shined it on the tires, all very, very flat. He moved it closer and pointed to the top of one tire. It had several slashes in it, obviously done with a large, very sharp knife. By someone who was very, very angry.

## 17

The local police arrived to take a statement, but neither one of us gave them any suggestions of who could have knifed Bean's tires. Really, the list of possible suspects was just too long. They asked the hotel security guards for security camera footage to see who might have been close, and promised to let Bean know if they found anything useful.

An un-uniformed Bobby arrived, shaking hands with the Urbana police and saying he was just there as a friend to give us a lift home. After the tow truck came and went, with the sad little Honda loaded on it, he gestured toward his car, luckily not a patrol car. Sitting in the backseat of those made me feel like a criminal.

I got in the back, exhausted, which didn't stop Bobby from confronting me. "What a coincidence," he said in a sarcastic tone. "You have an incident at the reunion of the murder victim."

"Isn't it?" Bean used a mild tone but gave Bobby a *back off* look.

"I can't believe I have to ask this," Bobby said, looking at me in the rearview mirror. "But haven't you learned anything from that threat on your van?"

"Obviously not," I said. "I'm tired and I'm going to close my eyes back here. You two go ahead and fight."

Bobby started in, saying that having Bean encourage us amateurs would end in disaster. I ignored him, going again through the people we'd talked to at the reunion and wondering who we'd angered with our questions.

Maybe someone who was really good at hiding their feelings.

The next morning, Honor called my cell before I left for work. She sounded horrified at the incident with the tires. "Everything got a little muddled later in the evening, but at some point I realized you had left," she said. "And this morning I heard what happened to your car. That's terrible!"

It probably got "muddled" because of the martinis she'd been drinking. "It's just tires." I tried to calm her down. "No one was hurt."

Her voice rose. "But that means someone from the reunion was trying to warn you off!" And then it dropped dramatically, like she was telling a ghost story. "Maybe someone didn't believe you weren't investigating Faith's murder. Which means the killer was *at the reunion*!"

"You don't know that," I said. "You're jumping to

conclusions. You said yourself that it had been talked about on Facebook, so anyone who heard about it and not even been connected to Faith's murder could have done it."

"How can you be so blasé?" she asked. "The killer knows what you're doing." She gasped. "Maybe he knows that I'm helping you!"

"I'm sure that's not true," I said. Of course, she was a total blabbermouth, so maybe the whole town of Urbana—and Frederick and West Riverdale—knew.

I certainly felt uneasy after we hung up. This warning seemed both impulsive and violent. Someone had been carrying a knife and jabbed it into Bean's tires over and over. What would have happened if Bean or I had been out there? Could it be the same person who had bashed in my car?

Erica came down to the kitchen with the notes Honor had sent over, highlighting everything she remembered about Faith's bullying back in high school. "Can you go over these today and fill in anything you and Bean learned last night?" She dropped them on the table and poured a cup of coffee.

"Sure," I said. I glanced at them while taking a sip and realized someone was missing from the reunion. "Wade Overton didn't show up."

Erica looked at me. "It could be a simple explanation, but given what happened last night, perhaps we should ask Detective Lockett to follow up with that." She drank some coffee.

"Do you think we can get away this morning to drop in on Nancy's neighbor?" I asked. Faith's sister-in-law might not have told us the whole story, and we hoped Nosy Neighbor knew something more.

"The one you thought you saw hiding behind the curtain?" she asked. "The timing will be tight with the opening, but let's do it."

W̲e opened up the store and waited for Kona and Kayla to arrive before leaving. I drove the rented minivan and had to move aside the folder of papers from Phoenix so Erica could sit in the front seat. "I haven't had time . . ." I told her, feeling vaguely guilty even with everything we had going on.

"No rush at all," she said.

We drove up to Nancy's neighbor's house. She must have been looking through the window again, because she came to the door before we could even knock.

"I knew you'd be back," she said. "My name is Celia Diamond. Come in, come in. Would you like some tea? I'm so sorry that I don't keep coffee here any longer. Not enough guests who enjoy it, I suppose."

"Tea would be wonderful," Erica said. "Can I help?"

"Oh, no." She bustled over to pat two chairs opposite the one she'd been sitting in by the window. Her hands were gnarled with arthritis. "Have a seat and I'll be out in two secs!" Her delight in having visitors was both infectious and a little bittersweet.

The sunlit room was filled with overstuffed furniture in various shades of lavender, looking cozy and inviting. An ancient black poodle with a gray face lay in a dog bed in the corner. He lifted his head for a moment before going back to sleep.

Photos of her family and the poodle in younger days covered the walls, along with framed Playbills from Broadway musicals and photos of their chorus lines.

"Are these photos of you?" Erica asked.

"Oh yes," Celia called out from the kitchen. "So nice of you to ask. I had a lovely time during my theater career. I was a gypsy, in the chorus, on Broadway for years." She poked her head out. "Never a leading lady, I'm afraid, but I could kick higher than a Rockette."

"How nice," Erica said, fascinated by the pictures.

"So you two are looking into that nasty woman's murder?" she called from the kitchen. "Erica and Michelle, right?"

I turned with wide eyes to Erica. "Um, where did you hear that?"

"Oh, I don't get out as much as I used to, but I know people who know things." She said it with a little laugh. "Almost as good as the Google." We heard teacups rattle. "I used to be in a creativity class with your neighbor Henna, when her name was Carol. And Beatrice Duncan, you know her. She was the director of the Boys and Girls Club forever, but now she helps out at her son's hardware store. Anyway, we go way back. I taught tap-dancing to the kids. Until my knees got too bad. But I call Beatrice and Henna all the time. I like to keep up on things. Keeps my mind fresh."

That was the best reason I'd ever heard of for gossiping. I'd have to remember that when I got to be her age.

She appeared in the doorway, holding an overloaded tray, and we both jumped up to help. She shook her head. "Just sit, dears. I got this, as they say." She poured tea for all three of us and sat down. "You go ahead and take all the sugar and milk you like."

She watched us prepare our tea, probably so she'd know next time. "We were hoping to find out what you know about Faith Monette. And how close she was to Nancy and Vaughn," I began.

The change in her expression was instant, as if a happy puppy had been scolded. She shook her head. "That Faith. There was just something wrong with that girl. A bad egg, as they say."

"Did you know her well?" Erica asked.

"No, but I talked to plenty of people who had just awful encounters with her," she said. "And that poor brother of hers. Knowing what she was and having to explain her nastiness away his whole life. It's no wonder Nancy pulled a gun on her."

What? "That was a couple of weeks ago, right?" I was amazed at how casual I sounded. I knew we hadn't gotten the full story out of Nancy. She'd still been so angry at Faith during our conversation.

She nodded, seeming to enjoy the drama while still empathizing with how Nancy was feeling. "Nancy just had enough," she said simply. "To tell you the truth, I would have done it a lot earlier."

"Nancy only told us a little of that day," Erica said. "What happened to bring her to that point?"

"Well she didn't tell me much either, but from what I understand, Faith had secretly friended Nancy's daughter on Facebook and arranged to take her out when the parents weren't supposed to be home. But luckily Nancy canceled her plans at the last minute and then, you know, Faith showed up."

"Why do you think Faith did that?" Erica asked.

She shrugged. "Well, if there's any bit of humanity in her, she just might want to know something about her family, her own blood. They kept her away from her niece her whole life. But I suspect it was to drive Nancy crazy and just cause more misery in the world. That's what made her happy."

"How did Nancy react?" I asked.

"Ooh, it was intense." She gave a theatrical shiver. "I saw her slam the door in Faith's face. And then Nancy opened the door." She paused dramatically. "With a *shotgun* in her arms."

"A shotgun?" I couldn't imagine that ultra-suburban mom brandishing a big shotgun like Annie Oakley.

"Yep," she said. "And this part I could hear clear as day. Nancy yelled that if Faith came anywhere near her family again, she'd shoot her and bury her where no one would find her. And that no one would look for her because no one would miss her or mourn her."

"What did Faith do?"

"She ran. She hightailed it out of there as fast as she could. And then she squealed away in her car." She took a breath. "It was very exciting."

"What did Nancy do next?"

"Well, it's almost like she came to her senses, like she'd been driven right out of her mind for a minute. She looked around to make sure no one had seen her act like that, and closed the door quick."

"Does she know you saw her?" Erica asked.

"I don't think so. I'm very discreet," she said with a humble expression.

Hmm. Probably not as discreet as she thought.

"But Nancy did pop over to tell me why it all happened, so maybe she suspected," she admitted.

"Did Faith ever come back?" I asked.

"No, but something weird happened." She leaned toward us and spoke in a conspiratorial tone. "For a while I thought Nancy had a stalker."

"What caused you to think that?" Erica asked, writing in her notebook.

"There was a man sitting out in front of her house several times. Right under that tree." She pointed out the window.

I got to my feet and looked outside. It was a great location for a stakeout. Shade from the tree would not only keep the car cool but would also make it more difficult to see who was inside. "When was that?"

"It started the day after the big scene with Faith," she said. "I thought it might be Faith herself, but I could tell it was a man."

"What did you do?"

"The first time, I didn't do anything. He could have been eating lunch or a worker or any number of things. But the second time I got annoyed. He thought he could fool us with a different car. So I walked right out there to tell him to move along."

I couldn't imagine this little old lady confronting a potential stalker. "What did he do?"

"He saw me coming and peeled out," she said with pride.

"Did you get his license number?" Erica asked.

"Oh no, dear," she said. "My eyesight isn't good enough for that."

"Did you ever see him again?"

"I sure did. He came back in another car, a big van, and I called the police."

"What happened?"

"Nothing," she admitted. "By the time they got here, he was gone."

"What did he look like?" I asked.

"It was hard to tell, but I got the impression that his hair was dark and he was kinda, I don't know, slouchy."

"Slouchy?"

"Yes. I pay a lot of attention to posture and he did not have good posture." She shook her head.

I slowly straightened my spine to sit up properly.

This woman was a gold mine.

Somehow, another hour flew by as we listened to Celia regale us with stories from her Broadway days. We learned that sometimes a lot more drama and shenanigans happened backstage than onstage.

Celia couldn't see well enough to drive and was looking into an assisted-living home. "One of those places with old people who still have spunk enough left to party."

She said that Nancy often drove her to the store, or picked up things for her, so if we needed her to find out anything, she could ask Nancy for us. She looked around. "I'll miss this house," she said. "But change is good. I'm excited to see what comes next."

I thought of something to ask. "Did you happen to notice if Nancy and Vaughn were home last Sunday night, the night of Faith's murder?"

"Oh, I'm sorry. I don't know," she said. "I was watching an *NCIS* marathon." She fanned her face with her hand. "Ooh, that Mark Harmon."

. . . . . . . . . . . . .

It seemed like the whole town, plus a lot of nearby towns, had come through the huge orange-and-black-balloon arch for opening night of the West Riverdale Halloween Festival. Erica and Yvonne dashed around, coordinating last-minute issues, while volunteers helped small children at the carnival games. Screams were emanating from the haunted house. During the many run-throughs, we'd reminded the more gung ho volunteers that enthusiasm was important, but we didn't want to give anyone a heart attack.

Oscar allowed Dylan to work in the haunted house, as long as he arrived in his costume so customers wouldn't know who he was.

Luckily, Reese was in community-event mode, rather than rabid-dog attack mode, taking photos of families in costume and writing down names. She was wearing a witch's hat. I was proud that I kept all of my comments about the appropriateness to myself.

The only way for Erica to manage the festival, and for me to help, was on-site. Besides, we didn't want our assistants to miss all the fun, so we decided to close early for the week of the festival. We posted a sign that said, "Chocolate Emergency? Come to the Spooktacular Halloween Festival at the Boys and Girls Club. *If you dare!*"

I wasn't sure about that last part of the sign, which Kona had painted in red ink slashed across the sign and made to look like dripping blood, but I decided to see what kind of feedback I got before replacing it.

Kayla and Kona were hard at work at the Chocolates and

Chapters booth, which was positioned right outside the haunted house. Kayla had made a sign that said, *Haunted house gave you the chills? Chocolate frogs will help!* They were certainly doing a brisk business selling the bags of the little yummy creatures, which we'd made with milk, dark and green-colored white chocolate.

The centerpiece of the festival was the haunted house. Everyone agreed that it was the scariest one ever, even beating out the Mayhem Mansion of 2013, when the slime machine had gone out of control and spewed green gunk all over the gym. Kids had panicked and tracked it everywhere. Yvonne said she still found dried green globs in odd places.

Attendance was booming at all of the carnival games, with little kids huddling around the duck pond to pick up the masked ducks and win a prize, tossing beanbags into mouths of assorted monsters, and bowling small pumpkin-painted balls into ghost-shrouded pins. The teens lined up to shoot basketballs painted to look like zombie heads in the hoop, fling darts at ghost balloons, and throw rings over the bottles with glowing green goo in them. I tried that one. It was impossible.

I'd gone simple with my costume this year, using the same mad-scientist wig, glasses and white lab coat from a few years earlier. I was pulling a tray of bat-shaped chocolate lollipops out of the coolers when my cell phone went off. I ignored it until I heard phones ringing all around me. My phone rang again, and I answered it with a sinking feeling.

It was Quinn, who was working at the entrance. "The police are here. They're looking for Dylan. I think they're going to arrest him!" Quinn said, sounding like she was crying.

"Where is he?" I kept my voice low.

"Zombie room," she said, sniffling.

"I'll get him," I told her. Inside I cursed the rule we'd made to have the students keep their phones turned off when they were in character. I wasn't sure what I was going to do with Dylan, just that I needed to protect him.

I dashed into the Boys and Girls Club through a back entrance and was immediately dumped into the surreal world of the prison of nightmares, with bloodied zombie inmates screaming and reaching through bars to get me.

Luckily, Dylan was at the front of the room, and I recognized him right away, even though the fog machine was working overtime. The sound effects were way too loud, so I grabbed his arm and led the way to the quiet room.

I closed the door behind him, muting the screams and loud bangs coming from the other rooms. "The police are here looking for you," I said. "I'm pretty sure they're here to arrest you. Call your dad."

He pulled out his phone without question. "Dad," he said, his voice urgent. "The police are after me. Can you"—his voice broke—"call the lawyer or something?"

I put my hand on his arm while he listened to instructions from his father.

"Okay," he said, and hung up.

"What do you want to do?" I asked, half wondering if we should make a run for it to Mexico.

Dylan took a deep breath. "He said to go quietly and not answer any questions."

I thought of the scene that would happen if this poor boy was arrested in front of his friends and everyone else at the festival. And Reese was out there. I shuddered. "Hold on," I said. "Wash your face and take off that costume. Let's try a different way."

I called Lockett while Dylan went to the sink. "I hear you're looking for one of my volunteers."

"Where is he?" His tone was no-nonsense and urgent.

"I'm sure you don't want a huge scene at the festival. Just think what Reese would do with the photos of you arresting a mummy." Dylan was removing his zombie costume, but I was hoping to delay Lockett in case the police had already made it to the zombie room. "I'll bring him down to the station."

"When?"

"Fifteen minutes. He needs to get out of his costume." Dylan had already peeled it off and was in basketball shorts and a West Riverdale High T-shirt.

"Fine," he said.

And then the door to our little sanctuary opened.

Lockett stood outside with Bobby, both of them grim and determined. "Let's go."

I paced the lobby of the police station, still fuming at the police. They'd allowed Dylan to walk out with just Lockett and not handcuffed, but they said there was no way they were letting me bring in a murder suspect alone. I'd called Erica, but I knew it was impossible for her to leave until the festival closed.

Of course, no one would tell me what evidence they'd found that justified arresting Dylan. How could one super-hero key ring and a Facebook account lead to this? At least they weren't questioning him until his lawyer arrived. I wondered what the heck was keeping Marino. He was probably helping some hotshot politician and couldn't be bothered with a small-town kid.

I glared at Bobby, but he was ignoring me. He was even avoiding Bean, who had joined me to provide moral support but seemed to be in hyperobservant mode, listening intently and following everyone's movements.

Then Oscar came running in. He went right past me to the counter. "I confess," he said to Bobby. "I killed that woman."

## 18

"Oscar." I jumped up to grab his arm, my heart in my throat. "You don't have to—"

He shook me off. "I confess. Now let my son go."

Chief Noonan stuck his head out from his office, not looking anywhere near as surprised as I was. Had they planned this? "Mr. Fenton," he started.

"You have to release Dylan," Oscar said. "Now."

"It doesn't work that way," the chief said. "Come into my office." He turned to Bobby. "Send in Detective Lockett."

Then Antony Marino walked in the front door. He looked at Oscar being led by the chief to his office and then turned an accusing eye on me. "What the hell is happening here?"

. . . . . . . . . . . . .

t took well over an hour to sort out, but after questioning Oscar, the police released Dylan. I'd stayed at the police station, texting with Erica, who couldn't leave her duties at the festival, and Quinn, who was keeping the comic book club updated by text. I had no doubt that if Dylan remained in custody, they'd show up at the police station in their costumes soon enough. We did not need the added chaos of students in their superhero, zombie and mummy costumes descending on the police station.

Marino jerked his head for Bean and me to join him as he led a shocked and scared Dylan out of the building. We stopped on the street, out of earshot of any prying police ears. "I'm calling in a top lawyer to represent Oscar Fenton," Marino said. "Dylan insisted."

"Thank you," I said and then turned to Dylan. "Would you like to stay with us until this is sorted out?"

"Mr. Fenton suggested the same thing," Marino said. "I understand they have no family close by?"

Dylan didn't say anything.

I touched his arm. "We have an extra room," I said. "But if you want to stay somewhere else, it's okay."

He shook his head, not meeting my eyes. "It's fine."

Marino nodded his approval and turned to Dylan. "*Do. Not.* Discuss this case with anyone, however well-intentioned." He sent Bean a stern look. "Especially reporters."

He turned to me, and I tried to look innocent.

"Michelle, I'll be calling at least once daily and expect you to answer the phone immediately," he said, and turned away before listening to my "Of course."

Bean walked us to my rental minivan. "Let me know if you need anything." He looked intensely curious but was holding back on bothering Dylan with any questions.

I unlocked the car and Dylan got in. He stared straight ahead and then his face crumpled. He pointed down the street. "My dad's truck." It was parked halfway down the block. "I don't want to leave it there."

"Can you get Oscar's truck to my house?" I asked Bean.

"I'll take care of it," he said.

I got in and started the car, having no idea what to say to Dylan other than "It will be okay. We'll figure this out."

He looked back at the police station, as if trying to see his dad. I hoped they would hold Oscar in the comfortable cell they had at the West Riverdale station instead of transferring him to the Frederick jail. I started the car, and just as I was about to pull out, Reese knocked on the window on Dylan's side.

We both jumped.

"Dylan, what do have to say about your father's confession?" she yelled, as though we couldn't hear her through the glass. "Did he take the fall to save you from prison?"

I drove out of there as fast as I could, then opened my window and yelled back, "Get a life!"

It took me several blocks to settle down and realize my tantrum wasn't helping anyone, especially Dylan.

I looked over at him and his face was white.

"I'm really sorry that happened," I said. "Can you do me a favor and breathe deeply a few times?"

He did as I suggested, and color flooded back to his face.

"She's just the beginning, isn't she?" he said quietly. "It just keeps getting worse and worse."

There wasn't anything I could do to make Dylan feel any better, except try to find some lead that the police had missed. It was time to ignore Marino's orders not to ask questions. "Do you have any ideas who the real murderer was?"

He shook his head.

"None?"

"No," he said, and I believed him.

"Do you know why they arrested you?" I wasn't sure I wanted to know the answer to that one.

He pulled his knees up and wrapped his arms around them. "The DNA test came back on the necklace," he said.

"What necklace?" I asked.

He nodded. "The one my dad gave her." He closed his eyes as if in pain. "It had her . . . blood on it."

"Where did the police find it?" My voice was trembling.

"In the secret drawer in my dad's desk. In the workshop," he said. "I put it there." His face was so bleak, my heart ached for him.

My heart stopped for a moment and then started thudding. I so didn't want to know what that meant, but I forced myself to talk calmly. "Let's start at the beginning," I said. "You set up the fake Facebook account."

He gave a shaky nod. "And then I scheduled a meeting with her. Like, she thought she was meeting my dad at Green Meadows."

Oh man. This could be bad. "Why did she agree to meet?"

"I said I—I mean, my dad—wanted her help finding a house to buy." He bit his lip. "I thought if she was interested in his money, she wouldn't say no."

"Why did you want to meet with her?" I asked.

"I just wanted her to know we knew what she was up to and if she didn't leave my dad alone, we were going to call the police." He shook his head, as if he couldn't believe how stupid he'd been.

"Then what happened?" I drove slowly, the dark car feeling like a safe refuge from the real world.

"We almost chickened out. And when we got there . . ." He took a deep breath. "She was dead. Her face, her everything, was bashed in."

"What did you do?" I asked.

"We backed away, but then I saw the necklace on the floor," he said. "My dad used to make them for my mom, and I couldn't stand for it to be there." He paused and then whispered, "I went back in and took it."

"And that's how your key ring was left there?"

"I think so," he said.

That must have been why there were so many footprints at the scene, and why Lockett had thought there might be more than one murderer.

We pulled up in front of our house and I turned the car off. It was a struggle to keep my voice composed and empty of judgment. "Why didn't you tell anyone before? We could have helped you."

"I thought my dad did it," he whispered. "And then, it all got so messed up. And I didn't want anyone to know anything," he said. "And Tommy said we could get in trouble for desecrating the body. And obstruction of justice. And other stuff."

"Does your dad know?"

He nodded.

I had to ask. "And there's no chance your dad . . ."

"No! That night, we drove around for a while, and when I came home my dad was in his workshop. But I was afraid to talk to him. I found out later he'd finished a set of cupboards he'd just started that day," he said. "He was definitely home the whole time." He looked down, red with shame. "I can't believe I doubted him even for a minute."

"So he's just trying to protect you now with that confession," I said, tears coming to my eyes.

He nodded and then put his forehead on his bent knees. "How did I screw everything up so bad?"

"Okay," I said, taking a deep breath. "First, have you told Marino all of this?"

He gave a small nod.

Wow. "Why hasn't he done anything with this information?"

He lifted his head. "He said his first job is to make sure I don't go to jail, but I told him he has to make sure everyone knows my dad is innocent too." He paused. "Or I was going to show the police the video."

"Video?" I asked, even more shocked than from his other revelations.

"Trent was wearing a GoPro—you know, a video camera on his head," he said. "We wanted her to confess that she was a fraud, so we could show my dad. And he caught, like, the whole thing."

For the first time, I felt a ray of hope. "It's all on tape?" Maybe the video would contain evidence to clear Dylan and Oscar.

He nodded.

"Why didn't any of you tell the police? Especially after you knew your dad didn't do it?" I asked.

"We made an oath," he said, as if it made total sense.

That must be a pretty strong oath. "Did Marino see the video?" I asked.

He shook his head. "He said it wasn't time yet."

"Well it's time now," I said. "Where's that tape?"

Much as I wanted to see the recording, I didn't want any chain-of-custody issues. Even though that might be ruined already. I called Marino as soon as we got inside. He blustered on about me questioning his client, but I told him he could come and look at it first, or I'd take it to Detective Lockett myself. He ordered his driver to turn around and come to our house.

I called Erica, who was shutting down the festival. "They have a video?" she asked, sounding grim. "I'll bring Tommy, Quinn and Trent to our house."

I bet this time she wouldn't take no for an answer.

Tommy's hearse arrived first, and Quinn and Trent spilled out. They all had the remains of their zombie makeup around their hairlines and in the creases of their necks. Trent carried an iPad.

Quinn looked the most guilty, although each of them expressed varying levels of remorse as they moved into the kitchen.

While I had to admire their loyalty to Dylan, they could all be in serious trouble with the police. Even if they thought they were protecting their friend's dad, what made them think that holding on to key evidence that could have cleared up this case, and possibly led to an arrest days ago, was in any way okay?

I automatically got everyone hot cocoa, this time with fresh mint leaves, while we waited for Marino to join us.

The teens stayed quiet, and Erica and I didn't harass them with questions. Tommy and Quinn sat on the couch with Dylan in the middle, while Trent perched on the armrest.

Marino's limo arrived and he stepped out, minus his double-breasted suit jacket. "Everyone go outside," he demanded as he walked up the stairs. "Except Dylan and whoever made the tape."

We all followed his orders, instinctively staying in the circle of light from the porch lamp. Moths flew against the bulb and the kitchen windows. Marino kept Dylan and Trent in the living room, away from all of our prying eyes.

Tommy and Quinn looked scared, knowing this was do-or-die time for all of them. I had no words to comfort them.

But Erica did. "Whatever happens," she said. "We're on your side."

Quinn nodded tearfully and Tommy looked away.

"It'll be okay," I said.

Marino came out, holding Trent's iPad. "Erica and Michelle. Follow me."

We walked with him to his car, where he had to wave off his driver, who had already leapt to his feet and opened Marino's door for him. The driver nodded and got back inside.

"If either of you question my client again, I will throw him into protective custody far away from here," he said. "Do you understand?"

We both nodded.

"I'm taking the tape to Detective Lockett," he said. "It does not help Oscar, but that's not my concern. As long as the police do not believe that Dylan and his friends are award-winning actors, it does succeed in clearing them of murder. Which is my one and only goal."

I felt a wave of relief, but then Erica had to ask questions. "How does it clear them?"

He raised his eyebrows at her, annoyed at being challenged. "The video clearly shows that until they arrived, there was only one set of shoe prints at the crime scene."

"Do you expect the police to file charges over obstruction, or anything else?" she asked.

"If they are feeling vindictive, they might, but I'll make it clear that they were frightened and devastated children when they made that decision," he said. "And that a reasonable jury would most likely feel the same way."

He stared at Erica. "However, until the police have arrested the killer, this is not over," he said. "That video clearly shows the badly beaten body, which demonstrates just how angry and possibly deranged the murderer is. Your brother is quite fond of you and would be very upset if something untoward were to happen."

Holy cow. He talked like Erica.

His eyes moved to mine. "And you too." He turned to get into the car, his driver popping out like a jack in the box. "Both of you need to be careful."

I t took a long time for any of us to get to sleep that night. Tommy, Quinn and Trent all looked like they wanted to stay with Dylan, but Erica convinced them they had to go home and tell their parents what they'd done.

Erica often paced deep into the night. I usually found the sounds of our century-old house creaking relaxing, but tonight I knew her steps were tinged with worry.

Dylan was quiet in the guest bedroom upstairs, but I couldn't imagine that he was able to sleep either.

My alarm woke me from a deep sleep, feeling way too early, and for the first time in ages, I didn't want to go into the store. Chocolates and Chapters was my home away from home, but I was dreading the gossip that was bound to surround us.

I made myself drive down Main Street and saw that a light in our store was already on, welcoming me and my bad mood.

Kona and Kayla were already there, opening up both sides of the store. They came over to give me a hug. "You okay?" Kona asked.

I shook my head. "It's a mess."

"Why don't you hang in the back today and we'll handle the Sunday hordes," Kayla suggested.

I gratefully escaped to Erica's office and made the mistake of checking out Reese's blog. She obviously had no qualms about falsely accusing her neighbors one day and then expecting them to buy her stupid paper the next. *Sins of the Father?* screamed her headline, twice the normal size. *The citizens of West Riverdale are wondering if we will ever know the truth about the brutal murder of Faith Monette.*

The only "citizen" she was talking about was Reese herself.

I forced myself to read the whole thing, but luckily, she knew even less than we did.

The comments section at the bottom was gratifying, for once. More than one citizen of West Riverdale told her to "Leave the boy alone," along with a "Shut the hell up, you vindictive jerk," which was my favorite. The last one said it all: "Reese Everhard, what is wrong with you? Haven't you heard of innocent until proven guilty?"

Unfortunately, that wasn't how the Internet worked.

Erica came in late, and waited until the last minute to wake Dylan. "He promised to stay in the house until his friends come over," she said.

I told her about Reese's article, and she opened the offending website on her laptop and gave a gasp of dismay.

Something new had popped up. Reese had ignored the angry comments of her previous article and doubled down on the nastiness right away: *Why are the organizers of the Halloween Festival allowed to harbor a suspected murderer? Citizens of West Riverdale are asking if they should be in charge of such a family-oriented event.*

And then she had a photo of the high school kids in full zombie makeup and poses. *Would you send your child to a haunted house with someone like this?*

Could she be more horrible?

I took a deep breath, feeling even more of an urgency to figure out who the murderer was and get the shadow of the "suspect" label off of Dylan. And Oscar. Where could we find out more about this mess?

"Maybe we need to eat at the Ear for lunch," I said.

We certainly didn't have to worry about too much gossip ruining the day. In the first hour, we had only one customer, a diehard who bought her current favorite and scurried off with her head down as if making sure no one saw her.

Erica and I left for lunch early, leaving the subdued Kona and Kayla in charge.

The Ear had earned its nickname decades before when the neon stopped working in the curves of the "Bar" sign for O'Shaughnessey's. The owner and bartender, Jake, had a knack of listening without judgment to all of his customers. He heard a lot and was often willing to share his knowledge with Erica and me.

Marino called us for a status update on Dylan and to say a colleague had agreed to take Oscar's case. He'd be meeting with Oscar later in the day.

Erica called Dylan to let him know.

"Is he okay?" I asked.

"He took it well," she said. "His friends are coming over and I ordered pizza." Dylan had decided to stay away from volunteering at the Halloween Festival, which made sense to everyone. We put off deciding what he'd do about school on Monday.

We walked in right before the lunch rush in an effort to avoid as many fellow West Riverdale citizens as possible. A few morning drinkers sitting at the other end of the bar ignored our arrival. I wondered if they'd been there all night. The dining area was empty, the familiar scent of stale beer and peanuts now marred by the smell of disinfectant coming from the open restroom doors.

"If it isn't the keepers of the town juvenile delinquents," Jake said as he walked through the swinging door from the kitchen carrying a drying rack full of glasses. Jake was good-looking in a casual, plaid-shirt kind of way. Women often fell for his friendly customer service, but he was utterly devoted to his wife and kids. "Which one of you is Fagin and which one is the Artful Dodger?"

"Hilarious," I said glumly as we sat on the stools at the bar.

He had already changed his chalkboard to say, *Sunday Happy Hour 4–7 p.m. Because Monday is coming too soon!*

One of Jake's multitudes of female cousins came out of the men's bathroom pushing a mop and wearing a surly look on her face. Bathrooms must not have been her thing.

We'd memorized the simple bar menu long ago, but I picked one up from the metal stand anyway. "What's the latest on our current disaster?" I asked, not even bothering to pretend we were there for anything but information. Although Jake knew I couldn't resist his baked potato skins.

He set down the rack and came to stand in front of us, managing to look sympathetic and amused at the same time. "Beer, wine or something more potent?" he asked. "Or just lunch and gossip?" He saw me check out what he had on tap. "Michelle, you'd love this Sorry Chicky by Burley Oak Brewery."

I sighed and passed. "Just an iced tea for me. And potato skins." It was going to be a long day. And night.

"Greek salad, please," Erica said. "And iced tea."

"Coming right up," Jake said, and yelled the order through the window to the kitchen.

"How are Sydney and Alex?" Erica asked. Even in our sorry state, she was polite.

"Kids are doing great," he said.

I got right to it before he started one of his kid's soccer-gymnastics-swimming stories. "So our store is empty today. Does that mean people actually believe Reese's BS?"

"Hell no," he said. "Don't worry. It'll blow over soon and they'll be back."

His cheerfulness rubbed me the wrong way. "How do you know?" I said, my tone a lot more churlish than I intended.

He raised his eyebrows. "It's just a knee-jerk reaction to the whole drama. Deep down, they know that you two are just helping. But there's a small part of them that's worried. Like, if they were wrong about Oscar, or even worse, Dylan, then what else are they wrong about?"

"So they're staying away from us and our store until they see how it all shakes out?" I asked.

He pursed his lips. "I think so."

Erica added. "I think there's a bit of social pressure being applied. Mean-girl bullying, if you will."

That made me even madder. "They think they're going to stay away from our store until we fall in line?"

Jake shrugged noncommittally, as if he didn't want to talk too badly about his friends and customers.

A few men in dusty construction clothes came in, talking about a pickup football game that had gotten nasty. I didn't recognize them and they sat on the other side of the bar.

"What have you heard about the murder?" I asked after he took their food orders and gave them their drinks.

He shook his head, all of his cheerfulness gone. "What a mess, right?"

"What do you mean?" I asked.

He hesitated before offering, "Some of them are saying that even if Dylan didn't do it, he's hiding something."

"Like what?" I demanded.

He looked distinctly uncomfortable. "That maybe he . . . moved the body or something."

Suddenly, I was so livid I felt buzzing in my ears. "He's just a boy!" burst out of me.

The construction workers stopped their conversation to stare at me.

Erica put a hand on my arm. "Do you know anyone who knew Faith?" she asked, sticking with our original mission to find out what information had filtered through Jake's scores of customers.

He shook his head. "I think we're too far from her stomping grounds."

"What about people who dated Oscar?" I asked. "Before Faith."

Now he looked truly troubled. "This is really awkward."

"Why?" I asked.

"I heard something, but I'm not sure if it's true," he said. We waited.

"Yvonne, you know, at the Boys and Girls Club?" he said. "Folks are saying that she was spying on Dylan and Oscar for Gilly, his mom."

"Yvonne?" Erica asked. "Why?"

"I assumed it was because they were friends, but you'd have to ask her," he said. "That's not the point. She kept sending information down to Florida, until . . ."

"Until what?" His reluctance was driving me crazy.

"Until she dated Oscar."

19

Once again, our visit to the Ear resulted in information we didn't want to know about a friend. We'd heard that Yvonne might be passing on information about Oscar and Dylan to Gilly, but dating Oscar?

Jake had also heard that Oscar dumped Yvonne when she confessed to being his ex-wife's friend and informant. And that's when Oscar tried online dating and met Faith. We all knew where that had ended up.

"What a tangled web," I said, finding solace in my caramels. I might as well eat them, because no one was buying any today.

We decided to take advantage of our lack of customers to go over the investigation. Erica brought her laptop over to sit at the counter. "This new information demonstrates two things: That even though Gilly now lives in Florida, she knew enough about what was going on in Oscar's life to be considered a suspect. And that Yvonne had a connection to both Oscar and Gilly that she seems to have kept hidden. What was her reason?"

"We need to talk to Yvonne," I said. "But we can't get to Gilly." I paused. "Maybe we should let Detective Lockett know about that arrangement. He might find it interesting enough to talk to Gilly himself."

She looked thoughtful. "We'll hold off on that until we talk to Yvonne tonight at the festival," Erica said. "Let's discuss the suspects again."

"Good idea. I'm getting them all confused." I stuck out my index finger. "Let's start with our latest. Yvonne just inched onto the list, although we have no evidence of any kind other than gossip from Jake. Two, Newell and/or Ullman. They were cleared by Lockett, but people with that kind of money and connections could hire people to do their dirty work."

"But neither one seems to have a strong motive," Erica said.

"We're also not done with Nancy and Vaughn. Besides the whole sibling-rivalry thing, which *had* to have made him angry his whole life, his wife must be a little nutty to pull out a shotgun like that. Maybe she's capable of worse."

"What about Faith's high school friends?" she asked.

"I wouldn't exactly call them *friends*," I said. "But unless the upcoming reunion triggered something . . . homicidal in one of them, why would they be driven to something so extreme a decade later?"

"Faith was on the Lost Classmates list for years," Erica

noted. "Perhaps someone hated her enough to go after her just when she was 'found' again."

I bit my lip. "It's something we have to consider, but it just seems so farfetched."

"Chuck?" Erica asked, going through her list.

I sighed. "I think we should take Lockett's cue that he just stole her stuff, since there's no evidence he did the actual murder."

"If he was sloppy enough to keep her electronics, he'd have to have left some kind of evidence that he killed her," Erica said. "What about Freddy, the pawnshop guy?"

"As far as we know, he had no motive either," I said.

"And we know it wasn't Dylan or Oscar," Erica said firmly, and then frowned. "Zane and I still have a lot of files to go through. Now that everything is out, the comic book club wants to help, so we're splitting up the workload and sharing the files with them. Maybe one of them will see something we missed." She closed her laptop. "In the meantime, I think we need a plan to bring our customers back in."

"Those traitors," I muttered. "We should just move. That would show them."

Erica's eyes widened. "That's a marvelous idea. Like when a sports team threatens to change cities in order to get a new stadium." She pulled out her phone. "I'm calling Jake."

"Great idea," I said.

"Hi, Jake. I was wondering if you could do us a favor."

He must have given her a cute comment because she smiled. "Perhaps you could mention to a few of your customers that Chocolates and Chapters may be forced to move. To Frederick, for example."

I could hear his laughter across the counter. He knew exactly what we were up to. They exchanged good-byes and she hung up. "That should do the trick," she said with satisfaction.

Then she pulled out the file from Phoenix.

"Did you read all that already?" I asked. I'd glanced at a few of spreadsheets but was too anxious to go through everything, knowing that a legal agreement was waiting for me at the end.

"Yes," she said. "It all seems in order."

"In order?" I asked. "In what way?"

"Phoenix presented his case that our financials should be merged. We'll save money and, after the initial hassle, time and energy in the future." She handed me the legal agreement. "I signed the papers but, of course, they don't take effect until you sign them," she said.

I couldn't help my stunned expression.

"I know this step is hard for you, and I completely understand if you're not ready to take it."

"Okay." My voice came out as a little squeak.

Then Zane joined us at the counter and I shoved the papers back into the file. He usually stayed in the back, but we had no customers for him to hide from. "I found another website where she had an account," he said. "And under Interests, it says she volunteers at the Gentle Giants Draft Horse Rescue Farm."

Erica Googled the organization and I came around to see what she found. Their website popped up with photos of Clydesdales scrolling by. A video started with tear-jerking music and interviews with their management. We watched as happy horses played in fields, and listened to devoted volunteers tell us why they saved these large horses from slaughter and abuse.

"Looks like we need a field trip," I said.

I t didn't take long for the news of our threatened move to spread. May popped her head in first. "Did I hear correctly?" she asked. "You guys are moving?"

I put on my sad face while I sat at one of our many open tables, tapping my fingers. "We're just concerned," I said, laying on the guilt like a neglected mom. On steroids. "It seems like our customers don't believe in us. Maybe we should make room for another store they'd enjoy more."

May hadn't known me long enough to figure out my tactics. "Don't you worry," she insisted. "They'll come around." She was about to pop back out, but changed her mind. "Can I get a latte? And some Champagne Milks?"

As soon as she left, my cell phone rang.

It was Iris from the diner. "You're movin'?" she asked.

"What do you mean?" I asked in a guilty tone, as if she'd caught me.

"People jes started flappin their jaws that you're up and movin'. Course I tole 'em to shut their pie holes. No way you guys was leavin'." I imagined her coming to our defense, waving around her skinny tanned arms for emphasis.

"Who did?" I asked. "What did they say?"

"Said you were lookin' at hightailing over to Frederick and I said no way. You ain't city folk." She inhaled deeply. Must be on her cigarette break. "But I also tole 'em it was their own damn fault for listening to dat Reese witch." The last line was yelled, as if she was directing it into the diner.

"We're not moving," I said.

"Good," she said. "Then git yer ass in here soon, ya hear?" She hung up.

That afternoon we had a trickle of customers coming back in, sheepishly requesting their favorites. I used my *being gracious only because you're my customer* face, so that they knew I wasn't happy with them, which seemed to cause them to buy even more.

Someone should take this Mom Guilt marketing tactic, write a book, and go national with it.


"Yvonne? Do you have a minute?" We were in the middle of the Halloween Festival but I left Kona in charge of the booth and tracked down Yvonne so Erica and I could discuss her relationships with Oscar. And Gilly.

"Of course." She brushed her hair back from her face. "Anything for you," she said with a smile.

I led the way through the wild prison room, the screens and booms shaking the walls. I opened the door to the break room. No Erica.

She must be dealing with some festival crisis, so I was on my own.

"You know Dylan is staying with us, right?" I asked, glad the noise was muted.

"Of course," she said, sounding a little less enthusiastic. "Everyone knows."

"We—I mean, I—need to ask you some questions." I paused. "About Gilly."

Her eyes widened. "How could I help you with that?"

"We know you're still in contact with her," I said, sounding more sure of myself than I really was.

"That's not true," she said flatly.

"But you were," I said. "Until you started dating Oscar."

Her face turned bright red. "How do you know about that? Did Oscar tell you?"

"No," I said. "But people know. I just need to ask you if Gilly knew that Oscar was dating Faith."

She took in a deep breath, understanding where I was headed immediately. "Gilly didn't do it. She couldn't. She lives so far away . . ."

"Let's start at the beginning," I said. "Why did you keep in touch with her and let her know who Oscar was dating?"

"Because it wasn't fair!" she said, outraged. "They just ripped her out of their lives. As if she didn't matter at all!"

I took a step back at her vehemence, wishing I'd waited for Erica.

She put her hand to her head and tried again in a more rational tone. "You're not a mother. You can't understand."

"From what I do know," I tried gently, "Gilly ripped herself out of their lives."

"She didn't have a choice," she said. "Not after . . . everything became public."

"The affair," I said.

"She was so exposed. And it was all so humiliating for both Oscar and Dylan," she said. "She punished herself by going away."

I kept silent.

"But she never thought they'd totally cut her off," she said. "So I let her know what was happening in their lives.

I even sent her photos sometimes. What I'd want to have if I was in her situation."

"Did she ever come up here from Florida?"

She shook her head. "I don't think so," she said. "They're not doing too well financially . . ."

"And?" I prompted.

"And I'm not sure how their relationship is doing either," she said.

*What a mess*, I thought. But I had to get my questions answered. "Why did you and Oscar stop dating?"

She let out a big sigh. "We shouldn't have even started. Maybe we both felt betrayed or something. We got close and then one thing led to another . . ." Her voice trailed off. "And then before it got serious, I told him that I'd been talking to Gilly. And he dumped me."

Her misery was apparent. "It was better that he learned it from you."

"You'd think so," she said, "but I still ended up alone."

"Did you tell Gilly what happened?" I asked.

She nodded. "But she already knew."

"What did she say?"

"That I got what I deserved," she said. "She dumped me too."

"I'm sorry," I said, and then went for it. "If Gilly knew about you, she must be in contact with other friends here. Did Gilly know about Faith?"

"I don't know," she said. "She wasn't talking to me anymore, but maybe she has someone else telling her what was going on with Oscar and Dylan." Her phone beeped and she looked at it. "I have to go."

Erica rushed in as soon as Yvonne left. "Sorry I missed

your talk," she said. "Janice misplaced some costumes, but I found them in the main office."

I told her what Yvonne had told me. "I think we need to let Detective Lockett know about Gilly," I said. "It's not like we can go down to Florida and talk to her ourselves."

Erica took a moment to consider all the possibilities. "I agree. Can you call him now?"

I sighed. "Sure." He wasn't going to be happy with us. Again.

O ur guilt tactics continued to work. A small crowd had gathered outside before opening on Monday. I hadn't even noticed since I'd been in my usual chocolate-making storm in the kitchen.

Normally, I'd ask Kona to open early, but our customers didn't deserve it after staying away the day before. After the initial rush, we had our normal ebb and flow of customers until after school ended, when the high school kids flooded the shop. It took me a while to realize that it was a show of support, or perhaps they hadn't known that the adults in town had been staying away.

Dylan had come with us to the store, hiding in the back as much as possible. I was running to the back kitchen to bring out more Raspberry Specials when I saw someone sneaking down the back hallway toward Erica's office.

It was Reese.

"What are you doing back here?" I demanded. "This is not public property."

"I was just looking for . . ."

I got in her face, at least as much as I could with someone who was half a foot taller than me. "You were looking for Dylan. Weren't you?"

Over her shoulder, I saw Dylan stick his head out of the doorway and then go back in.

"No!" she squawked. "And even if I was, haven't you heard of freedom of the press?"

"Haven't you heard of trespassing? And harassment?" I pointed out the front door. "Get out."

She grumbled the whole way to the front door. I might have even heard her say, "You'll be sorry."

By the time we closed up early for the festival, we'd sold out of a lot of varieties, especially Ghoulish Grapefruit Milks with their fresh grapefruit zest, Black Currant Darks in the shape of black cats and with a dash of Cointreau, and our Full Moon Coins with vanilla bean–flecked ganache. Luckily I'd set aside plenty of other chocolate for the booth, but Kona was going to join me early the next day to restock our shelves.

Erica popped her head into the kitchen the next morning just as Kona and I were finishing replacing the run on Halloween-themed chocolates we'd had the day before. "The manager of volunteers at that Gentle Giants horse rescue place can show us around this afternoon."

I looked up at the clock and blinked while I thought about the schedule. "It's Tuesday, right? Kayla will be here at one," I said. "I can go then."

I sent a questioning glance to Kona, who seemed to stop short of rolling her eyes. "Yes, Mom. We'll be fine all by ourselves."

"No parties," I said in a fake stern-mom tone.

"Sure thing," she said as she bent down to add a coffee bean to the last Mocha Surprise.

"Perfect," Erica said and popped her head back out.

"You need to get your private investigator license or something," Kona said. "Then you'll get paid for all this."

"You trying to get rid of me?" I asked.

"Oh yeah," she said. "And then your vast empire will be mine, all mine." She ended with a villainous laugh.

"Be careful what you wish for," I told her. "Hey, how's your class going?"

Kona had started taking an online business class, and wanted to have her own store someday. If I allowed myself to think about it, I worried that I'd lose her. Her website was doing great, but it wasn't the kind of business she wanted long-term. She'd assured me that it would take years for her to learn enough to move on, and she'd promised me it wouldn't be a chocolate shop. I wouldn't want to compete with her.

"Great!" she said. "Getting straight A's on everything so far."

"Of course you are," I said, feeling like a proud parent.

The drive to Gentle Giants Draft Rescue Farm took us through Frederick and the downtown section of Mount Airy. Their Main Street looked so much like West Riverdale that I had to do a double take. They even had a statue of an early mayor on horseback in the center of a tiny fountain like we did.

"I haven't had a visit from Lockett in a while," I said. "Has he said anything about Gilly?"

She shook her head. "Nothing yet. And Bobby's not talking either."

Dylan was spending the day with Colleen, who had been approved by Marino.

We continued through town and back out to the countryside to the farm. It was picture perfect with rolling hills, a barn in the background, and horses grazing together at one end of the huge pasture.

We drove up the long driveway, past the *Gentle Giants Draft Horse Rescue* sign made with horseshoes, and parked near the barn. Inside an enclosure a woman wearing a hoodie covered by a green Gentle Giants windbreaker brushed a reddish-brown horse taller than an SUV.

"Hello," she said when we got out of the car. The unexpectedly appealing smell of horse manure blanketed the air, bringing back memories of a summer camp I'd gone to for a few years before my parents died.

"Hi," Erica said as we walked over. "Are you Glenda?"

"Yep," she said. "Come on over and meet Sweetie Pie."

We reached through the worn fence to tentatively pat the horse, who turned an eye on us as if to say, "You have no idea what you're doing, right?" He could star in a Budweiser commercial with that long mane and tail, and long tufts of cream-colored hair covering his hooves, like horse Uggs.

"We were hoping to talk to you about Faith Monette," Erica said.

Glenda stiffened. "The police were out here earlier asking questions about her. You with them?"

"No," I said. "But we've trying to help a friend."

"I'll tell you what I told them," she said. "She called

herself Faylinn Moyner and she volunteered here for about a year. She said she saw a video online and wanted to help. After a few months she slimed her way onto our fund-raising committee and suddenly I'm getting emails and phone calls from people who donated money and never got a receipt."

"They gave the money to Faith?" Erica asked.

"Yes," she said. "She created a fake website with a Donate button and just stole the money."

"That's terrible," I said. "Did you get any money back?"

She shook her head. "It was gone."

"Did the police investigate?" Erica asked.

"Yep," she said. The horse threw his head around and snorted as if he was disgusted too. "Nothing came of it."

"How much money did she take?" I asked.

She shrugged. "We only know of the people who contacted us for a receipt. A few thousand for sure. Best I could do was report the website and have it taken down."

We thought for a moment and then I asked, "Is there anything else about her you can tell us?"

Her face looked hurt for a moment. "I just didn't get it. She was so good with the horses. I could tell she loved them. Why would she steal from them?"

"Any ideas?" Erica asked in a gentle tone.

"My husband has a theory," she said. "Have you heard the story about the fox and the scorpion?"

"No," I said.

"You see, a scorpion needs to get across a river, so he asks a fox to carry him. The fox replies that he can't because the scorpion will kill him. The scorpion says he wouldn't because then he'd die too, so the fox agrees. Halfway across the river, the scorpion bites the fox. As he's dying, the fox asks, 'Why? Now we're both going to die.' And the scorpion says, 'I couldn't help it. It's in my nature.'"

That was a sobering thought.

"So it was in her nature to steal from people, and even though she loved these horses, she just couldn't help herself?" I asked.

She shrugged. "I just don't know. After I got a few calls, she came out on her normal day to volunteer and I confronted her. She looked kinda speechless, like she didn't know how she got caught. And I told her to never come back. My husband says it's nonsense, but I saw it."

"What?"

"She looked devastated," she said. "She started to leave but stopped for one last look at the horses. I'm pretty sure she was crying."

"Did you ever see her again?" I asked.

"No," she said. "But I think she came by to see her favorite horse, Beechem. I came out a few mornings and found pieces of apple in his stall. I think she visited him at night."

"Is he still here?" I wasn't sure why I asked.

"No. He was adopted," she said. "By a really nice man."

"Do you remember his name?" Erica asked.

"Sure," she said. "We actually don't get a lot of men adopting our horses. His name was Wade Overton."

**20**

Wade Overton? Why did his name keep coming up?

I tried to remain calm but this seemed like critical information. "He has a farm?"

Glenda shook her head. "He needed a place to board him and we recommended a place. We keep track of our horses to make sure they're not being bought for meat."

I wanted to say "Yuck," but at the last second I changed it to "That's terrible."

"He wasn't sure which stables would take such a big horse, so he asked for a referral," she said. "I was happy to tell him one of my favorites."

We patiently waited for her to give us the address of the farm, along with how to get there. She explained that our GPS would take us in a much longer way, and we'd hit a gate that the farm never opened, if we didn't listen to her.

We followed her directions, getting nervous with the one-lane road she'd recommended, but sure enough, we were soon at the barn of yet another horse farm.

"Hello?" we called out, but no one answered.

"Seems deserted," I said.

We walked over to the opening to the barn and called out again. "Hello?"

"Hello?" A male voice answered from halfway down the barn, the contrast from the outside light to the inside making it too dark to see who it was.

"Hi," I said, taking a few steps in. "We're looking for the manager." I blinked, trying to make out the face of who I was talking to.

"You can find her at the main house," he said. "Hold on. I'll come out and show you."

"It's okay. I see it," Erica said, and headed up the slight hill to the large ranch house.

His voice sounded vaguely familiar. I could see the darker shadow of a man against the light coming through cracks in the barn behind him. But it wasn't until he hit the patch of light coming from the open door that I recognized him.

Wade Overton.

I gasped. "Wade?" I scrambled to figure out what to say to him. "What are you . . . ?"

He smiled. "Don't worry. I know who you are."

"What does that mean?" I tried.

"You should see your face." He threw his head back in laughter. "I'm not a complete computer idiot. When you told me what happened to Faith, I looked online and saw that article about you and your friend."

"Oh," I said, cursing Reese internally and wishing Erica was here.

"It's cool," he said. "I hope you figure it out. That dude has to pay."

"I'm so confused," I said, and this time I wasn't trying to use my ditzy ploy. "Why do you have Faith's favorite horse?"

He shrugged, pulling his sunglasses from the back of his shirt collar. "Look, I already told the police all this, but since you guys are on the same side, I'll tell ya."

I was all ears.

"Like I said, Faith came into the shop a while ago, but the truth was that I got up the nerve to ask her out," he said. "And she said yes. We went out a few times, real casual, and then she told me she needed someone 'more ambitious.'" He used finger quotes, and laughed again, but this time, it had an edge.

"That must have made you feel terrible," I said.

"Nah," he said. "I get it. I've certainly heard *that* from chicks before." His expression was totally bland.

"You weren't mad?" I wasn't sure that was something you got over so easy.

"I get it. That whole *need to be taken care of* thing women have."

Whoa. Sexist much? "Why didn't you tell me that to begin with?" I asked.

He looked a little sheepish. "I wanted your business. I thought if you knew we'd dated, you wouldn't take her word for it that I was a good mechanic."

"So why do you have Beechem?" I still felt like I wasn't getting the whole story. I started walking back to the stall he'd walked out of, and my eyes adjusted quickly to the semi-dark.

"When we were going out, she had some problem with his adoption, so she asked me to adopt him in name only," he said. He patted Beechem's face over the gate. "She paid for everything and I just had to put my name on the certificate, or whatever it's called. Easy-schmeasy. I didn't think any more about him until, you know."

I stayed back. Beechem was huge. "Are you going to keep him?" I asked.

"Can't afford it," he said, stroking his mane. "To tell you the truth, I was thinking of selling him, but the contract doesn't allow that, so he's going back to that adoption place."

"Gentle Giants?"

"That's the one," he said. "Did they point you this way?"

"Yes," I said. "Really nice folks. Do they know he's coming back?"

"Not yet," he said. "I guess I should let them know, so they can prepare." He seemed a little wistful. "He's paid up until November fifteenth."

I saw Erica returning alone at the end of barn and decided to press my luck. "So you didn't make enough money for Faith? That doesn't sound very nice."

His eyes narrowed. "I don't think it was a matter of money, but more like doing something special with my life."

"Okay." I nodded like that made sense.

He gave me a rueful look. "I always knew she was outta my league, but the whole thing was good for me. Now I'm thinking of going to college. Go see what I missed. Can't hurt, right?"

Was this someone else Faith influenced to better his life?

Erica came up beside me, and I introduced them. She didn't seem surprised to see him. "I'm sure the police asked you this already, but where were you the night she died?"

He laughed. "They did. And I told them I was in the can, sick as a dog. The guys from the garage ate at Wally's Shack. My buddy and I split the seafood sampler and we both regretted it. All night."

"Did you tell the restaurant?" I asked.

"Hell yeah. Soon as I could get outta the bathroom, I called them. They said it was a bad batch of clams. A few folks had the same problem, especially my friend." He tapped on his phone. "Here's his number if you want to call him."

"Thanks." I dutifully typed the number into my phone.

"Sorry I can't help. I sure hope you get the guy."

"What do you think?" Erica asked as I drove back toward West Riverdale.

"I'm not sure," I said. "Maybe if he hadn't lied the first time I met him, I'd believe him." I told her about our conversation in detail. "He seemed perfectly reasonable, but something . . ."

"I'll text Zane to send over anything he has on him," she said as she pulled out her phone.

On the way back, we drove by a billboard advertising the Marines.

Erica read my mind. "Have you heard from Leo?"

I bit my lip and shook my head. I assumed he'd check up

on me once he heard the news about the minivan, but he hadn't even sent a text.

"You have a key to his apartment, right?" she asked. "Why don't you take a drive over there after you drop me off?"

When we got back to the store, Erica went over to her side and I checked in with Kona before trying Leo's cell one more time. It went straight to voice mail. Again.

I couldn't stay away anymore. I drove over to Leo's apartment, grateful to see his motorcycle in his parking space, even though it was caked with dirt. He'd never have allowed that a few weeks ago.

I didn't even knock, just let myself in. "Leo?" I called out.

He sat on the couch, looking even more gaunt. He didn't even look up. My heart gave one big thump and then raced.

I sat beside him on the couch, moving slowly, and tentatively touched his hand.

He blinked, his face drawn with exhaustion. Whatever he'd been doing all these days, it hadn't been sleeping. Or eating.

"Can you talk?" I asked.

He gave an almost silent snort. "Yes."

"Can I get you some water?" I asked, and then got up to go to the kitchen and was glad to see that even though his sink had dirty dishes in it, his clean glasses were still lined up with military precision in the cupboard. I turned on the faucet and poured him a glass, grabbing ice from his freezer. "Have you been working?"

He shook his head.

I sat down and handed him the glass, with a little push to encourage him to bring it toward his mouth. "Have you seen your therapist?"

He nodded.

"Worst day?" I asked, my voice turning rough.

Two tears spilled over from his eyes, making their way down his face, a silent acknowledgment of the turmoil he was going through.

I couldn't remember the last time he'd cried. Not when he'd fought through so much pain in physical therapy. Not when he'd adjusted to his prosthetic leg. Not even when his commander had survived several battles in Afghanistan and succumbed to pancreatic cancer a year after he returned home.

I hugged him tight, trying to send my healing thoughts into his whole being. "It's going to be okay," I whispered. "It really will."

He took a deep breath and the tension in his shoulders relaxed just a little.

I tried again. "Worst day?"

Slowly, he shook his head.

Relief inched through me.

"Is this about Star?" I asked, hoping not to step on any emotional land mines.

His hands clenched. He didn't answer.

"Is she okay?" I asked.

He shrugged.

"Did you break up with her?"

He shook his head, but his eyes looked hopeless. He cleared his throat. "I'm no good for her."

I never felt the need to tread as carefully as I did now. "You're the best person I know."

His mouth pulled to one side as if to say it wasn't true.

I laid one hand on his cheek. "Leo. You are." I enunciated every word. "The absolute very best. You *deserve* her."

He pressed his cheek into the palm of my hand almost unconsciously.

"You do." I talked louder, willing him to really hear me. And to believe me. "And she deserves you."

He shook his head again.

"Are you afraid?"

He hesitated before nodding. "I might have already lost her."

I put my forehead to his forehead and squeezed both hands to his cheeks.

"Get her back," I said.

I stayed long enough to make Leo oatmeal from a packet and watched him eat it. Then I ran to the grocery store and bought every comfort food I could think of, along with the basic staples, and rushed back. He was in the shower, which I took to be a step in the right direction.

By the time he came out, in what looked like clean clothes, I'd washed the dishes and made a very strong pot of coffee. I handed him a mug after adding a lot of cream and sugar. "This will help," I said.

"Thanks," he said, still not looking at me.

"Are you going to be okay?" I asked.

"Yeah," he said, his voice still too quiet. "Thanks." He cleared his throat. "I'm better. You can go to work, or whatever."

"Okay," I said, not feeling very sure. "You'll let me know if you need . . . anything."

He nodded. "I just have some thinking to do."

"Oh, now we're in trouble," I joked.

He grimaced, trying to give me a smile that didn't quite work.

"Want to come over for dinner?" I asked.

"Maybe," he said.

"I'll pick up Zelini's," I said. "Meatball subs?"

He shook his head. "Not tonight."

"Tomorrow?" Of course, I was supposed to work the festival, but I'd get someone to cover for me.

"Probably," he said.

I hugged him good-bye, feeling like he still wasn't back on track, and worried all the way back to the store.

Erica was waiting for me. She asked, "Is Leo okay?"

"He's a little better," I said. "Dylan still at Colleen's?"

"Yes," she said. The school was letting Dylan work from home for a while, and his friends were always around when they weren't at the festival. It was weird having teen boys around, especially when there was usually more than one at a time. Besides eating all our groceries, they took up so much space. Dylan usually slept in the guest room upstairs with at least one of his friends bunking down on the couch. Like a nonstop sleepover.

"Did they get breakfast?" I asked. Listen to me, momming a bunch of teen boys old enough to pick up a bagel if they needed it.

"Yes," she said absentmindedly. "Jolene and Steve are coming over." She looked over my shoulder. "Speak of the devil."

Steve opened the door for Jolene with an elaborate bow, and she walked in holding a bunch of papers. I was about to excuse myself, when Steve said, "Hi, Michelle," and walked with me to the counter. Jolene sat down with Erica to go over Dylan's homework assignments. Erica had emailed all of his teachers; she'd definitely make sure he kept up on his schoolwork.

"I can't stop thinking about this mess with Oscar," Steve said.

"He's going to be fine," I said. "Marino got him a lawyer—"

"That's not it," he said. "It's just not fair what people are saying about him. He's one of the best dads I know." He shook his head as if trying to make sense of his thoughts. "Oscar is the kind of dad who would do anything for Dylan. After the craziness with Dylan's mom, he turned down a job in Atlanta to keep some kind of stability in Dylan's life. Even though they both had to deal with all the nasty gossip here. He absolutely wouldn't risk hurting Dylan by killing someone."

"I understand." He was preaching to the choir here.

But he wanted to get his thoughts out. "You know, my own dad wasn't bad, but he wanted me to take over the family business and hated that I wanted to be a teacher. He made it very clear." He gave a little laugh. "I'm not sure if he was madder about that or that Jolene was black. But eventually he fell in love with her like everyone does."

He looked back at her discussing homework assignments with Erica.

"My point is, Oscar will support anything Dylan decides to do or be. He would not risk Dylan's future by hurting a woman he just started dating, no matter how awful she was."

. . . . . . . . . . . . .

B ean called me the next morning when Kayla and I were preparing to open. "Truffles got out again." His voice was serious. "Can you help me find him?"

"I'll be right there." I told Kayla what happened and that I'd be back soon.

"No prob," she said.

I dashed out the back door and heard a meow. Coco was sitting in her spot. With Truffles, who launched himself at me as soon as I sat down. "What the—?"

I called Bean right away. "Truffles is here," I said. "With Coco." The kitten kept up some nonstop complaining.

He breathed out a sign of relief, and then realized that the kitten must have walked a couple of miles to get here. "Is he okay?"

"He's probably hungry and thirsty," I said. "But he's not hurt."

"I'll be there in a few minutes," he said. "With the damn cat carrier." He hung up.

I didn't want to leave Truffles outside and couldn't bring him inside the store, so I called Kayla to bring out cat food and milk for two. Truffles twisted out of my arms to attack both, but Coco took her time before settling down to eat.

I kept Truffles right next to me, so I could grab him before he tried to make another escape after his meal, and called May. "Coco's here," I said. "Is she allowed to be outside?" No way was I tattling on Bean that Truffles was here too.

May sighed. "Yes, the vet said she's healing well enough

from her surgery, but thanks for letting me know. I'm going to be worrying about that cat the rest of my days."

While I waited, Tommy's hearse drove up and Dylan got out of the car before it came to a halt. "What did you do?" he yelled from the parking lot.

"What do you mean?" I asked. There were so many things to choose from.

He ran over, stopping just a few feet from the porch and causing Coco to hiss, probably to protect Truffles more than me.

"You told the police that my mom did it?" His frantic voice matched his face.

"No," I said. "I just . . ."

He took a few shaky breaths, his shoulders heaving. "You sold out my mom."

21

"Dylan, I didn't," I insisted. "I suggested that Detective Lockett have someone ask her a few questions. That's all."

He stared at me. Tommy got out of his car, but stayed back beside it.

"You know we're trying to help you," I said carefully. "And your dad. I found out . . . someone was telling your mom what you and your dad were doing."

"Well, she was questioned by the Miami police," he said. "I hope you're happy."

"Does she have an alibi?" I asked.

He actually grabbed his hair and pulled on it. "Yes!" He groaned. "She was in freakin' Miami."

"Okay, then," I said. "So it's fine."

"No, it's not!" he said. "You brought her back into our lives! For no reason!"

Luckily Bean drove up, right to the porch. He didn't seem to realize anything was wrong until he got out with the cat carrier. "Everything okay?"

I stood up and put Truffles inside his little cage, where he immediately began to protest. "It's okay, right, Dylan?"

He turned around to walk back to the car and spoke over his shoulder. "Yeah. Just fine."

Tommy gave me an apologetic look and got back in the car.

"What was that about?" Bean asked as they drove away.

I told him about my conversation with Yvonne and Dylan's confrontation.

"If he doesn't calm down soon, you can always send him to stay with me," he said.

I doubted that Marino would allow Dylan to stay with a reporter, but I kept that to myself.

After Dylan's tantrum, he'd texted Erica—not me—that he would hang out with Colleen again. Erica had kept in touch with Colleen throughout the day to make sure he was okay. He didn't go back to our house until after we'd left for the festival, and Tommy stayed with him.

Tommy was sprawled on the couch, snoring like crazy, when we let ourselves in that night, and his hearse was parked in front. Erica even checked to make sure Dylan was safely in his room, worried that he might be mad enough at us to break the rules, but he was asleep.

The were both still asleep the next morning. I groaned while putting on my running shoes. It was an overcast and gray Thursday, and I was not in the mood for exercise. Only knowing that I was never in the mood before I actually ran made me finish tying my laces and head down to the street.

It took until the second mile to feel less like I was lifting cement legs and more like my muscles were made for this. I fell into my long-distance rhythm, where my breathing evened out and my legs pumped effortlessly. I pushed everything out of my mind, by placing one foot down on the pavement, over and over.

At the end of the fourth mile, I approached my house and saw that Tommy's hearse was gone and an unfamiliar car was parked in its place.

I picked up speed.

Oh no. It had a Florida license plate.

It had to be Dylan's mom, Gilly. What was she doing here?

I ran in the front door. "Dylan!" I was so panicked that I didn't give him a chance to answer, calling out, "Dylan!" again until I heard him say from the kitchen, "Yeah?"

I stopped in the doorway, heaving. Dylan sat at the kitchen table with his mother.

She looked at me with her lip curled. I wasn't sure if it was because I stank from sweat or because I had been acting like a lunatic.

I looked around and saw that someone had made coffee. Had Erica served Gilly coffee and made herself scarce? What was she thinking?

"How did you get here so fast?" I asked her breathlessly.

"It only takes fifteen hours to drive here," Gilly answered. The *you moron* was silent but intended. "And there's no need to scream like that. I'm his mother, not a criminal." She was a tiny woman, shorter than me and way skinnier. She had designer jeans and a cropped shirt, looking pretty chic for someone who had driven all night.

I was hoping she'd let me off the hook for that misunderstanding. If I wasn't already red from exercise, I'd have blushed at her words.

"Mom," Dylan said, as if he was incredibly embarrassed by her behavior. And she'd been back in town less than an hour. It might be a new record in the Humiliation by Mom game.

Erica came downstairs. "Michelle, have you met our *guest*, Gilly?"

"Yes," I said. "I was just about to ask her why she was here."

"Why, that's pretty obvious," Erica said in a *get off her back* tone. "She's here to visit her son in his time of need. Like any mother."

"Actually," Gilly said, her face determined, "I'm here to take my son home with me to Florida."

"Gilly," Erica said, way more kindly than I would have managed. "I'm sorry, but that's not possible. He's under our protection, and you have no grounds to take him."

"I'm his mother!" Gilly yelled.

"Mom!" Dylan yelled back.

"That is true," Erica said. "But you gave up your legal rights in that regard, and taking him anywhere, especially across state lines, will just make the situation worse. Especially for Dylan."

"I'm not going to freakin' Florida," Dylan said, his eyes defiant.

With that, Gilly seemed to collapse within herself. I grabbed her, just as she was about to slide off the chair, and eased her head between her knees, getting some blood back into her brain.

Erica held her other arm. "Dylan," she said. "Get some water."

We both sat on either side of her, holding on to her cold hands as she tried not to outright faint. She took several calming breaths, until she was able to sit up and take the water from her son, who looked on anxiously.

Her eyes watched him, haunted with remorse, and a longing so intense I had to look away.

There was no win-win situation here, but I knew Gilly was no threat to Dylan.

Back at the store, I grew even more worried about Leo. He hadn't called me back about the Zelini's dinner we'd talked about. I tried Star again.

She answered right away. "Yes."

"Uh, hi, Star," I said, stumbling at her unfriendly tone.

"I can't help you," she said. "Your brother dumped me."

I sucked in a breath. This was really bad. A major step backward. "When?" I demanded. "That makes no sense. He loves you."

"Yesterday," she said. "You haven't talked to him?"

"No," I said, panic crawling up my spine. "Can you tell me what happened?"

She paused a moment and I could hear her draw in a deep breath. "He called to tell me that he didn't love me, and I was moving too fast for him. He wanted to take a break."

"What a jerk," I said. "He's making all that up."

"I don't think so," she said. "He meant it."

"What did you tell him?"

"What do you think?" she said, her pain coming through the phone. "I told him he doesn't get to 'take a break.' We're either together or we're not. And that he better not come anywhere near me again or I'd kick his ass."

I thought about Star's biceps. She could totally do it.

I couldn't get the look on Gilly's face out of my mind even while I tried to track down Leo.

We'd allowed her to spend a few hours with Dylan, and he'd texted that she left to find a motel and that he was staying at the house until Quinn came by after school.

But part of me wondered how far Gilly would go to protect her son. Would she eliminate someone she thought of as competition?

My worries didn't matter. According to the Florida police, she had a solid alibi. But I was still keeping my eye on her.

Then I got a message from Bean. *I think Leo is fishing*, he texted.

Why hadn't I thought of that? I tracked down Erica in her office and told her about Star. "Bean said Leo might be fishing. I'm heading up to Cunningham Falls."

"Want company?" she asked.

I shook my head. "I just need to find out what's going on in his head."

"Zane found out something disturbing about Wade Overton's Internet use," she said. "Do you want to go over it before you leave?"

I groaned, feeling overwhelmed. "Do I have to?"

She didn't give in to my juvenile whining. "He's made a bunch of sexist comments, anonymously, of course."

I remembered the way he'd talked about his ex-girlfriends as "chicks" and his belief that all women wanted to be "taken care of." "Did he seem angry?"

"It's not clear," she said.

"Maybe you can ask Bobby about that," I suggested. "Shoot. I never called Wade's friend to confirm his alibi. I can do that on the way to the cabin."

I told Kona what I was up to, and she gave me a sympathetic hug and wished me good luck. Everyone loved Leo. Why couldn't he feel that?

I was filled with nostalgia on the drive up into the hills surrounded by trees with red, orange and yellow leaves. My family used to rent a cabin and spend a week there almost every summer. It was rustic, but Leo and I had loved splashing in the water, climbing the rocks that had seemed like mountains back then, hiking through the woods and fishing.

I stopped at the country store that had a small restaurant attached, picking up the cheeseburgers and French fries that had been a tradition with my parents. I tried Wade's friend but it went to voice mail.

Leo often rented the same cabin, and I knew his favorite fishing spots. As I arrived, I walked over to his regular cabin, and sure enough he was sitting on the small wooden steps, his head in his hands.

"Leo?" I asked.

He raised his head, looking miserable. He didn't even seem surprised to see me.

"Worst day ever?" I asked, my voice trembling.

He didn't even crack a smile. "Not even close." His grim voice was alarming.

I sat beside him and wrapped my arms around him. "Not even on the inside?"

"It's pretty bad on the inside," he admitted.

"I'm worried," I said. "You're having a hard time getting back to, I don't know, being yourself."

"What self?" he asked.

"The Leo you've been the last year or so."

"I'm not sure who he is." His voice was barely a whisper.

I had no idea how to handle this conversation, but maybe it was time for tough love. I used a gentle voice. "I can tell you who he's not. He's not the Leo who clings on to a weird sense of overprotectiveness."

He pulled away, looking a little mad.

"He's not the Leo who's so afraid to lose something that he lets go of the most precious person he's ever known."

"You're the most precious," he retorted.

"Okay, second most precious," I said, trying to make a joke.

His face twisted.

I took a deep breath. "You may have forgotten, but I know who the real Leo is. He's the man who fought for his life in a field hospital in Afghanistan. He's the man who fought through the pain to learn how to walk again. And he's the man who has fought to push back the darkness to get to a sunny place. Like this one." I looked away from his face and gestured to the sun glinting off the water. He followed my gaze.

"I know that darkness is in your head, not out here. But that sunny place is in there too."

We sat for a minute just looking at the peaceful scene. Then a fish jumped out of the water, causing a splash. For some reason it made us both smile.

"I just—" He stopped. "I wouldn't make it back again if something happened to you."

"Nothing is going to happen to me," I said. "But if it did, you would be okay. You really would."

His frozen face returned.

"Because moments like this, just sitting in the sun watching a stupid fish jump, they make it all worth it. Those days will be there no matter what."

His expression softened, but misery still shone through.

"You know how you joined the Marines because you wanted to protect innocent people?" I asked. "Dylan is an innocent kid, and I'm protecting him the only way I know how."

He shook his head, not liking the comparison.

"You know how you ride that motorcycle even though it makes me crazy?" I asked.

He nodded, knowing where I was going and not liking it.

"That's how I feel when I'm trying to figure out who the bad guy, or girl, is," I said. "Like you're riding your Harley down a country lane, full throttle, with the wind whistling by you."

He didn't respond.

"Like when you kiss Star and your head explodes," I said. "Those moments make the worry and the pain and the fear of life, of living, all worth it."

Leo bit his lip, and put his head on my shoulder as if exhausted beyond endurance.

I angled my head to look into his face.

"Get her back." I nudged his head with my shoulder. "Don't be too afraid to go after the best thing that ever happened to you."

"How?"

I pulled a ring box out of my pocket.

"What is that?" he asked, his voice a croak.

"Open it," I said, even though we both knew what it was.

He followed my order and our mom's engagement ring gleamed in its velvet base. The sun caught the small diamond and made it sparkle.

"That's for you," he said.

"No, it's not," I insisted. "It might not happen for me." The image of Bean down on one knee flashed through my mind and I banished it immediately. "But it could happen for you. You need this ring, right now. How could Star resist you *and* this ring?"

He shook his head, even as he stared longingly at it.

"Mom and Dad would have *loved* Star." I closed his hand over the box and squeezed. "It's meant to be. I know it."

"And you know everything?" he asked, sounding more like himself. He looked out at the water again, clutching the box. "How . . . ?"

I knew he meant *How can I make that leap of faith?* and not *How can I convince her?* but I went with the easier question. "I think the man who rides a motorcycle with one leg can figure that out. But a grand romantic gesture coupled with that ring and an explanation that you were a big chicken should do the trick."

. . . . . . . . . . . . .

The sun seemed to shine a little brighter when I headed back to West Riverdale. Leo had stayed behind, saying he had a lot to think about. This time I knew his thoughts were taking him to a better place, especially when he dove into the meal I'd picked up.

I thought about my mother's ring. Just a stone and metal, but a symbol of so much more. Love and a lifetime commitment. The necklace Bobby gave Erica. They might not have used the "L" word yet, but maybe they didn't need to. The necklace was enough.

I looked down at the file of papers on the front seat and realized that I'd been almost as big a chicken as Leo. I pulled over and read them through. The legalese was clear—this agreement would mean our businesses would officially become one business. Tied together no matter what came down the path. Success. Failure. Global shortage of sugar or paper. Erica and I would be in it together.

I signed and initialed everywhere that Erica had, not using my normal chicken scrawl, but looping my letters and making my name large and my commitment unambiguous.

"There," I said out loud, alone in my car. "I did it." I felt a rush of pride, and I started the car and headed to Phoenix's house, wanting to see my decision through.

His home was a charming farmhouse that had been haphazardly added on to over the decades. He had completely renovated it, not just upgrading things like the antiquated plumbing and electric, but also lopping off a rickety addition to create a more balanced appearance. I'd looked forward to reading his renovation updates in his newsletters, where he'd always had a cheerful take on what I would've considered disasters. He'd held a huge housewarming party when it was completed, inviting his clients from all over.

I turned into his driveway, right behind a brown UPS truck that had stopped at a gate blocking the entrance. The driver put in a code and the gate opened. I hurried to squeeze in before the gate closed behind me and followed the truck to the house.

"Hi!" I said cheerfully as I jumped out to put my papers in the mail slot. "Want me to ring the bell for you?" The chance of Phoenix being home during the day was low, but I knew UPS drivers were expected to ring the doorbell just in case.

"Sure," he said, hustling over a couple of small boxes and several large envelopes with the UPS logo. "I need a signature."

The door opened and Detective Lockett stood in the doorway, barefoot. He looked as stunned as I felt. "What are you doing here?"

"Good morning, Roger," the UPS driver said. "Can you sign for these?"

Lockett took the package and signed the electronic form. He scowled at me until the driver was back in his truck.

Roger? The UPS driver knew Lockett by name?

"You're living together," I said. "I guess you *are* serious."

He sighed. "Yes, nebby. We're engaged."

"Cool!" I said. "When's the wedding?"

Lockett shook his head. "You never stop with the questions." His phone rang and he answered it while staring straight at me. "Lockett." He listened for a moment. "Fine." He hung up.

He gestured to the papers I still held in my hand. "Want to do something with those?"

"Oh yeah," I said. "Sorry. I was excited to give these to Phoenix and stopped by on an impulse."

He snorted. "That'll always get you into trouble."

Bean called when I was on my way back to West Riverdale. "Hey, I have another possible overnight in Baltimore. Can I drop Truffles off with you?"

"Sure," I said, looking forward to spending time with the fluff ball.

"Now?" he asked. "My timing is tight."

"I'm ten minutes away from home," I said, "but Dylan's there."

"That works," he said.

It looked like our shared kitten custody was working out just fine.

He called me back. "Dylan's not here. I used my key and put Truffles in the living room."

My heart sank. "Are you kidding me? He's supposed to tell us when he leaves. Is the security system on?"

"No," he said.

"Gilly." I sped up. "I'll call him. Can you wait there?"

I took a minute to dial Dylan's number before taking Tommy's shortcut to get home faster. I'd just hit the bumpiest part of the dirt road when I saw Oscar's truck traveling off the road.

Way off the road.

In fact, it was heading down the driveway toward my neighbor's lake.

"What is he doing?" I said out loud and then realized the truck was picking up speed.

22

"No!" I screamed uselessly inside my car and accelerated down the road, looking for any break in the brush that would take me toward the lake.

I lost sight of the truck behind some trees and then I saw the faint outline of an unused driveway. The back of the minivan fishtailed as I turned too fast, dirt shooting up behind me. A hill rose in front of me, blocking my view.

I slammed my thumb down on my cell phone and listened for the beep indicating sound activation. "Call Bean," I yelled.

"Calling Bean mobile," the mechanical voice said back to me. The sound of the phone dialing on speaker setting made me almost sob with relief.

"Hey," Bean answered.

"Oscar's truck is heading right for the Dunbar lake," I yelled. "I think Dylan is driving it."

"I'll be right there," he said.

I crested the hill in time to see exactly what I was afraid of. The truck was already in the water, the front slowly sinking.

My foot automatically went to the floor, the engine roaring until I braked to a stop at the dock. I jumped out and yelled, "Dylan!" before bounding into the water, wading with my knees high until I was forced to swim. The windows were open and the cabin of the truck was filling with water fast.

Dylan was unconscious, the water rising to his chest, and I could see blood in the water. I held on to the side of the truck bed and yanked on the door. It didn't move.

It was locked. I reached in and unlocked the door, and this time I put my foot against the side of the truck and pulled with everything I had.

The door opened with a groan but the truck shifted even more, and Dylan's whole body pitched forward, his face right in the water. I started sobbing.

I tried to pull him out, but the door started to close on us both. This time, I held the door open with one foot, grabbed Dylan under the arms and pushed off.

We were free of the car, and suddenly strong arms grabbed Dylan.

Another wave of panic went through me before I realized it was Bean. "You okay?" he asked, swimming backward on his back and keeping Dylan's face out of the water.

"Yeah," I said, my chest heaving as I followed them.

Soon we both were able to touch the muddy bottom of the lake and make our way to shore.

Bean immediately put Dylan on the ground and checked his vital signs. "He's breathing," he said. "You did it. You saved him."

Sirens blared in the distance and I collapsed beside Dylan, trying to get my breath back. "Why is he unconscious?"

"I don't know," he said. "His lungs are clear." He went to the trunk of his car to retrieve three blankets. "Did you see what happened?" He handed me a blanket and unfolded another to cover Dylan.

"I was too far away," I said. "But it doesn't make sense."

Bean used the third blanket as a pillow under Dylan's head.

His hand came away bloody and he looked at me. "He was hit on the head. Dylan didn't do this."

The next half hour, time seemed to have warped, moving unbelievably fast and then in slow motion.

Bean tried to get me to go home and put dry clothes on, but I refused, standing and shivering while Dylan was placed on a backboard and taken away by ambulance. The EMTs seemed most concerned about his head injury.

One thought made it through the fog. "Where's Truffles?" I asked.

"At your house," he said. "Erica's got him."

Chief Noonan took Bean aside to ask him questions. I could hear the succinct tone of his answers but not his words, and the feeling that this couldn't be real swamped me.

Detective Lockett tried to question me but I couldn't seem to focus, while Bobby put up the crime scene tape, his face set, and the crime scene techs worked the area around the dock. A tow truck arrived and slowly pulled Oscar's truck out of the lake, the high whine of the winch making me jump.

Water poured out of it and I completely missed Lockett's question again, trembling at the sight of the murky water and the memory of the fear. What would have happened to Dylan if I hadn't been here?

"Why don't we go to your house to continue this," Lockett said for the third time. He sounded like he was being kind, but he probably was tired of me not being able to concentrate.

I nodded. "I can't drive."

"I'll take you home and Junior will bring your car around," Lockett said. He walked over to let the chief and Bean know where we were going and then led the way to his car.

A small group had gathered at the beginning of the driveway leading to the lake, their cars parked halfway off the dirt road. Junior lifted the crime scene tape high and we drove under it. Reese had her camera raised to take photos but stopped to stare at me, openmouthed.

"You know Dylan didn't do this," I said as we drove the short distance to my house.

Lockett's face was grim. "We're looking at all of the possibilities."

Erica met us on the porch, holding Dylan's cell phone in a plastic bag. "I didn't touch it," she said as she handed it to the detective. She gave me a hug and then turned me around by my shoulders to push me inside. "Shower and warm clothes. Now. And ignore those pitiful meows from Truffles. He has food and water upstairs in my room."

I cracked a smile and followed her orders. As I was putting on thick socks, Bean knocked on my door. "You okay?" he asked when I opened it.

I nodded even though I felt far from okay. He pulled me into his arms and held on. "You scared the crap out of me," he said, his voice rough.

"I didn't really think," I said. "I just jumped in." I shivered again at the thought of poor Dylan in that water.

"I get that." He placed a kiss on the top of my head. "I just don't want to lose you."

I held on tight. "You won't."

Lockett was waiting for me in the kitchen with the chief when I returned. "Please sit down," he said, and after the day I had, I was happy to listen to him. Erica handed me hot cocoa and I wrapped my hands around the mug.

"I need you to start at the beginning," he said, his voice gentle.

I explained everything, from Bean's phone call to pulling Dylan out of the truck.

Lockett looked right at me. "Dylan sent a text to his father, confessing to the murder and saying that he was going to kill himself."

I sat up straight. "It's not true."

"How do you know?" he asked.

His tone wasn't challenging, but I responded as if it was. "The real killer sent that text," I insisted, my voice shrill. "And then he hit Dylan on the head and drove him into that lake. He wanted to send everyone in the wrong direction."

"Did you see anyone else besides Dylan near the truck?" he asked.

"No," I said. "But the truck was far away. And there were trees in the way."

"Was there enough time for someone to send the truck into the lake and escape without you seeing them?" he asked.

I shook my head, feeling helpless. "I don't know. I was focused on helping Dylan. There are lots of bushes there. Someone could have easily hidden."

Erica laid her hand on my arm. "It's clear that there are enough questions to not accept this confession at face value, Detective. And if the real murderer truly intended to frame Dylan, then he might try to hurt him again. Dylan needs round-the-clock police protection."

Lockett stared at her for a moment. "I agree."

"And perhaps we should let everyone believe the suicide note," Bean suggested. "To make sure whoever did this thinks we've all fallen for it."

Lockett nodded, his face thoughtful.

"Can we see Dylan?" I asked.

"Gilly's with him." Then, as if understanding how much we needed to make sure Dylan was safe, he added, "You can't ask him any questions, not one, until we talk to him. Do you understand?"

I nodded, and this time it wasn't a lie.

Information about Dylan's suicide attempt spread like wildfire throughout West Riverdale and I had to turn off my phone to avoid all the gossipmongers who wanted to tell me they'd known Dylan was the killer all along.

Reese's blog was especially gloating, pointing out Erica's

and my failure to recognize a murderer right under our nose. Of course, Jolene and Steve sent reassuring texts, saying that it was all horse-hooey and our fine police force would figure out the truth.

Bean drove me to the hospital. Erica could not pass on her festival responsibilities to anyone else and told me to keep her updated. Gilly was kind to us, even though she had to believe this wouldn't have happened if she'd taken Dylan to Florida. We all kept a quiet vigil in Dylan's room. His friends took turns hanging out in the lounge at the end of the hall. Invariably, they spent their time on their cell phones, doing whatever teens do to stay occupied in an intense but somewhat boring atmosphere.

Junior had parked himself on an uncomfortable chair right outside the room, looking like a teen himself in a baseball cap and jeans. His alert expression and immediate analysis of anyone who entered the hall was the only thing that gave it away: this boy had police protection.

After a couple of hours, I realized I wasn't doing any good to anyone. Or perhaps my penance was over. Bean and I headed home.

Erica joined us after closing down the festival. We were all exhausted but not ready to sleep when we heard a knock on the door. I seriously considered ignoring it.

"Open up, Serrano." It was Lockett.

I ran over to let him in. Poor Lockett looked exhausted. I took a minute to make him a coffee before asking, "Did you learn anything new?"

"A text was deleted from Dylan's phone," he said. "It told him to come outside if he wanted to set his dad free."

I bit my lip, not wanting to cry in front of Lockett, but

the emotional roller coaster of the day was getting to me. "Dylan would do anything to help his dad."

"And that text proves he didn't try to commit suicide," Erica said.

I shivered. This was one bad dude. Even if the first murder was some kind of impulsive attack, this was premeditated.

"Did you notice anyone watching your house?" Lockett asked. "This person had to be waiting for the right time to make a move."

We'd been on the lookout ever since the Great Hearse Car Chase, but had never spotted anyone again. I shook my head. Could we have missed something like that? Then I remembered what Chuck had said. "Chuck mentioned that someone was following Faith, and Vaughn and Nancy's neighbor also said someone was staking out their house. Could it all be the same guy?"

Lockett's eyes narrowed. "We'll look into it."

Erica and I had decided that the best thing for our investigation was to wait for Dylan to regain consciousness and ask him who did this to him.

Friday passed in a blur, and Dylan was still unconscious on Saturday, worrying everyone. I stopped by the hospital on the way to working at the festival. Gilly looked exhausted, but hopeful.

Word of the festival must have spread to other towns, as everyone decided West Riverdale was the place to be on Halloween. The place had been packed with costumed families since noon, and the volunteers were stretched to the max keeping up with the crowds.

An adult clown was pretending to browse my chocolates while feasting on the freebies. The white gloves picking up the brown chocolate samples were making me uncomfortable.

Phoenix stopped by. "How are you holding up?"

"Good," I said, as Kayla rang up a small box of truffles for a grandma dressed up like the Fairy Godmother with her granddaughter dressed as Cinderella.

"Bippety-boppity-boo!" Kayla said to them.

"Hey," I said to Phoenix. "I hear you're engaged."

He smiled. "Yes I am." He put his arm on my shoulder and gave it a squeeze. "And you signed the papers. That was a very good decision."

"I hope so," I said. "But don't change the subject. When's the wedding?"

Phoenix laughed. "You'll be among the first to know." He waved and moved on to the next booth.

Quinn ran up to my booth, breathless, and inside I started quaking. "Dylan?" I asked.

"No," she shook her head. "I just found something. "

"What?"

"Zane brought us"—she looked around, but the only one around was Clown Guy—"*her* emails to help him go through and I noticed that someone used the same phrase in a comment on that stupid article Reese wrote *and* in an email to Faith."

"What phrase?"

"He called her a 'bright light.'"

Oh man. That was in the reunion slide show too.

"Who was he?" I asked.

"I don't know," she said. "Faith used the code name BCH.

But she didn't save any of the emails with him in her files. Then a month later, she put BCH in her Dud category."

That didn't make any sense. She'd saved every email from every single one of her targets.

But maybe he wasn't a target. Could BCH be the man Chuck said Faith fell in love with? The one who had lied about owning a business?

BCH. "Bucky Central High," I said out loud.

Wade Overton had admitted that they'd dated and she dumped him? Could it have been more serious than that? Could he have lied about owning the garage instead of being an employee?

"Her high school?" Quinn asked.

I created a little timeline in my head. "Do you know when she put him in the Dud file?"

She shook her head. "A couple of months ago?"

She didn't need to check. I was certain. "You found something very important. I have to call someone." I looked around for Erica, but she must have been putting out a fire somewhere else. My clown customer was gone without buying anything. But he'd be back. Once they tasted my truffles, they always came back.

Quinn looked pleased that she might have helped.

"Where are you supposed to be working tonight?" I asked her as I dialed Honor.

"Kids' grape-eyeball room," she said. "To keep the little monsters from eating them."

"Good luck," I said as she headed off to her assignment. I shuddered to think of the germs on those things regardless of how many times we rinsed them during the afternoon. "And thanks for that info," I called after her.

Honor answered the phone. "Hi, it's Michelle, Benjamin's assistant."

"Oh, you," she said.

"I have a very important question," I said. "Can you tell me who submitted the 'bright light' comment for Faith's memorial slide?"

"Sure," she said. "Hold on."

I waited impatiently until she picked up the phone again. "It was Wade Overton."

Wade Overton?

   The only person from Buckey Central High School who actually liked Faith.

I called Lockett but he didn't answer.

Shoot. I left a message. "When Dylan wakes up, show him a photo of Wade Overton," I said. "I think he did it!"

I saw that I had a voice mail and hit the button to listen, sticking my finger in my other ear to hear better. It was Wade's friend, returning my call. He left a stumbling message that yes, he's shared a seafood platter with Wade, and they were both incredibly sick. He said he'd spare me the details, but very, very sick. Almost as an afterthought he added, "I didn't see Wade eat none of them clams, but he got the bug anyways."

I blinked and listened to the message again. Had Wade faked being sick to create an alibi?

A group of elementary school kids swarmed the free samples, and the moms picked up a few boxes to make up for it. I checked them out, not sure what else to do with this information.

I looked at my phone again, willing Lockett to call me back.

Then I got a text from Quinn. *911. Meet me in hangout room.*

What the heck was she doing in there? I dashed inside, funneling through the mass of zombies, mummies and for some reason, a zombie nun, and opened the door.

The clown stood there, holding Quinn's upper arm tightly with one hand and a hunk of two-by-four wood left over from the guillotine construction with the other.

Wade Overton.

"Close the door," he demanded, his eyes angry and mean behind the clown makeup.

"There's no way to get out of this," I said, trying to remain calm, but my heart raced at the scared look on Quinn's face. "Let her go and I'll tell the police to go easy on you."

He scowled, the look made even scarier with the goofy clown getup.

"I heard her," he said. "She's the only one who figured it out. And she told you. All I have to do is get rid of you two."

"You can claim temporary insanity or whatever with Faith. But this is premeditated. This is life without parole." I took a step closer and he wrenched Quinn's arm up, jamming it into her shoulder and causing her to cry out.

I backed up. "Don't hurt her! She has nothing to do with this. She's innocent." I had to make him talk more. "The police know too much," I said. "They know that Dylan's suicide attempt was faked and when he wakes up, they're going to show him a photo of you."

He flinched, as if I'd hit a nerve.

"She must have caused you so much pain for you to be so angry," I said, trying to sound sympathetic when all I wanted to do was scream at him to let Quinn go.

"I loved her!" he yelled, unconsciously pulling on Quinn, making her whimper. "I would have done anything for her and she dumped me for a freaking old man!"

"She didn't love him," I said. I looked around for any kind of weapon but the only thing was a plastic witch's broom in the corner. I took a sliding step closer to it.

"No!" he said. "She said she loved me but Mr. Rich Man put her in his will and she said she had to marry him to get the money."

"She wouldn't let you take care of her?" I asked, trying to sound appalled.

"No, so I took care of *him*," he said. "He dumped her like I knew he would and she still didn't come back to me." He took a deep breath that caught like a sob halfway through.

Oh man. Why hadn't we seen it? Wade was a mechanic. Of course he was responsible for Newell's "accidents."

"Did she say why?"

"No," he said. "But that bitch was right back on her dating sites in a second."

"Did you try to get back together with her?"

"I did everything. Sent flowers, candy. I even gave her my mother's ring, and she sold it!" He narrowed his eyes. "And then I figured out that I was going about it all wrong. She needed to be shown who was boss."

"You followed her?" I asked, remembering that Chuck had said Faith thought someone was stalking her.

"Yes," he admitted, his eyes narrowing.

"She told her friend that she used self-defense to take care of the person following her," I said.

He pulled back on Quinn's arm, causing her to cry out, and I yelled, "I'm sorry! I'm just trying to figure out why you had to hurt her."

"Because she deserved it," he growled.

"Okay," I said, my throat so tight I didn't know how words were getting out. "So you saw her on her way to meet someone that night."

"Yes," he said, sounding defiant.

"And she talked to you, or hit you even. And you had to hit her with a bat."

"Yes," he said. "She said she was going to meet that guy at Green Meadows and he was going to buy a house for her."

I took a chance. "Her high school friends said she could be incredibly mean when people didn't do exactly what she wanted them to do. Was she mean to you?"

"Yes!" he yelled. "She said she was going to marry him, because he could afford to give her what she needed. Well, I showed him. And her."

"She taunted you, and you snapped," I said, trying to make it sound reasonable. "The police will understand that and go easy on you."

He narrowed his eyes.

"But only if you let Quinn go."

"That's not going to happen," he said. "She knows too much."

"The police know all this, Wade," I said. "They know

about you dating Faith. They know about the horse. They know you tried to kill Newell Woodfellow."

I saw the door handle turn and panicked that one of the kids would barge in, unknowingly putting themselves in danger too. I screamed, "No!"

The door exploded inward and what seemed like the entire cast of every superhero, zombie and mummy movie came through that door, swarming over Wade in a flood of angry teens out for blood.

Wade was forced to let go of Quinn and his weapon, and was subdued by the horde of punching and kicking teens until he was flat on his face, with Tommy leaning hard in the middle of his back, Wade's arm twisted up between his shoulder blades.

Tommy looked up at Quinn, who had simply stepped back against the wall and watched the whole thing in awe, like me. "You okay?" he asked her. When she nodded, he added with satisfaction, "Guess I'll have to tell my mom that those tae kwon do classes came in handy."

I t didn't take long for Detective Lockett and Bobby to arrive on the scene and arrest Wade. He looked utterly defeated, hunched over in the police car wearing a dirty white T-shirt and underwear, with some of the clown makeup sliding off to show where punches had landed. The police had stripped him of his costume while looking for weapons.

It took hours to sort out those who had actually seen something and get their statements. Tommy and a few others were invited down to the police station for a more intense interview. Trent had seen Clown Wade grab Quinn and drag her into the quiet room, and he'd texted everyone he knew, gathering the costumed cavalry. Word had spread fast and the gang of teens had come to the rescue.

Erica stayed behind to close up the festival, and then joined us at the police station, which hadn't had such a boisterous crowd since the ill-fated St. Patrick's Day parade of 2012. The hall was a chaos of excited and proud teens in colorful costumes.

Lockett and the chief had already taken my statement, but invited me back into the interrogation-slash-lunch-and-dining room to let me know that Dylan was conscious and had positively identified Wade as the one who had hit him over the head. He didn't remember anything after that, not even almost drowning in the lake.

Oscar was out of jail, and had gone directly to the hospital.

Wade had confessed to everything, blaming Faith for driving him to kill her, and dumping her body at the Green Meadows Estates to implicate Oscar. Lockett said he'd be in prison a long time.

Erica and I opened up Chocolates and Chapters a little early the next day, offering a day-after-Halloween discount. It seemed like the whole town had decided our shop was the place to be, to discuss the excitement of the night before and celebrate the comic book kids being the superheroes they'd always wanted to be.

The teens took over the stairs in the bookstore side, laughing and pushing one another as they retold their parts of the story.

Dylan had been released from the hospital, and he sat in the middle with a bandage on his head. In between acknowledging his friends' comments, he stole glances at his parents, who sat together at one of the tables in the back. They barely spoke, content to see their son safe.

Gilly was sticking around West Riverdale for a while. She told Erica that she realized her embarrassment over her affair was something she could handle after almost losing her son. She was hoping that she and her new husband could move back close enough to be in her son's life.

Bean was sitting at the counter, as if he didn't want to be far from me. He'd driven home from Baltimore in the middle of the night to make sure I was really okay, and stayed with me for the first time. Of course, Bobby had stayed right upstairs, not wanting to be far from Erica either. It made for an awkward breakfast.

Leo opened the door to Chocolates and Chapters, and I was delighted to see him holding the door for Star. Then he announced, "We're engaged!" to the whole room.

Star laughed, looking up at him with a dazzling smile and so much love, she shined. She held up her hand with a sparkling diamond for everyone to see.

I burst into tears and made my way around the counter to hug Star first. "Oh my God! I'm so happy!"

I grabbed Leo and hugged him tight. "Good job, big bro," I whispered in his ear at the same time he said, "Thanks, sis." I clung to him, so grateful that my big brother was back.

Over his shoulder, I saw Bobby exchange a shocked look with Bean. Bobby's hand seemed to unconsciously pat his front pocket as if making sure something was still there.

In the din of many congratulations, I could've sworn Bean said, "That sonofagun stole your thunder."

Leo pulled back a bit and I looked into his beaming face.

"Best day?" I asked him while Erica and the customers gathered around Star to see the ring.

He grinned at me, his eyes full of happiness. And hope. "So far."

# RECIPES

• BY ISABELLA KNACK •

## ✹ Passion Fruit Vanilla Ganache
(YIELDS 120 PIECES)

### Vanilla Milk Chocolate Ganache

*¾ cup heavy cream*
*¼ cup glucose syrup*
*1 vanilla bean pod*
*2 cups milk chocolate, chopped*
*4 teaspoons butter*

### Passion Fruit Ganache

*6½ tablespoons heavy cream*
*⅓ cup passion fruit*
*6½ tablespoons glucose syrup*
*2¼ cups white chocolate, chopped*

*2 tablespoons butter*
*1½ cups dark chocolate, chopped*

### Preparing the Vanilla Milk Chocolate Ganache:

Combine the heavy cream and glucose in a saucepan. Scrape the vanilla bean into the mixture, and then drop in the scraped pod. Bring to a boil. Remove it from heat and pluck out the pod.

Pour the cream mixture over the milk chocolate. Using a spatula, stir in small circles to emulsify. Add the butter and stir until it is incorporated into the ganache.

Spread the ganache onto a baking sheet lined with plastic wrap. Place it in the freezer for about 10–15 minutes.

### Preparing the Passion Fruit Ganache:

Combine the heavy cream, passion fruit and glucose in a saucepan and bring to a boil. Remove from heat and pour the mixture over the white chocolate. Using a spatula, stir in small circles to emulsify. Add the butter and stir until the butter is incorporated into the ganache. Pour the mixture immediately on top of the Vanilla Milk Ganache and spread. Allow to crystallize overnight.

Remove the ganache from the sheet pan and plastic wrap. Cut it into rectangles. Melt the dark chocolate in the microwave at 30-second intervals. Dip the rectangles into the dark chocolate and place them on wax paper. Chill in the refrigerator for 2 hours.

# ✸ Irish Cream Ganache
(YIELDS 100 PIECES)

*¾ cup heavy cream*
*¼ cup glucose syrup*
*1¾ cups dark chocolate, chopped*
*4 teaspoons softened butter*
*2 tablespoons Irish Cream liqueur*
*premade chocolate molds (available at candy/*
*    baking shops or online)*

Combine the heavy cream and glucose syrup in a saucepan and bring to a boil. Pour the hot cream mixture on the chopped dark chocolate and let sit for 2 minutes in a bowl. Using a spatula, stir the mixture in small circles until it emulsifies. Stir the softened butter into the ganache until it's incorporated. Add the Irish Cream liqueur, stirring until the mixture is homogeneous. Pipe into premade chocolate molds. Chill for two hours.

# ✸ Peppermint Patties
(YIELDS 24 PATTIES)

*2¼ cups powdered sugar*
*2 tablespoons softened butter*
*2 teaspoons peppermint extract*
*2 tablespoons cream*
*12 ounces melting chocolate wafers*

In a mixing bowl, combine the powdered sugar, butter, peppermint extract and cream. Beat them with a paddle attachment until the mixture comes together. Turn the mixer speed higher and beat until the candy comes together and is light and creamy. When you touch it, it should be soft but not at all sticky. If it seems sticky, add a little more powdered sugar, a few tablespoons at a time, until it's no longer sticky.

Scrape the candy paste out onto a long piece of plastic wrap, and form into a thin tube, about 1½ inches in diameter. Wrap it well in the plastic wrap and twist the ends so that they stay in place. Chill the candy until it is very firm, about 45 minutes.

Once firm, use a large sharp knife to slice off rounds about ¼ inch thick. Melt the chocolate wafers in the microwave at 30-second intervals, and stir between each 30 seconds until melted. Dip the candy slices into the melted chocolate, covering completely, and place them onto wax paper. Chill in the refrigerator for one hour.

ALSO AVAILABLE FROM NATIONAL
BESTSELLING AUTHOR

# Kathy Aarons

# THE CHOCOLATE
# COVERED MYSTERIES

## Death is Like a
## Box of Chocolates

## Truffled to Death

## Behind Chocolate Bars

"[A] delectably devious mystery...any lover of chocolate
and books will find this story the perfect combination
of savory, sweet, and deadly."
—Jenn McKinlay, *New York Times* bestselling author of
*Dark Chocolate Demise*

"Aarons's deft blend of delicious chocolate and tasty
mystery will delight the reader's palate."
—Victoria Hamilton, national bestselling author of
*Death of an English Muffin*

kathyaarons.com
penguin.com